KT-557-350

05226748

A Fine Dark Line

BY JOE R. LANSDALE

The Hap Collins and Leonard Pine Novels

SAVAGE SEASON
MUCHO MOJO
THE TWO-BEAR MAMBO
BAD CHILI
RUMBLE TUMBLE
CAPTAINS OUTRAGEOUS

Novels

ACT OF LOVE
THE MAGIC WAGON
DEAD IN THE WEST
THE NIGHTRUNNERS
THE DRIVE-IN: A B-Movie with Blood and Popcorn, Made in Texas
THE DRIVE-IN II: Not Just One of Them Sequels
COLD IN JULY
CAPTURED BY THE ENGINES
TARZAN'S LOST ADVENTURE
(with Edgar Rice Burroughs)
FREEZER BURN
THE BOAR
WALTZ OF SHADOWS
BLOOD DANCE
THE BOTTOMS
THE BIG BLOW
A FINE DARK LINE

Juvenile

TERROR ON THE HIGH SKIES

Short Story Collections

BY BIZARRE HANDS
STORIES BY MAMA LANSDALE'S YOUNGEST BOY
BESTSELLERS GUARANTEED
WRITER OF THE PURPLE RAGE
ELECTRIC GUMBO
A FISTFUL OF STORIES
ATOMIC CHILI: The Illustrated Joe R. Lansdale
THE GOOD, THE BAD, AND THE INDIFFERENT
VEIL'S VISIT (with Andrew Vachss)
PRIVATE EYE ACTION, AS YOU LIKE IT (with Lewis Shiner)
THE LONG ONES
HIGH COTTON

Anthologies (as Editor)

BEST OF THE WEST
NEW FRONTIER
RAZORED SADDLES (with Pat LoBrutto)
DARK AT HEART (with Karen Lansdale)
WEIRD BUSINESS (with Rick Klaw)

Nonfiction

THE WEST THAT WAS (with Thomas W. Knowles)
THE WILD WEST SHOW (with Thomas W. Knowles)

A Fine Dark Line

Joe R. Lansdale

Weidenfeld & Nicolson
LONDON

First published in the United States of America in 2003 by Mysterious Press,
a division of Warner Books, Inc.

First published in Great Britain in 2006
by Weidenfeld & Nicolson

1 3 5 7 9 10 8 6 4 2

© Joe R. Lansdale 2003

All rights reserved. No part of this publication may be
reproduced, stored in a retrieval system, or transmitted, in
any form or by any means, electronic, mechanical,
photocopying, recording or otherwise, without the prior
permission of both the copyright owner and the above publisher.

The right of Joe R. Lansdale to be identified as the author of
this work has been asserted in accordance with the
Copyright, Designs and Patents Act 1988.

A CIP catalogue record for this book
is available from the British Library.

ISBN-13 9 780 297 84559 1
ISBN-10 0 297 84559 4

Printed in Great Britain by
Clays Ltd, St Ives plc

Weidenfeld & Nicolson

The Orion Publishing Group Ltd
Orion House
5 Upper Saint Martin's Lane
London, WC2H 9EA

The Orion Publishing Group's policy is to use papers that are natural,
renewable and recyclable products and made from wood grown
in sustainable forests. The logging and manufacturing processes are
expected to conform to the environmental regulations of the country of origin.

www.orionbooks.co.uk

In memory of Cooter.
Brave, True, and Noble Protector.
Friend.
Family dog.

Although movies, music, and certain events listed here did take place in 1958, I have condensed the release dates of some of these to fit my story. Forgive me this transgression. The town of Dewmont and the Dew Drop Drive-in are my creations, and to the best of my knowledge do not exist, and if they do exist, they bear no relationship to my fictional creation. Some parts of this novel are inspired by autobiographical events, but they serve only as springboards and are not meant to represent true events or real persons.

—J.R.L.

PART ONE

The Dew Drop Drive-in and Concession, 1958

1

M Y NAME is Stanley Mitchel, Jr., and I'll write down what I recall.

This took place in a town named Dewmont, and it's a true story. It all happened during a short period of time, and it happened to me.

Dewmont got its name from an early settler named Hamm Dewmont. Little else is known about him. He came, gave his name to the place, then disappeared from history.

Dewmont, during its early days, was a ratty collection of wooden huts perched on the edge of the Sabine River in the deep heart of East Texas, a place of red clay and white sand, huge pines and snake-infested wetlands.

There are faded photographs in the Dewmont library of a scattering of pioneer hovels on the river's edge as viewed through the lens of a primitive camera. You wouldn't think much would come of this beginning, besides maybe a hard rain and a slide into the river, but through the years, and into the twentieth century, these shacks gradually inflated into a town as the great trees went down and were turned to lumber.

Later the town swelled into a small city of about one hundred thousand, but these events happened earlier, when my family, the Mitchels, moved there at the tag end of the 1950s.

Before we moved to Dewmont my daddy had been a mechanic in a small town of three hundred, appropriately named No Enterprise. One day he came home sick of working beneath cars, lying on cold cement and creaking creepers. He made an announcement that surprised us all. Including Mom.

Daddy loved movies, and somehow he heard about the Dewmont drive-in being for sale. The original owner, not long after opening the theater, had died of a stroke. His family was anxious to move some place west, as debt was clinging to their butts like feathers to tar.

So, Daddy collected our life savings, and using it as a down payment, hauled my mother, who he called Gal, me, my older sister, Caldonia, and my dog, Nub, on over to Dewmont.

Dewmont was mostly a long street with brick buildings on either side of Main Street, including our competition in the form of the Palace Theater, an indoor place.

I remember when we first arrived it was a hot clear day and above was a blue sky dotted with clouds, and you could look down Main Street and see cars parked at the curb and people moving about, and way and beyond, tall trees.

Our drive-in, the Dew Drop, was set just inside of town across from a ritzy residential area.

I'm sure adults in the ritzy section frowned on the nearby drive-in and its catering to the town's great unwashed, or for that matter, their own children who came to us at a dollar a carload.

The Dew Drop was one of those drive-ins where the screen was a residence. These were rare structures, the screens usually being nothing more than a sheet of wood or metal fastened between a large frame, but the builders of the Dew Drop had been progressive and had gone all out.

The Dew Drop's screen was actually a thick building designed to look on the outside like a Western fort. Painted across it was a mural of well-feathered Indians on horseback being pursued by cavalry in sharp blue uniforms and crisp white hats. There were snowy puffs of smoke to show gunfire coming from the pistols and rifles of the soldiers, and one Indian was obviously hit and falling from his horse, to neither ride or scalp again.

Hanging inexplicably above all this on the roof, fastened to a metal frame, was a huge, ocean-blue dew drop, looking as if it were about to drip and explode against the roof, drenching the world.

On the other side, where the cars faced the screen, the wall was white and served as the screen. Above it, this side of the dew drop was painted green, and not a pretty green, but a color that made me think of a puss-filled blister. I wondered why it had been painted at all. At night, when the movie showed, it was lost in the darkness above the reflected light on the screen.

Inside the movie screen, our home, it was pretty normal. Downstairs was a kitchen, living room, bath, and Callie's bedroom. Connected to our living quarters was a concession stand that served hot dogs, popcorn, candy, and soft drinks. Shortly after taking over, we added fried chicken and sausage on a stick to the menu.

On the second floor were two bedrooms, one for me, one for Mom and Dad. I was ecstatic about that. Our old house in No Enterprise had one legitimate bedroom, and me and Callie slept in the living room at night on pallets. Here at the Dewdrop we had our own beds, our own privacy, which was great since I had recently discovered the joys of masturbation.

Though I hadn't exactly figured out what it was all about, it beat playing checkers against myself.

Above all this was yet another floor, a kind of attic with stairs that led to the roof of the drive-in where the great dew drop resided.

Up there on the roof, you could see the cars coming in, and if you walked to the other side of the roof, you could see what made up our backyard: speakers on posts in tidy rows, and at night, cars and lots of people.

Next to the drive-in structure was a padlocked toolshed, and to the side of that was a playground with a teeter-totter, swings, and a slide for when the kids got bored with the movie. All of this was surrounded by a fence. Mostly tin, with some chain link near the swings and seesaws.

———

I WORKED at our drive-in during that summer with Caldonia. A black man named Buster Abbot Lighthorse Smith, who had worked for the previous owner, ran the projector. He was old, sullen, strong-looking, said very little. Mostly did his job. He was so quiet you forgot he was around. He came walking in an hour before the show, did his work, put the film away when it was over, and left.

My mother and father opened the drive-in Monday through Saturday, except during rainstorms or the dead of winter. Even in East Texas, it sometimes got too cold for drive-in patrons.

For that reason we closed a week before Christmas, didn't open again until the first of March. During that time Daddy did repairs on speakers, hauled in fresh gravel, painted and carpentered.

When he wasn't doing that, if he needed the money, he did mechanic work on the lawn of the drive-in. He hated that, longed for the day when he would no longer turn wrenches and listen for air blowing through a leaky manifold.

Daddy loved the drive-in as much as he hated mechanic work. He liked to sit out front sometimes on Sundays, when it wasn't open, in a metal lawn chair, and I'd sit on the ground beside him, usually tormenting ants with a blade of grass. He'd stare at those cowboys and Indians on the front side of the screen as if he were actually watching a movie.

I think in his mind's eye they moved. And maybe it was just the idea of owning his own business that fascinated him. Daddy hadn't come from much, had about a third-grade education. He'd scraped and scrapped for everything he had, and was proud of it. For him, owning that drive-in was as good as being a doctor or a lawyer. And, for the times, for his background, he felt he was making pretty good money.

At thirteen years old, I was the youngest of the Mitchel clan, and not a sophisticated thirteen at that. I was as unaware of the ways of the world as a pig is of cutlery and table manners. I thought sex came after the number five and before the number seven.

Sad to say, I had only recently gotten over believing in Santa Claus and was mad about it. I had been told the truth by kids at school six months before we moved to Dewmont, and had fought a hell of a fight with Ricky Vanderdeer over the matter. I came home with a battered cheek, a black eye, a limp, and a general ass whipping.

My mother, upset over the beating, and a little embarrassed that a child my age still believed in Santa Claus, sat me down and gave me a speech about how Santa may not be real but lived in the hearts of those who believed in him. I was stunned. You could have knocked me over with a wet dog hair. I didn't want a Santa in my heart. I wanted a fat, bearded man in a red suit that brought presents at Christmas and could squeeze through a chimney or a keyhole, which was how Mother told me Santa came into our home, not some nothing living in my heart.

This realization led me to the immediate conclusion that if there was no fat, jolly old elf in a red suit that came by magical sleigh, then there was no Easter Bunny hopping about with colored eggs either, not to mention the Tooth Fairy, one of the few mythical creatures I had honest suspicions about, having found one of the teeth she was supposed to have claimed for a quarter lying under my bed, probably where my mother, the real Tooth Fairy, had dropped it.

I had been set wise and I didn't like it. I felt like a big donkey's ass.

My ignorance did not end with Santa and assorted mythological creatures. I was no whiz at school either. Though I was smarter and better read than most kids, I was so bad at mathematics, it was a firing squad offense.

Having come from No Enterprise, a three-street town with two stores, two alleyways, a filling station, a six-table cafe, and a town drunk we knew by name, and who in a strange way was respected for his dedication to his profession, Dewmont seemed like a metropolis.

Yet, in time Dewmont actually began to feel sleepy. At least on the surface. Especially during the long hot summers.

The turmoil of the 1960s was yet to come, and Dewmont was way behind anyway. People dressed and conducted themselves like it was the 1930s, or at the latest, the 1940s. On Sunday men wore thin black ties and heavy black suits and hot wool hats. They always removed their hats when they were inside and they still tipped them at ladies.

Because air-conditioning was rare, even in stores, it was sticky-hot then, indoors and out, as if you had been coated in a thin film of warm molasses. In the summer, those men's suits rested heavy on their victims, like outfits designed for torture. The thin ties lay dead on sweat-stained shirts and the cotton in the shoulders of the suits shifted easily, making lumps; the material held sweat like a sponge holds water; the brims on the wool hats sagged.

In the late afternoons people stripped down to shirtsleeves or even undershirts and sat outside on porches or in metal lawn chairs and talked well after the fireflies came out. Inside, they sat in front of fans.

It didn't get dark during the summer till way late, and the sun, not blocked by tall buildings or housing developments, dipped into the East Texas trees like a fireball. As it died, it looked as if it were setting the woods on fire.

Certain kinds of language now spoken as a matter of course were rarely heard then in polite company. Even the words *damn* and *hell,* if women were present, could stun a conversation as surely as a slaughterhouse hammer could stun a cow.

The Depression was long gone, if not forgotten by those who had gone through it. World War Two was over and we had saved the world from the bad guys, but the boom times that had hit the rest of the country had not quite made it to East Texas. Or if they had, they hadn't stayed long. Came in with the oil field wildcatter for a financial quickie, then played out so fast it was hard to remember there had ever been good times.

There was rockabilly, or rock and roll as it became known, on the radio, but there was no abundance of rock and roll feel in the air where we lived. Just a clutch of kids who hung out at the Dairy Queen afternoons and evenings, especially thick on Friday and Saturday nights.

A few of the guys, like Chester White, had ducktails and hotrods. Most guys had pretty short hair with a pompadour rise in front and plenty of hair oil on it. Wore sharp-creased slacks, starched white shirts, and polished brown shoes, drove their daddy's car when they could get it.

The girls wore poodle skirts and ponytails, but the most radical thing they did was play the same tune over and over on the jukebox, mostly Elvis, and some of the Baptist kids danced in spite of the lurking threat of hell and damnation.

The colored knew their place. Women knew their place. *Gay* was still a word for "happy." Children were still thought by many best seen and not heard. Stores closed on Sunday. Our bomb was bigger than their bomb and the United States Army couldn't be beat by anyone. Including Martians. The President of the United States was a jolly, grandfatherly, fat, bald man who liked to play golf and was a war hero.

Being blissfully ignorant, I thought all was right with the world.

2

HERE WAS ONE KID I met after moving to Dewmont who I
made friends with. His name was Richard Chapman. He
was a little older than me, but in the same grade, because he had
failed a year.

Like Huckleberry Finn, Richard wasn't the sort that would
make a great adult, but he was one hell of a kid. He could ride
a bike faster than the wind, could toss a pocketknife between
his toes and not stick himself, knew the woods, could climb a
tree like a gibbon, and juggle four rubber balls at a time.

He had a shock of brown greasy hair, made greasier by
generous doses of Vitalis, sweat, and body oil. Richard combed
his mop straight back like Johnny Weissmuller, who he resem-
bled.

Richard's hair was constantly slipping out of place, and he
spent a good portion of his time flipping it back into position
with brutal jerks of his head, and knowing lice lived there, this
activity made you nervous. Still, at the time, having a cowlick

and a white spot at the front of my hair, I envied that greasy mop of his, along with his muscles.

My thought was, if Richard were in a plane that crashed in the jungle, he would survive and become someone like Tarzan. He would figure out how to hunt, build a hut, and fight natives.

I, on the other hand, would be eaten by lions, or beaten to death by monkeys within moments.

One Saturday morning Richard came over to watch television, see all the shows on *Jungle Theater.* While he watched, he held and mooned over my Roy Rogers cowboy boots. He had a thing for those boots; they were red leather and written on the pull-up straps in silver letters was "Roy Rogers."

Richard's family didn't have a TV. They had owned one, but when a storm knocked down their antenna and twisted it up like a pretzel, his father decided it was a sign from God, and sold the set to a sinner.

Even before the jungle shows finished, Richard held one of my cowboy boots against his foot to see if it would fit, and informed me he had to go, had to get back home and do chores and take a beating because he was running late and had left home without asking.

"Why didn't you ask?"

"Because Daddy would have said no."

"Then why did you come?"

"I wanted to."

"What about the beating?"

Richard shrugged.

Being accustomed to beatings, Richard wasn't overly frightened by the notion. He told me if he thought of himself as Tarzan being tortured by natives, he could make out tough enough to take it.

Richard pretended he was Tarzan a lot.

When Richard talked about chores, he meant grown-man

chores on Mr. Chapman's worn-out farm. I picked up my clothes and a few odds and ends like that, but Richard had to feed the chickens, slop the hogs, put hay out for cows, plant and harvest crops. He fixed fence and cut fence posts, and once dug a six-foot-long, twelve-foot-deep trench for their outhouse before breakfast.

His daddy made him slave as hard as the people he hired to work the fields. Usually, this was an unending cycle of one or two colored people, sometimes Mexicans, who, whether native to Texas or from across the border, were referred to as wetbacks.

These workers, migrants and transients—anyone who lived in Dewmont knew better than to work for Chapman—didn't last long on the farm, and were soon gone, fired either for laziness or religious infractions.

Mr. Chapman thought he was called by God and had set up a kind of church in his barn. Richard said he and the workers had to memorize passages from the Bible and listen to preaching from Chapman. Richard figured a lot of the workers who decamped left because of this, or they were just plain tired of so much work for so little pay.

This kind of life was alien to me. My daddy would get upset with me, and I had occasionally gotten an ass shining. But it was nothing savage like what Richard got, and I didn't live in fear of it or expect it on a regular basis. In fact, since the age of eleven I had not had a spanking.

Frankly, on this day, I wasn't concerned with Richard's chores or the whipping he would take. I was more disappointed I was going to have a full summer day, a Saturday, without anyone to play with.

After Richard left and the television shows were over, I vacated the comfort of our water-cooled window fan, went out into the blinding heat.

Me and Nub took to playing at the edge of the woods out back, just off our property, but not far from the drive-in fence. The fence was about eight feet tall and tin, supported by two-by-fours and two-by-sixes. It was designed to prevent sneaking into the theater.

The outside of the tin was to have originally been painted in a mural fashion, and someone had bothered to paint four long slices of it with colorful paintings of a flying saucer and little green men before they said the hell with it and painted the remaining expanse of back and side fence in the same green that adorned the dew drop symbol and gave hue to the skin of the aliens.

I was playing what I called Nub Chase. It was a simple game. I ran and Nub tried to catch me, and, of course, he always did. When he caught up with me, he'd latch his teeth into my blue jeans, and I'd keep trying to run, him hanging on my pants leg, growling like a grizzly bear. I'd drag him about for a while, free him, break and run again.

Dutifully, he'd charge after me, and we'd repeat this process, running the hundred-yard gap between fence and woods. We had been doing this much of the summer, along with other games like prowling the woods and throwing rocks into a pond I wasn't supposed to go near. The pond was large and the water was as green as our fence. Moss and lily pads floated on its surface.

I often saw large frogs bunched up on the pads and logs and along the bank. There was a kind of smell about the place that brought to mind something primitive, like a prehistoric swamp containing dead dinosaurs. I liked to pretend there were dinosaurs in there, in suspended animation, and that any moment one, awakened by a crack of thunder, or maybe a stroke of hot lightning on the surface of the algae-slick green pond, would rise out of there shedding water and begin a rampage through downtown Dewmont, hopefully taking the school out first.

I loved going there to see the frogs and the blue and green dragonflies. Once, I even came upon a fat water moccasin sunning itself on the shore, a frog's hind legs hanging out of its mouth.

But on this day, playing between fence and woods, running from Nub, I suddenly tripped and fell. It was a hard fall, and my ankle, where something had snagged me at the top of my black high-top tennis shoe, felt as if an anvil had been dropped on it. I sat down crying, rubbing my foot, easing off my shoe to see if it was worse than I thought. Once the shoe and sock were removed, I saw only a red mark turning purple at the top of my foot and along the ankle.

I rubbed my foot and Nub licked my toes. When I looked in the direction I had first stumbled, I saw something dark brown and sharp sticking up out of the edge of the ground.

I put my sock and shoe on, and leaving my tennis shoe untied, limped over to take a look. It was the edge of a metal box sticking out of the ground. I was immediately excited, thought perhaps I had discovered some kind of pirate treasure chest, the edge of a flying device from Mars, or perhaps, as in one of the books I was reading that summer, *At the Earth's Core,* by Edgar Rice Burroughs, the tip of a metal mole machine burrowing up from the surface.

I gave up on the latter idea immediately. It wasn't burrowing at all. It was just sticking out of the ground. Perhaps, I thought, it's the tip of the machine and it's stalled, and Abner Perry and David Innes from the novel are trapped down there and need my assistance.

Now, I didn't really believe this, any more than I believed a dinosaur would rise out of that old pond and crash and chew its way through Dewmont, though I should add there was always a part of me that *did* believe it and thought on some level, in some universe, in some far corner of my mind, that it was real. But for the most part I knew it was the edge of a metal box.

I attempted to dig around it with my hands, but the dirt and grass had become too entwined.

I went into the drive-in, used the padlock key hidden under a brick next to the shed, got a shovel out of storage, and went back.

When I returned to the spot where Nub and I had found our treasure, Nub had already begun to dig up the unidentified ground object. He had managed with paws and teeth to make pretty good progress.

I carefully pushed Nub aside, and ignoring my sore foot, I dug.

I had to stop and take a breather a couple of times. It was so hot it felt as if I was sucking down hairballs with every breath. I wished then I had filled and brought the army canteen my Uncle Ben had given me, and I even considered going to get it, but didn't.

I stayed at it, and pretty soon, the little box was free. It was about twice the size of a cigar box and it had a small, rusty old padlock holding it together. I tugged at the lock, and rusty or not, it was still firm; in fact, the rust may have only made it tighter. The keyhole in the lock was filled with dirt and roots.

A summer rain started up. One moment there had not been a cloud in the sky, the next the clouds rolled in and the rain started, soft and steady, giving the earth that sweet smell that either makes you want to plant or sin.

I knew I had to finish up whatever I was doing, because Mom would be wanting me out of the rain, and it was near lunchtime.

I thought about using the shovel to knock the lock off, but hesitated. I was afraid I'd end up breaking the shovel.

I decided the best thing to do would be to get a more serviceable tool out of the shed for the job. But when I got back to the shed with the box, I heard Mom calling me to eat.

I pushed the metal box on a shelf, put a greasy cardboard box full of electrical fuses and switches in front of it, went to wash my hands and eat.

Though I would not have imagined it right then, what occurred at dinner caused me to actually forget about the box for a time.

———

I SUPPOSE DADDY could have picked a more opportune moment to confront Callie, and it's my guess he would have had it not been an immediate and shocking discovery, but my father was not in any way like the fathers you saw on television in the 1950s, calm and collected and full of sharp wisdom.

We were sitting at the table waiting for him, plates of fried chicken, mashed potatoes, and gravy stacked in the center of the table, when he arrived holding something with a pair of tweezers.

I thought it was a balloon. It dangled limp from the tweezers and was tied in a knot at the top and was filled with something, and Daddy's hand shook as he held it.

He looked at Caldonia, said, "I found it in your room."

Caldonia turned red as Santa's suit, slid down in her chair. Even her ponytail seemed to wilt. "You couldn't . . ." she said.

But, he had.

Later we learned he had gone in Callie's room to shut her window against the rain, and had seen what he now held with tweezers. But at that moment, all I knew was here was a very upset man standing at the table with an odd balloon dangling from a pair of tweezers.

"You're only sixteen," he said. "Not married."

"Oh, Daddy," Callie said, and with the speed of the Flash, she leaped from her chair and darted for her room.

Still holding the thing with the tweezers, Dad looked at Mom, who stood up very slowly, put her chair under the table and left the room with a sob. Down the hall I heard her crying, and over that I could hear Callie wailing.

Daddy looked at me, said, "I'll just get rid of this."

Not knowing what it was he was disposing of, or what had actually occurred, I just nodded, and when he left the room I sat there bewildered. Eventually he returned. He sat at the head of the table and stared off into space. Finally he noticed me sitting there. He said, "You go ahead and eat, Stanley."

I filled my plate and started in, curious about what was going on, but in no way put off my feed. I was through my second piece of chicken when Mom came back and sat down and made a production of placing her napkin in her lap.

Daddy said, "You spoke with her, Gal?"

Mom's voice wasn't any better. "Some. I'll be speaking with her again."

"Good. Good."

She looked up at me, smiled weakly, said, "Callie won't be joining us for dinner. Would you pass the chicken, Stanley?"

3

IT WAS SUNDAY, and the drive-in was closed. Back then Sunday was taken seriously by Christians, and no legitimate businesses were open. Some Christians argued Saturday was the true day of praise and rest for the Lord, but the law thought it was Sunday.

For years there was a thing in Texas called the blue law, which meant there were certain items you couldn't buy on Sunday. Like alcoholic beverages. Or you could buy a hammer, but couldn't buy nails, a drill, but no bits. Anything that might lead to the successful completion of work. Someone saw you working, they looked at you as if you had just set fire to the courthouse while it was stuffed with pink-cheeked Girl Scouts and all their cookies.

As I recall, certain bathroom items were even considered taboo to be sold.

So, back then Sunday was not a day the drive-in opened. My parents were not churchgoers, and to the best of my memory, religion was never seriously discussed, least not from a theological standpoint.

Still, no matter what the family's beliefs, there was no question there was some sort of moral event at the heart of Callie's mistake. Enough that I heard Mother call on God. Twice. I think she was threatening him.

Daddy, realizing I was puzzled about the matter of the knotted balloon, tried to explain it to me that afternoon.

We were out back, inside the drive-in, under the awning over the front of the concession stand, sitting in chairs, looking at the green fence in the distance, watching what was left of the rain.

Daddy, without looking at me, said, "Son. Do you know what happened with Callie?"

"You found something in her room that shouldn't have been there."

Daddy sat silent for a moment. I glanced at him out of the corner of my eye, because, somehow, I knew this wasn't a face-to-face kind of conversation.

"In a way that's correct," Daddy said. "Son, do you know about the birds and the bees?"

Of course I did. Was he asking me the difference? Was this a bird and insect lesson? I said, "I think so."

"Well, there's a time for the birds and the bees. You should know what it's all about."

"Yes, sir."

"Well, Callie found out too soon. Or maybe she knew, but she got involved too soon."

"With the birds and the bees?"

"In a manner of speaking."

"You're mad about it?"

"Yes. I'm hurt. I'm a little scared."

I did look at him now. I couldn't help myself. Daddy,

scared? My daddy seemed to me invincible. Kind of man that would go bear hunting with a switch and make the bear carry the switch home for him. And here he was upset over some birds and bugs and a knotted balloon.

"Why, Daddy?"

"Because Callie is my little girl and I want the best for her, and she's too young to be involved with that kind of thing."

"Was she throwing them in her room?"

"Do what?"

"Water balloons?"

Daddy looked at me for a long moment, blinked, said, "Oh . . . Oh, I see . . . Why yes, son. She was. I can't tolerate that kind of thing . . . Tell you what. We'll talk later."

Daddy stood up and went inside.

I sat there for a while, then toddled inside, confused. Whatever our conversation had been about, I was certain of one thing: It wasn't a matter Daddy really wanted to discuss anyway.

———

IN THE NEXT FEW DAYS there occurred what seemed to me a series of random events. Oh, I knew Callie was in trouble for the water balloon, but it astonished me that Mom and Daddy told her she wasn't going anywhere for six months or longer, or "maybe forever," as Daddy put it, unless it was with the family.

Callie was also weepy all the time, and that surprised me. She normally took her punishment quite stoically, though it seemed to me she always got off lighter on everything than I did. She usually had Daddy wrapped around her little finger, but this time that wasn't the case. He was harder on her than Mom was, and Mom wasn't easy. She gave Callie all manner of odd chores, and would break out crying sometimes when she saw her.

Callie's boyfriend, Chester, who she had met the second day we arrived in Dewmont, and who was nineteen, stopped coming around soon after, due to Daddy and him having what Mom would refer to in later years as an altercation.

To be more precise, Daddy told him not to show his face there again. After a few days, however, Chester ignored him, coming up one Sunday afternoon wanting to talk to Daddy, as he said, "Like a man."

He came up in his black hotrod Ford, flame licks painted on the sides, got out, his hair sculptured into what looked like a black, overturned gravy boat. He had on a pink and black shirt and jeans with the cuffs rolled up, and a pair of, you guessed it, blue suede shoes.

Chester got out of his car slowly, like a visiting dignitary from the planet Rockabilly.

Daddy had already received word of his arrival, as I had been out in the front yard with Nub, messing about, and as soon as Chester showed, I rushed into the house to tattle.

I followed Daddy outside. Chester cocked his leg forward, tried to look like Elvis. He said, "Sir, I want to set you straight on something about me and Callie."

That was the wrong tone. Daddy's answer was to spring on Chester. Daddy's fist found Chester's mouth, and after that blow there was a sound from Chester like someone torturing a cat. Then Daddy was straddling him, beating him like a circus monkey.

Well, actually, had Daddy been serious, Chester would have never gotten up. Daddy was slapping him repeatedly, saying, "Getting any smarter, grease stick, getting any smarter?"

Chester's IQ didn't seem to be rising, but his voice had certainly jumped some octaves. After about five minutes of slapping it reached the level of the tenors in the Vienna Boys Choir, only less melodious.

And so, with Daddy straddling Chester under the shadow of the drive-in wall, trying desperately to raise Chester's IQ with repeated slapping, the morning passed. Or so it seemed. I do believe Daddy slapped Chester for about fifteen minutes.

Chester wailed for God to come down from the heavens and save him, and though God didn't show, Mom and Callie did.

Fearing Daddy would really lose it, turn his hitting into something more serious, Mom and me and Callie pulled him off. Daddy called Chester a sonofabitch while Chester limped for his car, his face red from slapping, his greasy hair hanging in front of his face, his ducktail mashed flat against his neck, the ass of his jeans dripping grass. His blue suede shoes still looked pretty good though.

"I told you not to come back around here," Daddy said. "Ever see you again I'll kick your ass so hard you'll have to hire a goddamn winch truck to crank it down so you can shit."

Nose bleeding all over creation, Chester got in his old Ford and gunned it out of there, the tires tossing gravel.

"What in the world has gotten into you?" Mom said to Daddy.

Daddy burned a glance at Callie, said, "It's what's gotten into Callie that matters."

"Stanley," Mom said.

Cops came around later. Daddy took them aside and talked to them. I heard one cop laugh. Another slapped Daddy on the back. And that was the end of it.

No one really liked Chester anyway, so it ended up he just had to take his beating and enjoy it like it had been a Christmas present he always wanted.

These were the kinds of things going on, and I didn't have a clue what they were.

———

THAT NIGHT, before going to bed, I started a book called *Treasure Island.* I had read pirate books before, but never anything like this. I read half of it before I fell asleep, but next morning, having read about that treasure, I was reminded of finding that rusty old box out back of the drive-in, and after breakfast I went to the shed to open it.

I found a crowbar, and by standing on the box, planting the bar in the loop of the lock, I was able with much huffing and puffing, and with the assistance of Nub barking and leaping, to snap it.

Inside there was a leather bag. In the bag, wrapped in what felt like a piece of a raincoat, was a bundle of brown envelopes tied up with a faded blue ribbon.

This wasn't what I had hoped for.

Disappointed, I replaced them in the box, took the box to my room, closed the door, sat on the bed with it.

I was a little nervous about that. One water balloon had really gotten Callie in trouble. I wondered what my fate might be.

I opened the box, removed the bundle from the bag, tugged the ribbon loose, took hold of the envelope on top. It was not sealed. I reached inside and pinched out what appeared to be a letter.

I read a bit of it and my heart sank. It was written by some girl and it was all moony-eyed stuff. I opened the other envelopes, skimmed the contents, put them all back in their place, closed up the box, pushed it under my bed.

———

ABOUT A WEEK LATER Daddy hired a big colored woman named Rosy Mae Bell. She was big and fat and very black, wore clothes that looked to be made from my mama's curtains, colorful rags around her head that she tied up front in a little bow. She looked a little bit like Aunt Jemima on the front of the same-named syrup. Or as we called it: surp.

Her job was to clean and dust and cook. This came about because of the drive-in work. Mom felt if she was going to work all night at the drive-in concession, and mess with me and Callie during the day, she ought to have some help doing the cleaning and cooking.

At cleaning, Rosy Mae turned out to be so-so, but when it came to cooking she had the skills of an angel. God's own table could not have been as blessed as ours. I could tell my mom was actually a little jealous of Rosy Mae, and when we sat down to an early supper—the drive-in opened at eight on summer nights, which meant we'd start real preparation about seven—she'd always find a small complaint to make about the biscuits or the gravy. But it was halfhearted, because Mom knew, just as we all knew, and as Rosy knew (though she always pretended to be in agreement with Mom), it didn't get any better.

Me and Rosy took to one another like ducks to june bugs.

During the day when Rosy was supposed to be cleaning, she often spent time with me telling me stories or listening to me tell her things I'd never even mention to my parents. A lot of the time she sat on the living room couch and read romance magazines. She could get away with this when Mom was running errands and Daddy was out front mowing the grass or out back picking up cups and popcorn bags and the like that patrons had thrown out their windows.

Along with that trash, another item that began to appear with some regularity among the toss-aways were those strange clear balloons like the one that had been found in Callie's room.

It was my job to sweep out the concession and the little porch veranda in front of it, and I would watch Daddy pick up the trash with a stick with a nail in its tip. He'd poke stuff and put it in a bag, but he always seemed to poke those balloons with a vengeance. It slowly began to dawn on me that those particular balloons had about them a mysterious, perhaps even sinister quality that I had not previously suspected.

Rosy Mae and I had a kind of deal. I'd keep watch for her when I was sweeping the veranda, or when I was inside the concession and could see Daddy out the windows. I also had such good ears Rosy Mae called me Nub's big brother. If I heard Mom coming home or saw Daddy finishing up, I'd step inside and call her name in a tone that meant she should get up, stash her magazine, grab a duster, start moving about.

And she was quick at it. The magazine would disappear inside the big paisley-colored bag she brought every day, and she'd start flouncing about with that duster. And to see that big woman flounce was something. She looked like a bear dusting her den.

———

ONE MORNING, Rosy Mae's day off, a Saturday, I was out on the veranda sitting by my daddy in one of the metal lawn chairs as he whittled on a stick and talked about the new Jimmy Stewart movie showing that night, *Vertigo*. He said that he wouldn't really get to watch it because he had so much work to do, and he hated that because he loved Jimmy Stewart, and thought on

Sunday he might just show it for the family and have friends over, but Callie couldn't have any of hers. She could watch, but her fun was to be limited.

I listened to this, liking the idea, especially about Callie not having friends over. I was really enjoying her punishment. I was also envious that she made friends easily. In the short time we had been in Dewmont she had made a lot of them. She was so pretty, so fun, all she had to do was show up and the boys were falling all over her, and the girls, though maybe jealous of her at first, soon warmed to her as well.

Well, most of them.

"Can I invite a friend?" I asked.

"Sure. Who?"

"Rosy Mae."

Daddy turned to me, said, "Son, Rosy Mae's colored."

"Yes, sir," I said.

He smiled at me. "Well, she's all right. I like her. But white people don't spend special time with coloreds. It's just not done. I haven't got a thing against her, you see. She's all right in her place, but if I invited some of our friends over, I don't think they'd want to sit with a colored and watch a movie."

"Why not?"

"Well, coloreds are different, son. They aren't like you and me. Good upstanding white people just don't spend a lot of time around niggers."

This was all something I should've known, I suppose, but in No Enterprise I had been sheltered. There, the only coloreds I had seen were those driving mule-drawn wagons with plows in the back.

And there was Uncle Tommy, who sharpened knives and fixed household goods. He lived down by the creek in a one-room shack with an outhouse out back. I knew the colored people I had seen were poor, but it wasn't until that moment I understood they were different, considered inferior to whites. And though I had heard the word nigger before, I realized now that it could be said in such a way as to strike like a blow, even if spoken to a white person.

It also occurred to me that Daddy and Mom didn't have any true friends in Dewmont, and they had most likely spent more hours with Rosy Mae than anyone they might invite.

Daddy, sensing I was disappointed, said, "If you want, you can invite a friend of yours. What about that Richard kid? He looks a bit like a hooligan to me, but I reckon he's all right."

"Yeah. Okay. Maybe."

"You think he has lice?"

"He scratches a lot."

"That hair looks buggy to me."

Richard was all right. I liked him. But I realized right then that I felt a closer attachment to Rosy Mae, and I had known her even less time than Richard.

Me and Rosy Mae did spend special time together. I didn't have to think about what I was going to say before I said it to her. I sure didn't tell Richard that I liked to read poetry, and I had told Rosy Mae that. And though she didn't know a poem from a cow turd, she understood I liked poetry and appreciated my interest in it, and even let me read one by Robert Frost to her twice. She had also seen all the Tarzan movies from the balcony of the Palace Theater, where the coloreds watched, and she had seen movies in the black theater over in the neighboring town of Talmont that I had never seen or even heard of. Black cowboys. Black gangsters. Black musicals. I had no idea those movies even existed. She called them "colored picture shows."

Aware of my pondering, Daddy said, "I just want you to know I haven't got a thing against Rosy Mae."

I thought, other than her being a nigger. I went in the

house, upstairs, lay on my bed and felt . . . odd. I don't know any other way to describe it. The information I received that day had struck me like a bullet, and it felt like a ricochet, meant for Rosy, received by me.

————

I HAD LEFT the door open, and while I was lying on the bed, Nub wandered in, jumped up next to me. Shortly thereafter, Callie came to the door. After the balloon incident, Daddy and Mom had swapped rooms with her, moving her upstairs, next door to me.

Callie was barefoot, had her hair in a ponytail, was wearing pink pedal pushers and a white, oversized man's shirt. Like most girls that age, she wore too much perfume. For that matter, three years later, I would wear too much cologne.

She leaned against the door frame, said, "Mom catches you with your shoes in the bed, and that dog, there's going to be some trouble."

"You ought to know about trouble," I said. "And she doesn't care about Nub. She lets Nub in their bed."

"Maybe she does, but you don't know a thing about me being in trouble, Stanley Mitchel, Jr. Not a thing. I didn't do anything. Now I'm grounded at the best time of my life. I'm supposed to be having fun."

"You aren't supposed to have those balloons in your room."

I rolled my head to look at Callie, saw that she had turned red.

"I'll have you know that it isn't what you think."

I wasn't sure what to think, but I didn't give away my ignorance. I said, "Yeah, whatever you say."

"Jane Jersey dropped that through my window . . . Well, at

least I think she did. Someone mean that likes Chester and doesn't want us to be together and wants to give me a bad reputation. Jane Jersey already has a bad reputation. Not to mention an ugly hairdo. You could hide a watermelon in that hair of hers. Actually, it looks like one of those wire fish traps."

"Why would you like Chester? He's creepy. He looks like a spaceman. I think I saw him in *Invasion of the Saucer Men*. He was the little monster on the left."

"You're just mean, Stanley."

"And you're telling me Jane Jersey came by and slipped that balloon in your window on a stick? I'm supposed to buy that?"

"Most of the girls I get along with, but a few are jealous. Jane is the most jealous. She used to go with Chester. I didn't break them up, though. They were already broke up. I met him at the Dairy Queen and we hit it off. It's nothing serious. He's just kind of fun. Different. Jane's been ugly to me because of it. Always frowning, telling me to leave her boyfriend alone. Her putting that rubber—"

"Rubber?"

"That's what the balloon is called, Stanley. It's not called a balloon. Politely, it's called a prophylactic. But her putting that in my room, or having one of her friends do it, that's just mean. I don't really know she meant Mom or Daddy to find it, but I think she wanted to show me she was getting what she thought I was getting. But I'm not. And if I was, I'd be smart enough to pick it up and get rid of it. And if Chester is getting what she says he's getting, I don't want any part of him."

I finally gave in. "And what is she getting that you're not?"

"Do what?"

"Jane Jersey. You said she wanted to show you she was getting what she thinks you're getting. What were you and her getting?"

Callie closed the door. "You really don't know about this, do you, Stanley?"

"I got some idea."

"No you don't. You keep calling it a balloon."

"Well it is a balloon. Kinda."

Callie laughed. "You don't have a clue."

"Well, I know Daddy's real mad. I know that much."

Callie sat down on the end of the bed. "Daddy's wrong. I think he knows he's wrong. He's just waiting to be sure."

"Waiting for what?"

"To see if I come up pregnant. To see if there was a leak."

"Pregnant? A leak in what?"

I know it's amazing, but I actually had no idea how pregnancy occurred. It just wasn't talked about then by parents or in polite society.

Callie, however, was versed in all this, and was not as skittish about it as Mom and Daddy. She said, "You want to know how a girl gets pregnant?"

"I guess."

"Well first, let me straighten you out on something. I'm not getting anything from anybody . . . Remember that part. You know those dogs out in the yard? The ones Daddy turned the hose on?"

"The ones with their butts hung?"

"Their butts weren't hung," Callie said. "The boy dog had turned, and that put them rear end to rear end, but it was his thing that was hung."

"His thing?"

"That's right. His doodle."

"In her butt?"

"In her pee-pee."

I was growing very uncomfortable.

"Let me explain it to you," Callie said.

When she finished, I was amazed. "People do that?"

"Yes."

"Why?"

"Because it feels good. Or so I'm told."

"Does it feel good with one of those balloons on? Is that what makes it feel good?"

"I wouldn't know if it felt good with one or without one."

"Ooooh, you and greasy Chester?"

"I didn't do anything. Let me tell you something, Stanley. I don't really like Chester that much. I mean, I like him, but not that way. He's a little on the stupid side. I like riding around in his car, but to tell the truth, I like Drew Cleves."

"Never heard of him."

"He's quite the big dog at the high school. He's a year ahead of me. He's handsome. On the football team. Very popular. Of course, I hate football. Even if I want to be a cheerleader."

"You haven't even started to school and you know all that?"

"Yes. Unlike you, I'm not obnoxious. People like me. Well, most of them. I guess I'd have to mark Jane Jersey off the list."

Since Callie was so forthcoming with information, I thought I'd slip in a question that had been bothering me.

"Callie?"

"Yeah."

"Daddy says Rosy Mae is a nigger. Is she?"

"That's a terrible word," Callie said. "Mom says never to use it. Daddy shouldn't say it. Rosy Mae is a Negro. Or colored."

"He says we shouldn't be around Rosy Mae unless she's working here."

"It shouldn't be that way, Stanley, but I guess it is. I haven't a thing against coloreds, but I doubt I'd be very popular hanging around Negroes."

"Is that why they don't go to our school? Because they're niggers?"

"Stanley, I'm going to spank you myself if you say that terrible word again. Coloreds do not like being called niggers. I may not be brave enough to spend time with Negroes, but I know it's wrong, and I know calling them nigger is wrong. And you should too. The world just hasn't caught up with the way we ought to be treating people, Stanley . . . What's that?"

"What's what?"

"That rusty old box poking out from under your bed."

"I found it."

Callie pulled the box out. "What's in it?"

"Just some letters."

"Where did you find it?"

Callie opened the box.

"It was buried in the backyard. Me and Nub found it."

"Buried? Wow."

I sat on the edge of the bed and watched Callie take out the bag, remove the letters, and untie the ribbon.

"Those are mine," I said.

"They belong to whoever wrote them. You just found them, you little goober."

"They're just love letters."

Callie read the first letter. When she finished there were tears in her eyes. "That is so sweet."

"I thought it was mushy."

"It's very sweet. And so old-fashioned. Did you see the date?"

I shook my head.

"It was written during the war. First year of it."

"That's a long time ago."

"I was born during the war. Nineteen forty-two. So it's not so long ago. It reads like a woman writing to her lover."

"You saying a guy kept those letters?"

"Well, it reads that way. I suppose they could be letters from a guy to a girl. Initials are used. M to J, so I don't know for sure. Maybe if I read more."

"How did it end up buried out there?"

"I don't know."

Callie pulled out another envelope, removed a letter. "It's signed M as well. I guess it was a pet thing with them. Just using the initials. Did you notice there are no stamps or addresses on the envelopes."

"What does that mean?"

"To me it means these were probably not mailed, but hand-delivered."

Callie began looking through the entire bundle. "Hey, not all of these are letters. Just the top four. The rest of these are torn-out journal pages, written on the back and front. And written crosswise too."

"Crosswise."

"They are written the way you normally write, front and back, then the pages are turned and written across. See?"

I took a look. Sure enough. I said, "How can you read something like that?"

"People used to do this to save paper, especially way back. You get used to reading it, I suppose. Where exactly did you find this?"

I told her.

"Let's go look."

I didn't have anything else to do, so I agreed. Callie put the letters and the journal pages back, pushed the box under the bed.

She put on shoes and we went outside. Out back I showed

her where I had found the box. Nub dug at the hole as if something might still be in it, then quit suddenly, charged into the woods, after who knows what.

Shortly thereafter, we heard Nub barking.

I called him, but he didn't come.

"It is strange that it would be buried right here," Callie said, "at the edge of the woods . . . Nub, shut up."

"Don't talk to Nub like that."

"He's giving me a headache."

I called him again, but he still didn't come. "Let's look," I said.

The woods were thick with pine trees and brambles. It was hard to follow Nub, but shortly we found him. He had his front feet against an old oak, his head thrown back, barking at a squirrel. All you could see of the squirrel was its tail blowing in the breeze.

I grabbed Nub by his collar, pulled him off the tree. His sharp little barks were making my back teeth hurt.

I said, "Hush, Nub."

"My goodness, Stanley, look."

I turned, didn't see anything other than Callie, but as I looked closer, I realized there were some old porch steps half submerged in the earth. Then I saw the outline of a house, a large house.

Looking closer yet, I saw where lumber had rotted and fallen to the ground and was mostly covered with pine straw and oak leaves.

Callie glanced up. "My God."

I looked. Shredded, rotted lumber hung from limbs like ugly Christmas decorations. There was a window frame with a broken piece of glass still in it, supported by a pine limb. A large piece of the roof frame was up there too. Even a blackened door where a limb had grown through where the door-knob had been.

Most peculiar was a circular iron staircase that began at the earth between two pines and wound upward to a height of thirty feet, intercepting pine boughs along the way, mixing between the railings until trees and stairs were one.

I examined the rusted stairway, saw that it was not actually touching the ground. It had been lifted several inches from the earth. I took hold of it and tugged.

"Don't," Callie said. "You'll pull it down on your head."

I climbed up a couple steps. "It's firm, Callie. I could go all the way to the top."

"Well, don't."

"You think a tornado got the house?"

"I don't know. This didn't happen a short time ago, but not a long time ago either. That big oak has been here for no telling how long, but those pines are young. The oak was probably in the side yard, but the pines, they've grown up since. Look."

Callie bent, picked up a fragment of lumber that had been partially hidden under the pine straw.

She handed it to me. It was less than a foot of jagged, blackened board. It crumbled in my hand, leaving my fingers black.

"A fire, Stanley. The house burned down, and pieces of the house were slowly pushed up by the trees as they grew. Isn't it amazing?"

"It's creepy."

"It was a big house, Stanley. I bet this is the center of it. The heart of the house."

"You mean it was a mansion?"

"Seems that way. If it was, could be the box wasn't buried at all. But in the fire it dropped through the burning floor-boards and in time got covered. Grass grew up around it, water washed dirt over it. Everything shifted. And there it lay until you and Nub found it."

Nub had fixed his mind on the squirrel again. It was running along a limb, looking down at Nub, making that peculiar chattering noise they make, slashing with its tail.

Nub managed to run up the slight slant of the oak's trunk, and was now perched on a low-hanging limb barking at the squirrel.

Callie laughed, said, "Get that fool mutt down from there before he falls on his head."

I called Nub, but he wouldn't come. I finally climbed up and got him, swinging by my feet from the limb and handing Nub to Callie. I squirmed back onto the limb and climbed down.

"You're such a bad dog," I said, petting Nub on the head.

As we went out of the woods, the squirrel chattered loudly, calling for me to return his playmate.

4

CALLIE WANTED TO EXAMINE the letters and the journal more closely, but it was almost time for supper, then it would be time to get ready for opening up the drive-in.

Saturday was our biggest night. It was the night Daddy was the most nervous. He took to wringing his hands and drinking baking soda mixed in water for his stomach.

If we had a big Saturday, we sometimes had our money for the week. Everything else, Monday through Friday, was just icing on the cake. But Saturday you had families and dates, the masses turned out to worship the gods on the big white screen.

Since Rosy Mae was off Saturdays, it had become our custom to have TV dinners, or hot dogs, or fried chicken from the concession stand. But this night, perhaps because Mom didn't want us to forget she could cook when she had to, we had a big dinner of roast ham, bacon-dripped green beans, brown gravy, and mashed potatoes so light and fluffy you could have tossed them skyward and they would have floated like a cloud. It was as if Mom were trying to compete with Rosy. And as amazing as Mama's food was, competing against Rosy was like trying to play against a royal flush with a busted flush.

We finished eating, and were about to go about our business, when we heard the front door open, which we seldom locked (though that would change), and we heard a voice call out, "You Mitchels in there?"

It was Rosy Mae, calling from the front door. She was leaning in, acting as if she had never been in our house before.

Mom called out, "Come in, Rosy Mae."

Rosy Mae came, stood in the doorway of the kitchen, clutching her paisley purse to her as if she were holding a kitten.

Her head rag was gone and her woolly hair was twisted up in braids that bounced about her head like sprung bedsprings. Her black face had patches of greater darkness around the eyes and her lips were swollen and there was a cut on her lip, red as original sin. Her dress was stretched at the neck and her right shirtsleeve was torn, ripped to the shoulder.

"My God," Mom said. "What happened to you?"

"I didn't want to bother y'all none, but I jes' didn't know where else to go. My old man, Bubba Joe, he done beat the tar out of me, and I guess I had it comin', sassin' him back and all, but he done scared me this time. Pulled a knife. He tole me he gonna cut me up."

Mom went to the refrigerator, broke open an ice tray, poured the ice on top of a cup towel, folded it up. "We'll see if we can bring some of that swelling down on your eye. Poor girl. Did you call the police?"

"Nawsum. Ain't no use in that. I done tole the po-leece before. They say it's a personal matter, and a nigger want to beat his woman, that ain't none of their business. Besides, we ain't married."

"Then you don't even have a license to fight," Daddy said.

"No suh, we don't."

"That's not funny, Stanley," Mom said.

Mom led Rosy Mae to a chair at the table, pressed the towel full of ice to the left side of her face, which was the side most swollen. At that angle, her hair looked like knotty snakes; she could have been Medusa.

"This is the worst spot," Mom said.

"Yessum, he hits me mostly with the right, so it's the worst. He hits pretty good with the left too. But he likes to hits me mostly with the right. And he got a ring on that hand."

"What in heaven's sake could this have been over?" Daddy said.

"I sassed him."

"About what?" Daddy said.

"What?" Mom said. "Like it matters what. You ought to be able to sass a man and not expect a whipping."

"Well, some women don't know their place," Daddy said.

"Stanley Senior," Mom said. "I'll tell you now, my place is pretty much where I put it. You hear?"

Daddy didn't answer, but it was plain from the color of his face that he was embarrassed, and it was plain from the slump of his shoulders he knew it was time to shut up on the matter. It was he who knew his place.

"A man ever hit me," Mom said, "he better never go to sleep."

She looked at Dad as if he might be considering such a thing. He looked back, shocked.

"Yessum," Rosy Mae said. "That's what I was thinkin'. I get him when he sleeps. I gots me an ole chicken axe out back under a bucket. I use it to kill my fryers, but I could kill him like a chicken if he was asleep. He have to be asleep. He a big man. I thought too I could throw lye in his mean ole face. Lots of niggers I know throw lye, and it sure work good. Put your eyes out, cut the color on a nigger's face . . . But I ain't got no heart to do neither . . . I don't know why I come here, Miss Mitchel. I jes' didn't know no other place for me to go. He prob'ly won't bother me at a white person's house. That's what I'm thinkin', see."

"You just sit there until you feel better," Mom said. "And let me fix you a plate."

"That's mighty nice of you, ma'am, but I don't know I ought to be sittin' here at y'alls dinner table and you fixin' me no plate."

"That's another thing," Mom said. "You work for us, you sit at the table from now on and take your meals with us."

I saw Daddy give Mom a look, but Mom gave him one back that could have sheared the horns off a bull.

"Callie, you get Rosy Mae a fork, knife, plate and napkin. Fix her a good plate. Stanley Junior, you get her ice tea."

Callie and I got the stuff and brought it over. When Callie set the plate in front of Rosy Mae, she patted her on the shoulder.

"Now, what did he hit you about?" Mom said.

"It doesn't matter," Daddy said. "You said so yourself. Just some sassin'.."

"No matter what, he didn't have call for this," Mom said. "But why he hit her matters to me. If, of course, you want to talk about it, Rosy."

"He hit me 'cause I ain't been givin' him all the money I make here. He wants it all, but he jes' gambles and drinks it. He been wantin' me to go out and do another little work, but I ain't doin' it."

"What little work?" Mom asked.

"Well now, Miss Mitchel, I can't talk on that with the chil'ren here."

Mom's eyes widened.

"Oh," she said.

"Yesum, that's the work. And I ain't gonna do it. He done run him some womens like that befoe, but I'm a good decent woman, and I ain't gonna do none of that. Not for no one. Even if'n they beat me. He gonna kill me fo' I do that."

"He beat you because you told him no?"

"I sorta made it a little too clear, sassy-like. He didn't 'preciate that none. He'll cool down, though. He always does. When he gets off the drinkin' a day or two and sobers up. Then he'll be pretty good for a time. It's 'round Fridays, when my payday come, that's when he gets all swirly-wigged. By Monday, Tuesday, he doin' better."

"That gives you maybe two good days a week," Mom said. "Rosy Mae, you don't need to go back to him tonight. You eat your dinner, then you're gonna sleep in the living room. I don't want you around that man."

Daddy was sitting with his mouth open, not knowing exactly what to say. Mom removed the iced towel from Rosy Mae's face, said, "Now, you go on and eat. We'll eat too."

Rosy Mae was tentative at first, but pretty soon hunger overtook her.

"How is it?" Mom asked.

"It really good, Miss Mitchel. Needs a little salt in them green beans, but it's real good and I thank you."

"Salt?" Mom asked.

"Yesum. Jes' a little, though."

When we were finished, Mom said, "Rosy Mae, you want, you go lay down in there on the couch. We got to open up the drive-in."

"Miss Mitchel," Rosy Mae said. "You gonna feed me and let me spend the night. I be glad to help you in the kitchen with the fried chicken. Anything you doin'."

"Well, there's no real cooking except the chicken," Mom said. "But sure. You can do that. But you get to feelin' tired or in pain, you come in and lay down on the couch."

"Thank you, kindly, ma'am."

"You're more than welcome, Rosy Mae."

Rosy Mae finished eating, went out to the concession's kitchen to help Mama fry chicken. I knew that was going to be the best fried chicken anyone ever had at the drive-in, or maybe anywhere else, and it would have just the right amount of salt.

Daddy sat at the kitchen table, looking in the direction of their retreat, an expression on his face like he had just awakened to find his old life was a dream and that his left foot was actually a cured ham.

Me and Callie finished eating, asked to be excused, told Daddy we'd be back in plenty of time to start helping with the drive-in work, went back to my room where we dragged out the box and Callie started reading from the letters.

"It's all from M to J. Were any real names mentioned?"

"I don't think so . . . I don't know. I haven't read all of that stuff."

"These last pages, they're out of a journal, or a diary . . . Well, this is odd."

"What's odd?"

"They're from a diary, but the diary seems to be the girl's diary. It reads in the same way as the letters. With it bound up and in a padlocked box, you get the idea it's something someone treasured, but wanted to keep secret. That makes me think it all belongs to one person, this J. I guess it could belong to the girl who wrote the letters and the journal, and she never sent the letters. You know. Wishful thinking . . . Or maybe J gave them back. That happens sometimes when people break up. Back then, during the war, letters were prized more highly than now, Stanley."

"How come there's just pages torn from the diary? Where's the rest of it?"

"That is odd, isn't it?"

Callie examined the journal closely. "Here's something interesting, though you may be too young to hear it."

"I've heard more lately than I knew there was," I said. "I don't believe a little more information will kill me."

"She's talking about sexual activity in the journal. She says . . . I don't know if I should read this to you. Maybe you should look at it."

She gave it to me. I read it. I said, "What's fingering?"

Callie turned red. "That's why I had you read it, silly. I didn't want to say it or explain it."

"Well, I read it, but now you explain it."

She did.

I said, "Oh," and gave it back to her.

"She's talking about what she and this boy, J, did. She says they did it out back in the woods, on a blanket. She doesn't say any more in detail, just that they made each other happy. That means they did it."

"Did what?"

"Oh, for heaven's sake, Stanley, you are dense. Remember about the dogs?"

"Oh, yeah."

I felt worse than when I discovered there was no Santa Claus. Here was something that was going on that everyone seemed to know about but me.

"You said they did it in the woods. You mean the woods where the old house was?"

"I don't know. I think the house would have been there when these letters were written. So probably not. I think M tore these pages out of her diary and gave them to J as a kind of memento. I think that's it, and that's why J has M's pages.

"I think maybe you've had enough of this for now. I don't want you blowing out a fuse. You're going to need a better hiding place for this than under the bed. Mom or Rosy Mae are eventually going to come across it . . . I'll be."

Callie was reading from the pages. I said, "What?"

"She thinks she might be pregnant . . . Listen to this. 'I'm sorry about the baby. But it will be okay. Things can be done.' She's talking about getting rid of it before it's born, Stanley. And here's more. 'Or we can learn to live with the idea. Having a baby around wouldn't be so bad.' "

"What do you mean, getting rid of it?"

Callie spent a few minutes explaining.

"You can do that?"

"Some doctors will do it, but it's against the law."

"So J must have lived in the house in the trees?"

"I suppose. It wasn't in the trees then, though."

"I know that."

"You can never be certain with you, Stanley. Thing to do, when we get time, is find out who owned the old burned-down house. That might help us decide who the box belongs to."

"That sounds great. Like a mystery. Like the Hardy Boys. Or Nancy Drew."

"It's interesting, Stanley, but it isn't exactly something that drives me to distraction. Understand?"

"Sounds to me like a murder."

"Guess it could be that," Callie said. "J didn't really love her like M loved him, and when she got pregnant, he decided to get rid of her. It could have happened that way. But if he hated her, why did he keep the letters?"

"He hid them?"

"Why didn't he just destroy them?"

"See," I said. "You are interested."

"I suppose. But that doesn't mean I'm nuts to figure it out. I'm just saying, since I got nothing else to do with my summer, maybe we can take a crack at it. Maybe not. We'll see. Come on. We got to help Mom and Daddy."

Callie went out. I put the box in my closet on the top shelf and put a folded shirt over it and my Davy Crockett coonskin cap on top of that.

———

THE LAST SHOWING of *Vertigo* finished well after midnight. It was like that in the dead of summer. It got dark late, so to make two showings, you had to go into early morning.

That night they packed the place. Everyone wanted to see the new Hitchcock film. I saw none of it, of course. I was waiting for our family get-together.

I spent time helping out at the concession, and when we closed at eleven, Daddy took position at the exit to make sure no one was trying to sneak in for the last hour of the movie.

It took about an hour to clean up, and Rosy Mae's disposition seemed much better. She even hummed a bit while she used woolen mitts to pour the grease from the frying pot into a barrel.

Rosy Mae washed the pot and other dishes, and when she finished, she asked if I wanted to go out front while she smoked a cigarette, as she was afraid of her man, Bubba Joe, and my mother did not allow smoking in the house by friend or relative.

Mom overheard us, said, "I wish he wouldn't go out front. It frightens me to think Bubba Joe might be out there. Why don't you go on the roof and let Stanley keep you company?"

"Yesum," Rosy Mae said.

We went upstairs, walked a slanted ramp that opened on to the roof by a trapdoor. We stepped out just below the giant dew drop.

The last of the cars could be seen filing out of the drive-in, their lights coming on, poking at the night. I could see Buster leaving the concession stand, his thermos in his hand, walking toward the exit, moving slowly by the cars as they exited. I thought I heard someone yell "nigger" from one of the cars.

Buster didn't look up. He kept walking.

Rosy Mae got out a can of Sir Walter Raleigh and shook some tobacco onto a rolling paper. She folded it quickly with one hand, licked, slipped it into her mouth, smooth as any cowboy.

She removed a big kitchen match from her wild hair, cocked her hip, struck it on the side of her dress, and lit up.

"Oooooeeee," she said. "I needed that."

She began coughing almost immediately.

"I don't need that none. Hit me on the back, Mr. Stanley."

I did, sharply.

"Thanks. It done went down the wrong pipe."

"You don't need to call me Mr.," I said. "I'm just a boy."

"Yessuh, but you a white boy."

"Call me Stanley."

"All right, Stanley."

"This man of yours . . . Is he dangerous?"

"Scares me. I know some niggers run the other way they see him comin'. I carries me a razor."

Rosy Mae reached into a fold of her dress and produced it, flicked it open. The blade lapped like a tongue, cut some darkness, flicked closed, went into her dress.

"He carry one too, though. And he done cut folks with his. I ain't never cut nobody. But I did threaten me a nigger with it once. He got on my wrong side, that's what I'm tryin' to tell you. But I don't want to cut nobody. 'Specially him."

"You love him?"

"I shuly do, Stanley. I do. I don't know why and shouldn't, but I do. I ought to take the ole chicken axe to him, but I won't. He don't do nothin' but make me crazy and sad. He messes with other women, drinks somethin' awful, plays them cards, shoots that dice all the time. He ain't no good at all."

"Then why do you love him?"

"I couldn't begin to tell, honey. I ain't got no reason. Men's got their reasons, and they reasons ain't much and don't last long. But a woman. She ain't got no real reason. She jes' does."

"But you're scared of him?"

"I am. I loves him, but I hates him too."

"Does he love you?"

"I don't know he loves nobody. He don't even love himself. And Mr. Stanley . . . Stanley. You got to love yo'self 'fore you can love most anything. Even if'n it's a flower, or some old bush you a growin'. You hear what I'm sayin'?"

"Yes, ma'am."

"You so polite."

"So you think he could hurt you?"

"I do. But don't jedge on him too hard. You know what the Bible say about not jedgin' least you be jedged yo'self?"

"I don't know," I said.

"Well it says that. Somewhere. Or so I been told by a preacher, but since he had his hand on my knee, I don't know he was tellin' the truth. I told him, you maybe ought not to jedge, but I sho ought to tell you to get yo' hand off my knee. And he did . . . Bubba Joe, he done had it hard, Mr. Stanley."

"Just Stanley."

"Yes, suh. He done been put down by the white mens hard."

"White men? How?"

Rosy Mae laughed. "Oh, chile, you just the sweetest thing. And don't know nothin', and that good right now, 'cause someday you'll know somethin' and you gonna be different. All coloreds be niggers then."

"I don't think so."

"I hope you right, honey. I truly do."

"How's he been put down, Rosy Mae?"

Rosy Mae sucked at her cigarette, blew smoke in a little white cloud that hung about her nose, spread, and faded.

"He a man, Stanley. Jes' like you gonna be when you grow up. Like yo daddy. He a man. And Bubba Joe, he treated like a boy. White man calls him boy, and he a grown man. Bigger than most men you ever see. He six three, weigh near three hundred pounds. Stong as an ox. And I tell you another thing. He a war hero."

"Really?"

"That's right. He go over there to Korea, and he a hero. Got him a wound that cause him to walk a little stiff. But when he come back, come into Dallas, he told to go to the back of the bus. Told he can't eat with white folks. He mean 'cause of them ways he been treated, Stanley. Way his family been treated.

"When he a boy, them Kluxers, they hear Bubba Joe's daddy stole a watermelon and a chicken 'cause his family hungry, and they take Bubba Joe's daddy down in them bottoms and whup him good. Then they take off his clothes, and they got this big ole cottonmouth in a tow sack, and they make his daddy put his foot in that bag with that snake, and they tie the bag around his leg and waist so he can't shake it off, and they tie his hands behind his back and leave him."

I had a sensation like someone rubbing an ice cube along the top of my skull.

"What did he do?"

"Well, Bubba Joe get this story from his daddy, and he tell it to me on one of his good times, when he's happy I'm with him. Say his daddy can't just stay in the woods till either he or the snake dies, so he try to walk home. He do all right at first, then the snake slip down to the bottom of the bag, and he step on it, and it gets its fangs hung in the bag. Now, he thinks he can walk on while the snake's hung up, and he do good for a time, then the snake works loose, and he bites Bubba Joe's daddy, and by the time he get to the house, he done been bit, three, fo' times."

"Did he die?"

"Might near. But they take him over to a colored man works on horses and such, and he cuts the leg off 'cause it done turned black as the bottom of a well, and swole up big as an oak tree trunk. Bubba Joe's daddy lives, but now he can't work no mo'. And he turns mean. He gave some of that mean to Bubba Joe. Coloreds got reason to be mean, but it may be worse on a colored man 'cause he don't never get to be no man 'cept in his own house, and he overdo it. He knows he goes out, he jes' another nigger. Some little white boy comes along, he got to step off the sidewalk. Little white boy can call him boy, and he has to grin and live with it. Wears on a person."

"Does it wear on you, Rosy Mae?"

"Yes, chile. It shuly does. But all that said, it ain't no excuse for doin' the wrong thing to people. They's lots of people ain't happy, but you don't get no happier makin' people unhappy. Least you shouldn't. Well, I done smoked my smoke. We ought to go on back down see there's anything we can do 'sides set a fire and rob a bank."

"Rosy Mae? Do you know anything about the house that

stood where those trees are?" I pointed in the direction of the pine stand beside the drive-in.

"That ole place belong to the Stilwinds. They a big important family, and they still 'round here. That house, burn down on the same night little Miss Margret Wood was messed with and murdered. And when it burn down, it burn up that young Stilwind girl, Jewel Ellen. Hard to believe how fast them pine trees growed up after that house burned down. That was in, let me see, nineteen and forty-five. 'Course, that ole oak and some of them elms and them sweet gums out to the side there, they always been there long as I can remember. They jes' bigger."

"Who was Miss Margret?"

"Why she a young girl then, about fifteen. I think me and her about the same age when that happen."

"Who murdered her?"

"Ain't nobody know."

"Was she murdered in that house?"

"Where you get such an idea? Miss Jewel Ellen die in that house. In the fire. Miss Margret, she killed over by the tracks. Someone do somethin' mean to her. And Mr. Stanley, you and me don't need to talk about what that was. That ain't for me and you to discuss. But I tell you she was laid out with her head put on them railroad tracks, an' that ole train come along and cut it right off. That's what I hear, anyway. They never did find her head. Say her ghost still wander down there, where the woods run close to the tracks. That's where she was murdered. They was this man say he thought he saw an ole stray dog runnin' along down there with that head in its mouth. But that could have been a wolf. Or a wolf's man."

"A wolf's man?"

"Mr. Stanley—"

"Stanley."

"Stanley. White folks don't believe this, lot of coloreds

don't. But I believes there's mens can turn themselves into wolfs and such. That a wolf's man. Like the movie with the wolf's man. I ain't sayin' no wolf's man got her head now, I'm jes' sayin' could have been. It might have been an ole stray dog or other varmints. It might have been smashed like a pumpkin when that train hit her. It might have been cut off 'fo she was put on the tracks. Ain't no one ever find Miss Margret's head. But they say her ghost down there lookin' for her head most nights and I believe that. I ain't never seen it myself, but I done hear on it plenty from them has."

"What started the fire?"

"Oh, chile, I don't know. I jes' remember it burnin' down and that sweet Jewel Ellen burning up."

"You knew her?"

"I know'd them all. My mama used to wash the mess out of that whole family's drawers, and that Miss Margret, she live on across town in the lesser part. You see, this here used to be money here. Right where the drive-in stand. Then money move on over there a ways. You know all them big pretty houses 'cross the highway?"

"Yes, ma'am. Well, I know they're there. I've never really looked at them."

"I don't know lookin' such a good idea. I look over there, I feel how that Lot's wife felt in the Bible when she looked back on stuff she wanted, and God turn her to that pillar of salt. 'Course, she least got to have it oncet. I ain't never had it none. Ain't never gonna. Ain't no need for God to turn me to nothin' for lookin' back. There ain't no lookin' back. Place I live ain't nothin' but a nigger rent house. I don't be lookin' forward or back."

"What about Margret?"

"Miss Margret live over on the other side of town, 'cross

them tracks. It's the place where the poor whites live, down by the swamp land. Their house set off a bit from the others.

"Miss Margret was poor, but seemed like she had it pretty good to me. My momma would have jes' wanted to move us up that much. For her, it would have been a castle. Miss Margret had a yard out back, even if it was wet land, and the house was painted up white and nice, and it was big enough she might have had her own bedroom. And Miss Margret, she jes' as pretty as could be. Had dark hair and dark eyes and this real pretty skin, and she smile, she got a big smile, and a big silver tooth right next to these front two.

"I use to see her 'round. She didn't have no daddy 'cause he run off when Miss Margret born. That's how I heard it. I think he was some kind of Mex'kin and white man mixed up, or some such thing, and her mama got some Indi'n blood."

"So they weren't really white?"

"Well, when you a colored girl, they white. Miss Margret look like she gonna grow up to be a movie star, she so pretty. I really liked that tooth, though I don't know white people would make no movie star out of some girl with a silver tooth.

"I hear her mama was kinda mean, though. Really don't know much about 'em 'sides little Miss Margret was nice. Both her and that Jewel Ellen was nice. That brother of Jewel Ellen, James Ray, he not always so nice. He pinch me on my bottom oncet. I'm on the street, carryin' white people's wash home to be done by my mama, and he pinch me on the rear end and laugh and say he give me money I do somethin' for him. I got away from there real quick."

I thought: M for Margret and J for James. Some of the mystery was coming together.

"Is James still around?"

"After they house burned down, he growed up, lived on the hill over there where the money is. Guess he still live there. He

own a big store downtown. Men's shop with suits and the little drugstore next to it, and the picture show. Colored can buy
hamburgers and get a pop out back the drugstore. Movie house
has a big upstairs and it's where the colored go. But, James
Ray, I don't really know so much about him. He don't 'vite me
over for supper, you see. All I remember was him wantin' to
pinch my bottom, and I wasn't but a girl.

"Come on, now. I don't want no one thinkin' I'm takin'
leave 'cause your momma been nice to me. Let's go down see
there's anything left we can do . . . And, Stanley, you tell me. I
shouldn't have mentioned that salt in them green beans, should
I?"

"No, ma'am."

"I know'd it when I done it. But I jes' couldn't helps myself."

———————

THAT NIGHT after the drive-in was closed and Rosy Mae was
given a place to sleep on the couch, I slipped out of my room,
leaving Nub to curl up on my bed, opened Callie's door, stuck
my head inside. "Callie?"

"What are you doing?" she said.

"I wanted to talk."

"You've talked to me more in the last two days than since
the time you learned to talk."

"I found out some stuff about the old house that burned
down."

"Oh . . . Come in."

I sat on the foot of her bed. Callie sat up in bed and turned
her face toward me. I couldn't make out her features completely. Her dark hair was undone and fell down to her shoulders. In the moonlight I could see a bit of her face and the horse

designs on her pajamas. The water-cooled fan beat the warm air into near submission.

"What do you know?" she asked.

I told her what Rosy Mae told me.

"That's kind of creepy, Stanley. To think a little girl burned up right over there."

"What's creepy," I said, "is that a little girl named Margret was murdered on the same night as Jewel Ellen Stilwind died, and her brother's name was James. Don't you think it's odd, Callie, that the letters we have are from an M to a J? Margret to James, who got her pregnant."

"It may not be connected at all. You certainly didn't even know how a girl got pregnant until I told you."

"I know now. Come on, it's interesting? Right?"

"Tomorrow, maybe we'll look into it. Right now, I got to sleep. I'm exhausted. Beat it."

I told Callie what Rosy said about Margret's ghost, about her missing head and the wolf's man.

"Oh, poo. I don't believe that. Coloreds are always telling ghost stories. Besides, I don't want to hear that right now. This whole thing is kind of scary to me and I don't want bad dreams. Now beat it."

"It isn't any harder for this to be connected, than believing someone stuck that balloon through your window when your bedroom was downstairs."

"Stanley, you little shit, get out of my room."

I beat it with regrets, knowing full well I shouldn't have added that zinger, not if I wanted Callie's help. But, heck, it was the brotherly thing to do; I couldn't help myself.

I didn't go right to sleep. I got the letters out from under my bed and looked at them. I read the journal carefully. Nothing in the letters or the journal mentioned Margret's last name. But I was convinced these letters had been to James and that Margret had torn out the journal pages and given them to him, maybe to keep her mother from seeing them, or as a gesture of some kind.

I put the letters and pages up, went to bed, dreamed of a decapitated girl walking along the railroad tracks, searching for her missing head. I dreamed too of a wolf's man, as Rosy called it, running through the brush with Margret's head in its mouth.

5

NEXT MORNING after breakfast, I pulled Callie aside and we walked out to the drive-in lot.

"Are you going to help me find out more?"

"Oh, I don't know."

"Last night you said you would."

"I didn't say for certain. It sounded like fun last night. But in the light of day, I'm not so sure. What if it is the same Margret? So what?"

"She was murdered. No one ever found the murderer. That's a real mystery, Callie. James Stilwind lives over on the hill with the rich folks. He might know something."

"You're just going to knock on his door and ask him about his burned-up sister and a murdered girl named Margret, and a boxful of letters he might have owned?"

"I hadn't really thought about what I was going to do. Not really. Are you going to help or what?"

"I'm not allowed to go anywhere. So what can I do?"

"But last night . . ."

"I forgot. I forget about it ten times a day because I didn't do anything. Then there was that crack about the balloon . . . So, just solve your own stupid mystery."

Callie crunched across the lot's gravel, back toward our house, which was an odd way to think about a movie screen thick enough to contain two stories, a roof view, and all the comforts of home.

I got my bicycle out of the storage shed, placed Nub over my thighs, and rode across the highway into the residential area where the rich folks lived.

For the first time I really noticed the houses there.

They were built along different designs, but all were big and fresh-looking, as if someone came daily to wipe them down from roof to porch. Some of the porches were big enough for a family of four to live on. All the other houses were equally as magnificent.

I put Nub down so he could run alongside me. I rode on through the neighborhood until the steep hill got to be too much, then I pushed my bicycle, checking the names on mailboxes. They were all neat mailboxes with black lettering, and not a one was different from the other in size and design. None of them said Stilwind.

I came across a girl playing in her front yard that looked to have not only been mowed, but manicured with nail clippers. She was sitting at a little table with chairs, a tea set, and dolls. She wore a pink dress and had a pink bow in her shiny blond hair. She looked as if she were about to go to church.

I called to her from the street. "Do you know where the Stilwinds live?"

"No. Why are you dressed like a nigger?"

"What do you mean?"

"Well, you're wearing those blue jeans with the cuffs rolled up."

"All the kids do."

She took a sip from her teacup, said, "Not around here. Your mama make you that shirt?"

"So what?"

"A feed sack and a Butterick pattern?"

"It's not a feed sack . . . It's plaid."

"I don't wear homemades, and I don't wear hand-me-downs."

"So?"

"That little dog looks like a mutt."

"You look like a mutt," I said.

"Well, I never," she said, standing up from her little chair and placing a hand on her hip.

I rolled my bike on, and when I was away from her, I glanced down at myself. My blue jeans were patched, and the shirt I had on was a little thin and faded in spots, but I looked okay. Surely the folks over here didn't dress up all the time, just to play or ride bikes.

I passed three teenage boys tossing a football. They were wearing jeans and tennis shoes just like me. But there was a difference. They looked as tidy and confident as bankers, and as the little girl had reported, they didn't cuff the legs of their jeans.

I was about to get on my bike and start riding again, when one of the boys tossing the ball in the yard called out to me.

"Who are you?"

I turned, looked at him. He was tall and blond. Probably seventeen or eighteen. He repeated himself. I told him who I was.

"You're kind of in the wrong neighborhood, aren't you, kid? You know what happened last time a white-trash kid came over here, bringing some little rat of a dog with him. I tell you what happened. He disappeared. Him and his little dog."

One of the boys, darker and stockier, walked closer to the edge of the curb. As he neared, I could smell his hair oil. The aroma was sweet and expensive, unlike the Vitalis on my head.

"They found that boy dead alongside the railroad track with his pants down and his little dog stuffed head-first up his ass," Stocky said. "The dog was still alive, 'cause when they came up on it, it wagged its tail."

He and the blond boy laughed.

I knew it was a big joke, but it made me uncomfortable just the same.

"I'm no white trash," I said.

"You aren't from the hill," the blond boy said, "so you have to be."

"I'm from the drive-in. Down there."

The blond boy grew serious. "Oh. Well, I go to the drive-in now and then. It's all right. No hard feelings. I take dates to that drive-in. I don't want to get in bad there. I was just kidding. You know how joking is."

The third boy, who so far had not spoken, walked over to the curb holding the football. He was tall and thin with brown hair, probably nice-looking. The other boys began walking back into the yard. He turned and tossed them the football. The blond kid caught it.

"Don't pay them any mind," he said. "They think they're funny. But they're about as funny as a screen door on a submarine. You just have to ignore them. My name's Drew. Drew Cleves."

I knew that name. It was the boy Callie had mentioned last night, that she liked. I decided not to mention that.

"You live here?" I asked.

"No. I live the house over."

"Do you know where the Stilwinds live?"

"Oh yeah. Top of the hill. Around the curve. Dead center where the street ends. But they don't really live there anymore. No one lives there. They have it for sale. But no one wants that house."

"Why?"

"They say it's haunted. I've heard all kinds of stories about it growing up."

"Does it look haunted?"

"Just a little run-down. But there was some kind of murder there. Or maybe it wasn't a murder. The story is kind of vague."

"Then the Stilwinds don't live in Dewmont?"

"Oh, they do, but just not up there. I don't know exactly where they live. Different places. There's several of them, you know. But I couldn't tell you where. Why do you want to know?"

"Just curious. Many years ago they used to have a house out back of our drive-in. Burned down."

"I've heard that," Drew said. "My father knew them then. I understand they built the one here not long after the fire. I've never really been that curious about it. Went up there once with Tatum, that's him."

He pointed at the blond kid. "We were maybe twelve. Don't tell anybody, but we broke out a back window with a rock. It's a little spooky-looking is all. Hey, I heard you say you're one of the new people. The drive-in owners?"

I nodded.

"I met your sister, Callie, at the Piggly Wiggly at the beginning of the summer. She's very pretty."

"Some think so. She tried to get a part-time job at the Piggly Wiggly."

"Did she get hired?"

"No. My parents say it's a good place to shop, though."

"I just get a candy bar and a Coke there now and then. My parents wouldn't be caught dead shopping at the Piggly Wiggly."

"Oh."

"Hey, that's them. I'd shop there if I shopped. I figure a loaf of bread tastes like a loaf of bread no matter where you get it."

"I suppose you're right."

"Callie's seeing Chester White, isn't she?"

"Not anymore. My dad doesn't like him. In fact, he beat him up."

"Your father made a good choice. To beat Chester up, I mean. He's not the best of people. Why did he beat him up?"

I decided to lie. "I don't know exactly."

"I'm sure he had a good reason. Hey, you ought to come over and throw the football around with us sometime."

"Sure."

"Now, if you want."

I thought, here's a boy who wants to see my sister bad.

"No, thanks," I said. "I'm going to see the house and go home. I got things to do later."

Drew stuck out his hand. I shook it. He said, "Nice meeting you. Give my best to your sister. And don't pay these mooks any mind. They don't know dog doo from a hairdo. The house . . . it's right at the top of the hill."

I nodded, went up the street pushing my bicycle, Nub trotting beside me, his tongue hanging out, dripping water.

Before me and Nub had gone very far it turned dark and the wind picked up. Glancing at the sky, I saw a huge raincloud had settled over us like a black umbrella. The wind was welcome though. It was cool and smelled of rain and there was a crackle to the air that made the hair on my arms stand up.

When we got to the top of the hill it curved slightly. I pushed my bike around the turn, and there, dead center, as Drew had described it, stood the Stilwind house. A FOR SALE sign with a real estate agent's name on it poked up in the front yard.

From a distance, it was not too unlike the other houses in the area, but as I grew closer I could see it was in great need of paint and the windows were specked with surprised bugs and water spots and the front door was swollen like a drunkard's belly. The hedges grew too high, losing design, and the cement walk along front, side, and back of the house was hairline-cracked in many places. The oak trees near the house were moving in the wind and waving their boughs against the roof with a sound like cats scratching in a litterbox. You could see where the wind-pushed limbs had torn loose shingles and tossed them in the yard like an old man peeling dead skin from his feet.

Still, the house was so magnificent on its wooded acreage I actually gasped. I got off my bike and kicked the kick stand out to support it, stood looking at the house.

Nub sat in the street and looked at the house with me, turning his head from side to side.

"What do you think, boy?"

Nub didn't seem to have an opinion.

I walked up the drive, climbed the steps, and knocked on the bulging door, certain, of course, no one would answer. Nub sat on his haunches, watching me, trying to determine in his little dog brain exactly what I was doing.

No one answered.

Me and Nub walked around back of the house, saw a massive heart-shaped swimming pool with a tall diving board. As I neared it, there was a burst of crows, like pieces of night exploding from the ground. They beat up to the sky, stalled, spread out and fled in all directions. They came together in the distance as if it had all been planned, and dissolved into the trees.

A dead armadillo was lying on the bottom of the empty pool. It was almost flat, the crows having helped themselves to the better morsels, picking at it along with weather and time.

Shrubs lined the remains of the tennis court, which had cracked and given way to yellow weeds and grass burrs. Beyond all this was a small pecan orchard and a great expanse of woods.

I walked to the back of the house and touched the back door. It slid open slightly and jammed where it had swollen at the bottom. I pushed harder and made enough room to go inside.

It was dark with patches of dirty light shining through the dusty windows. The place smelled. Beneath it all was that biting stench of rat's nests and mildew.

I slipped inside and Nub followed, staying close to my leg. My eyes became adjusted to the darkness, but the smell was almost overwhelming.

I noticed there were footprints in the dust. Some of the prints were from animals, like squirrels, maybe a coon, but there were human footprints as well. Little feet in narrow shoes. As we came to a wide staircase, I saw the prints went upstairs.

We stopped at its base and I looked up and considered, but decided against it. The upper floor was crowded with shadows, as if something had squeezed them all into one spot, fastened them there with a wrap of invisible chain.

I had the uneasy feeling that something lay at the top of the stairs, just where the steps curved to the upper landing.

Nub looked up the stairs. I saw the hair on his back stand

up like porcupine quills, then he growled. I strained to see if anything was there, but saw nothing, heard nothing.

Then a shadow, shaped like a crone in a Halloween carnival, fled along the wall and went away.

That was enough for me.

Softly calling Nub, we went away from there very fast. Outside the air was cool and sharp with rain. It flushed the stench of mildew, rat's nest, and discomfort out of my head. I dismissed the shadow as nothing more than a trick of the light.

I mounted my bike. Beneath that dark cloud, the aroma of rain in my nostrils, I started pedaling down, Nub running along beside me, his tongue hanging out like a small pink sock.

I zoomed along with the wind in my hair, raindrops striking my face. As I came to the bottom of the hill, my speed picked up, and before I knew it, the highway loomed before me.

I stepped back on the pedal with everything I had, putting the brakes on hard, but that big J.C. Higgins bike wasn't having any of that. The tires glided over the slightly damp cement and the Higgins turned sideways, fell over, dropped my leg hard against the concrete.

I skidded right out into the middle of the highway. There was a blaring sound so loud my hair stood on end. I saw the grillework of a Big As Doom Mack Truck bearing down on me, knew right then there was a good chance I was going to miss that planned showing of *Vertigo* with the family, and most anything else that would come up a second later.

In that instant I felt neither fear or regret, just resignation.

As I continued to slide, I glimpsed Nub out of the corner of my eye, running between me and the truck. The horn blared again and something smacked me.

PART TWO

Buster Abbot Lighthorse Smith

6

"YOU WERE LUCKY," Richard said.

It was three days after the accident. Richard Chapman was sitting in a chair by my bed writing his name on the cast on my left leg with a pencil stub he kept wetting by poking it into his mouth. His writing was slow and deliberate, so damp it was smeary.

"That probably won't be there long," I said.

"I'll write it again," he said. "Next time I'll use ink."

As he wrote, he leaned forward so his long brown hair hung almost to his chin. As it dipped toward my leg, Nub, who was lying beside me, sniffed the tips of it with a wrinkled nose. Considering Nub would lick his ass hour on end, yet seemed offended by the smell of Richard's hair, I assumed my friend's locks were fairly ripe.

"I was really lucky, I wouldn't have got hit at all," I said. "I wouldn't have a broken leg. My bike wouldn't be a bunch of bent-up metal. I wouldn't be spending most of what's left of the summer in a cast. I'm just glad Nub wasn't hurt."

"You could'a been smashed like a possum, truck that big."

"Driver saw me, slammed on his brakes. Nub ran past me and another car went right over him. Mrs. Johnson was standing in her yard and she saw it all, told Mom and Mom told me."

"Who is she?"

"She lives down from the drive-in a bit. Mom knows her some. She's the one came and got me and my bike out of the highway. Her and the truck driver. It wasn't his fault. I slid right out in front of him."

"Did you think it was all over, you seen that truck?"

"I didn't think much of anything. Not until the hospital anyway, and they were putting the cast on me."

"You really don't remember the in-betweens? Don't remember the truck running over your leg?"

"Nope. Truck didn't break my leg. I did it sliding on the road, that's what Mrs. Johnson says. I got a real bad case of concrete rash, that's for sure. My head got banged too. If I had been sitting up the truck would have knocked my head off. I just sort of slid under it and it passed over me, way that car did Nub."

"I got an arrow run right through my side oncet. I made it myself, sharpened it with my pocketknife, and I fell on it runnin'. It went right through the meat on my side. Hurt like the dickens, but I didn't get nothing but a hole in my side and some blood. I got over it quick. I had to. Daddy put me in the fields cutting down dead corn stalks with a scythe. He don't cotton much to foolish injury."

"I wish I'd got an arrow through my side. It beats this."

Richard finished writing his name, flipped his oily hair

back in place, and tossed the pencil onto my nightstand, atop a stack of comic books.

"You want me to bring you some more funny books? I want 'em back, but you can borrow 'em."

"Got any more *Batman*?"

"Naw, just them. I got some *Superman* funny books, though. I can't buy the new ones. They're a dime. But in the back of Mr. and Mrs. Greene's store, they got them with half the cover cut off. There might be some *Batman* there. They're just a nickel. I'll be checking when I get a nickel."

"Why are they cut like that?"

"They don't sell after a time, they cut off half the cover, send it back, they get their money back, then they sell the funny book anyway. For a nickel. Ain't supposed to, but they do. I got to hide all mine 'cause my daddy will tear them up. Actually, he takes them out to the outhouse and wipes his ass on 'em. He says they're devil's stuff. I thought about that, and I couldn't picture no devil reading a *Batman* comic book."

"He won't let you read comics?"

"He don't think you ought to read nothin' but the Bible. He calls all them books man-made book learnin'. He wants me to drop out of school I get a little older, go to work. He says that's what a man does. Reckon I will drop out."

"I'm surprised your dad doesn't want you to be a preacher."

"He don't want nobody but him to be a preacher. What's your daddy want you to be?"

"Whatever I want. He always tells me to find something I'd like to do for free and learn to make a living at it. I don't know what that is yet. Mama wants me to be a teacher."

"Your daddy lets her contradict him like that, tellin' you what to be after him sayin' do what you want?"

I was a little taken aback.

"Sure. He doesn't care."

"In our house my daddy runs things and what he says is how it is."

"I guess Mama runs things here."

"Your mama?"

"Daddy thinks he runs things, but Mama runs them."

"My mama don't run a thing. Daddy'll hit her in the mouth if she sasses back. He told me you got to treat a woman like a nigger sometimes."

"That doesn't sound right to me," I said. "No one should be treated that way."

"Well, I'm just sayin' what he said. Mama, she reads that Bible all the time, and that's the only thing Daddy gives her credit for. Hey, do you know Elvin Turner?"

"No."

"He beat up a nigger with a stick. It was just a little nigger, but Elvin beat him anyway because he said the nigger looked at him funny."

"I'm sure Elvin is proud," I said.

"He's pretty proud, all right, but I don't know Elvin could beat up much if he didn't have a stick. Even with that, that little nigger put up a pretty good fight . . . Got to go. My old man is gonna whup the tar out of me with a razor strap or that darn belt of his I don't get back in time to do chores."

"Thanks for loaning me the funny books, Richard."

"That's okay."

"Richard. Don't say nigger here. Rosy Mae might hear it and it might hurt her feelings."

"Oh. Well, okay."

"Something else. You ever heard about a ghost in the house on the hill?"

"Naw."

"What about by the railroad track?"

"The girl lookin' for her head? My daddy mentions her and her mother from time to time, and ain't none of what he mentions is good. Then again, he ain't got a lot of good to say about nobody less it's Jesus. I been down there at night couple of times, and it's spooky, that's what I'm tryin' to tell you."

"See any ghost?"

"Naw. But they say it's like a light that bounces around."

"I got this mystery going," I said. "It seems to have something to do with this girl."

"What kind of mystery?"

I briefly outlined it for him.

"I heard about that Stilwind house burnin' down from my daddy. He's talked about it several times. He worked for the Stilwinds, odd chores and stuff. But I didn't know the house used to be back there behind the drive-in."

"There wasn't any drive-in then. On your way home, go to the trees out back and look up. You'll see."

"I'll do that."

Richard left, scratching at the lice in his hair.

Rosy Mae came up a few minutes after Richard left. She had been living with us ever since the night she came in hurt and confused. She was still sleeping on the couch. She smiled big, said, "I swear, that Mr. Richard's momma need to hold him down and pour kerosene on his head and get rid of them bugs. Or get him some lye soap. I got me some I made from hog fat and lye and boiled mint leaves, and I'll give him a right smart piece, if'n he'll use it."

"He's all right," I said.

"He come to see you, didn't he?"

"Yes, ma'am."

"You is so polite. He bring them funny books?"

"Yes, ma'am."

"Then he all right, ain't he? He better than his daddy."

"How do you mean?"

"His daddy, he all the time nervous as a corn-fed duck on Christmas Day."

"Nervous?"

"Uh huh. He got that religion, and ain't a bit of it the way he understands it good to nobody but him. You know, twenty years ago, he a handsome man. But not now. He done let all that bitterness eat him up."

"What's he bitter about?"

"Lord if anyone knows. There's just some people like persimmons, they bitter when they born, sweet for a short time, then they go fast rotten."

Rosy Mae sat down in the chair Richard had occupied, picked up one of the comics from my nightstand, thumbed through it a bit. "I can read this and them movie magazines pretty good, but there's words I ain't never learned that throws me in books."

"I can help you learn to read better," I said.

"Can you now?"

"I can."

"I don't think I got the brains to learn more than I done learned."

"Sure you do."

Rosy Mae brightened. "Guess I can learn I want to. Learned to read them magazines, didn't I? Even if I got to skip and guess at some words. Learned to read what I read now so I'd know prices at stores and such. Had to learn so the white man down at the store, Mr. Phillips, don't overcharge me. He always adds a bit to colored people's stuff. 'Course, since we got to buy through the back door, it's hard to know he don't mark them prices up before we sees 'em."

Rosy Mae scratched at her woolly head.

"Either I gots me Mr. Richard's bugs, or I'm thinkin' I gots 'em. I'm gonna go down, wash up, and fix lunch. You want me to bring yours up?"

"If you don't mind."

"I will. And don't you lay up here now and starts to feel sorry for yo'self. You jes' got a broken leg. There's boys can't and ain't never been able to walk. You okay. You gonna heal up. You a little white boy with a good home and good mama and daddy. You could'a been me."

"All right, Rosy Mae. I won't feel sorry for myself. But there's nothing wrong with you."

"I thank you for that, Mr. Stanley."

"Just Stanley."

"Uh huh. You know your daddy done fixed your bike. He straightened out some of them spokes, got another bike from some junk, and he used them parts to fix yours. He done painted it up for you too. But it ain't that rust color no more. Now it's blue."

"That's great."

Rosy Mae went out, and contrary to her suggestion and my agreement, I lay there feeling sorry for myself, Nub lying across my chest, his eyes closed, one of his legs kicking as if he were having a bad dream.

Probably about the car that passed over him.

––––––––

OVER THE NEXT FEW DAYS I mostly stayed in my room with Nub. Daddy had Buster run *Vertigo* for a week, but never did have anyone over for a special showing.

I finally watched it from the veranda where there were speakers, and thought it was dumb. I could not believe anybody could be as stupid as Jimmy Stewart was in that movie.

Not long after that we got in a John Wayne cowboy movie. That one I liked.

My leg itched a lot and I straightened out a coat hanger to stick down in my cast to scratch. I carried that hanger with me wherever I went. I named it Larry.

Worse than the itch, however, was my head. It really ached. Not all the time, but often enough, and when the pain came it was like being hit all over again by that Mack Truck. It seemed as if there was a crack in my head and my brains were about to ooze out. But all I had was a big blue knot that pulsed like some kind of second head growing.

When my head wasn't killing me, I read Hardy Boys books, and when I tired of that, I managed the box out from under my bed and took to reading the letters and the journal again, this time more carefully, and completely.

I began to know something about Margret, began to feel certain she was the Margret that ended up dead, down by the railroad track, her head cut off. There were hints in the letters.

She talked about how at night she could hear the trains go by and how they rattled the glass in the window of her bedroom and how lonesome the whistle sounded and how much her mother drank and yelled at her. She wrote about her mother's "friends" and how her mother took them in and they paid her money. She never said what all the friends and money were about, but now from talking to Callie, learning about the world a little, it was all starting to click together fast.

I had also begun to notice an oddity. At night, when I lay down and closed my eyes to sleep, I had the sensation of someone being in the room. I felt cold all over, thought if I opened my eyes someone would be standing by my bed, looming over me like a shadow, perhaps the cronish shadow I had seen in the Stilwind house on the hill.

I feared whatever it was would take hold of me and drag

me with them across the fine dark line that made up the border between the world of the living and the world of the dead.

After a time, the sensation would pass, and I would awake exhausted, usually with the sun shining through the window, Nub beside me, lying on his back with his feet in the air, his head thrown back, his mouth open, his tongue hanging out.

This feeling was so intense I began to suspect someone was actually entering my room at night.

Callie?

Maybe Mom or Dad coming in to check on me because of my leg, just making sure I was okay?

Maybe it was the letters and the journal entries that had me feeling that way. Thinking about Margret (I no longer thought of her as M, because I was certain it had to be Margret) and how she died, down there by the railroad track, her head cut off, stories of her ghost wandering along the rails.

In the letters, Margret wrote to J, telling how she missed him, that she hoped to see him soon. She talked about the trees where she lived, big dogwoods, and how she heard that the dogwood tree was the one used to make the cross that held Jesus up. That the white flowers that bloomed on the dogwoods had little red spots inside, like the drops of blood Jesus shed. That this was God's message to remind us that Jesus had given his life on a dogwood cross.

This dogwood cross thing was a popular story of the time, though when I grew up and read about such things, I never found serious reference to it. Most agreed the crosses used by the Romans would have been made of almost anything but dogwood.

But Margret talked about all kinds of things like that. She was a dreamer, and I enjoyed her dreams.

There were pages and pages of the journal where Margret

mentioned the pregnancy, said how they could keep the child, raise it, as she said, "In spite of everything."

When I finally bored of the letters and journal pages, I put them back in the box and used my crutches to get me across the room to my closet. I put the box on the top shelf behind my cowboy hat and my Indian war bonnet, noticed something had eaten off the tips of the feathers.

Oh well, I didn't wear the bonnet anymore. I had outgrown playing cowboys and Indians. I had even stored my Davy Crockett coonskin cap away in my wooden chest. I now found the idea of running around the yard on an invisible horse with a racoon's hide on my head, or an Indian war bonnet, foolish.

I crutched back to the bed and lay down. I used Larry to scratch inside my cast, and gave up thinking about Margret for a while.

7

NEXT DAY I spent in a lawn chair pulled up next to the projection booth, residing in its shade, reading a book by Edgar Rice Burroughs called *Tarzan the Terrible*. Nub lay at my feet, snoozing.

I paused briefly to stretch, realized the sun was falling away. I was amazed to discover I had spent all day, except for a brief bathroom trip and time for lunch, in that chair reading.

Late as it had become, it was still hot as a griddle, and when I returned to my book, sweat ran down my face.

"You better get you a hat, boy. Only an idiot sits out in the sun like that."

I turned, startled. Nub raised his head for a look, lowered it again and closed his eyes.

It was Buster Abbot Lighthorse Smith, carrying two paper sacks. One was wrapped tight around a bottle. The lid and neck of it stuck out of the top. He was unlocking the projection booth, sliding inside.

He left the door open to let the heat out. He had a fan in there and he lifted it and sat it on a chair and turned it on. It could swing from left to right, but he had screwed it down so it wouldn't move. He sat in a chair across from it and opened the top of his paper sack, produced a church key, and popped the top off the bottle and took a swig.

"Shit," he said, when he brought the bottle down. "Don't ever take to this stuff, boy. Seen it knock many a nigger low, and it won't do a white boy no good neither. You put this in a Mason jar lid, bugs will get in it and die. That ought to tell you somethin'. So, you don't want none of this."

"No, sir."

He pulled the sack down and revealed an RC Cola.

"Had you fooled, didn't I?"

"Yes, sir."

But I could smell alcohol, and knew he had been hitting the liquor before arriving.

"I'm just kiddin'. Wouldn't want you to think I'm drinkin' on the job. Your daddy might not like that, and I wouldn't want to have to go find some job shoveling gravel in this hot sun. How's that book? That the one where Tarzan finds them dinosaurs, people that's got tails."

"You've read it."

"You think niggers don't read."

"I didn't say that."

Buster laughed.

"See you got you a plate by your chair. You eat out here?"

"Lunch. Rosy Mae brought it to me."

"That old fat nigger gal?"

I didn't know what to say to that, so I said nothing. I had never had a conversation with Buster before, and this one seemed out of character. He was usually broody and sullen, his brows knit up tight. But I guessed he'd nipped enough before arriving today to feel friendly.

Daddy knew he drank, but so far it had not affected Buster's job, and therefore had not been a real problem.

"You know today's my birthday?" he said.

"No, sir."

"Well it is. You know how old I am?"

"No, sir."

"Guess."

"Forty?"

He laughed. "You tryin' to flatter me, little boy, that what you're tryin' to do? I ain't seen forty in a long time. Try seventy-one."

"Try seventy-eight if you a day," Rosy Mae said.

She had come out of the house with a glass of lemonade for me. In spite of her size, way she walked, she moved silent as an Indian when she wanted to. I hadn't even heard the gravel crunch.

"You don't know nothin', woman."

"I know what you full of. You ain't seen seventy in at least eight or nine years."

"Well, I don't look seventy, now do I?"

"Sure you do. You look about a hundred and forty-five, you axe me."

"You go on back in the house. Me and the young man here was talkin'. This ain't none of your business. Why don't you get in there and fry up some chicken or somethin'. I could use some chicken myself. I ain't got nothin' but a bologna sandwich in this bag."

"And about two quarts a whiskey in you already, 'bout half a bottle of that there is RC, rest full of cheater."

"Now I was just tellin' the boy here to stay away from alcohol, wasn't I, boy? And he saw me open this bottle. Ain't that right?"

"Yes, sir."

"Why don't you get on in the house, Mr. Stanley. I got some cookies I done made fresh for you in there. I'll carry yo' lemonade back for you. You don't need to be hangin' around out here with this old man."

"Yes, ma'am. Happy birthday, sir."

"You damn right it's happy. Happy, happy, happy."

I slipped the Tarzan book into my back pocket, started crutching for the inside, Rosy Mae following, Nub dragging up the train.

As we went inside, Buster called out to Rosy, "Your ass looks like two greased pigs squirmin' up against one another in a sack, woman. But I want you to know I ain't got nothin' against pork."

"Least they happy pigs," she said. "Ain't nothin' happy about you."

"They so happy, why don't you take 'em out of the sack and let 'em smile, run around a bit."

"You ain't never gonna see these here pigs, you ole fool."

———

INSIDE AT THE TABLE, I said, "Is he really over seventy?"

"He been around long 'fo I was born. Around when my mama a girl. But he right, he don't look it. He look pretty good, actually. Got that white kinky hair and all."

"It's black, Rosy Mae."

"No, it's white, and looks better when he leaves it white, and he used to. He got to puttin' shoe polish on it now."

"Shoe polish?"

"That's right. Get up close, you can smell it. Makes him look smart he leaves it white. And he is smart, not like me."

"You're not stupid, Rosy Mae. I told you that."

"Well, I ain't educated."

"That's not the same thing."

"Thing about Buster is I don't like him."

"You sound like you like him."

"Do I? Well, he could be liked he didn't drink. I done had me a drinkin' man. I ain't gonna have me another. 'Sides, he too old for me. And he got a mean streak. Not bad as Bubba's, I guess, but I'm all through with them mean men and moody men."

"He doesn't sound like he likes you, Rosy."

"Oh, he likes me all right. I can tell."

Rosy Mae went away to attend to other matters. I sat drinking lemonade, eating cookies. I pulled the Tarzan book from my pocket and went back to reading, but I didn't read long.

I crutched outside, Nub beside me. I think he really wanted to stay inside in the fan-cooled room, but he followed me. He had that sort of dutiful stride he adopted when he was working against his will. Moving fast, head down, tail swinging. A dog on a mission.

It was near dark now and the movie would be starting before long. I leaned on my crutches and looked at all the speaker posts sticking up like runted trees, at the projection booth and the back fence, thought about what was beyond it.

Buster was sitting in my lawn chair with his RC. He called across the lot to me.

"You finally shake that old witch?"

I didn't want Rosy Mae to hear that kind of talk, so I started working my crutches, heading on over to him.

"Me and Rosy Mae are friends," I said.

"You are? Go over to her house a lot?"

"She lives here."

"Where you keep her?"

"She sleeps on the couch."

"Not good enough for a bed?"

"We don't have another bed. She's staying with us until she can do otherwise."

"How come she's stayin' with you?"

I didn't think that was any of his business, so I said, "She just doesn't have a place to live right now."

"What you mean when you say friends, is she waits on you, takes care of you. But that don't make you friends."

"It's her job. She gets paid for it."

"How much?"

"I don't know."

"Bet it ain't even half what a white woman would get to do that kind of work."

"I don't know any white women who do that kind of work."

"True enough. Now think on that."

"Well, I got to go back."

I turned to go, and Nub, who had once again lay down on the ground, stood up. He sort of let out his breath, seeming to suggest I was a boy who couldn't make up his mind.

"Hey, it's my birthday. I could use a little company. That dog, he's somethin' way he follows you around."

"That's Nub," I said. "He's a good dog."

"Yeah, he looks all right. Ain't nothin' like a good dog, is there?"

"No, sir."

"How'd you do that to your leg?"

I told him. I didn't mention that I went in the Stilwind house, but when I finished, he said, "You must have got scared up the house on the hill, way you're talkin'. Scared enough to ride out in front of a truck."

"I didn't say that."

"No, but I can tell. I always hear that house is haunted. Kids think that. It ain't though. You know what you saw?"

"I didn't say I saw anything."

"You saw old Mrs. Stilwind. She's crazy. Runs off from where she is in the old folks home, goes up there. Ain't no one gets in any kind of hurry to go fetch her. They know where she is. They go up there and get her when it pleases them. She comes to that house through the back, where the woods are. There's a trail, leads right to the old folks home. Didn't know that, did you?"

"You're sure?"

"I know coloreds work at the old folks home, wipe them old white asses and give them their green peas. They tell me about it. Now, I could be just yarn'n you, but which yarn sounds more likely? Think about it. Don't knowin' it could have been Mrs. Stilwind make what you saw up there less spooky?"

"I guess."

"Then you did see her?"

"I saw a shadow that looked like an old woman."

"You could have seen just what you thought you saw. Shadow of an old woman. Not a ghost. Life has some clear answers, and then it has things where the questions ain't even clear. Ain't like in a movie where it all comes together all the time. You know who Sherlock Holmes is?"

"I've seen him on TV."

"Read the stories. Mr. Sherlock Holmes got a sayin' go somethin' like this. Take away the possible from somethin', show that ain't it, whatever is left, no matter how impossible, is it. That's what he says. Or somethin' close to it. But you see, first you got to get rid of the possible.

"You got to look at a thing careful-like. If you done set to believe somethin', you got to know you likely to believe it even if there ain't no truth there. Followin' me?"

"Yes, sir."

"I'm just talkin', ain't I?"

"That's all right."

Buster paused as if considering a math problem. He took a drink of his RC, wiped his mouth.

"I want to tell you somethin', boy, and keep it quiet. I been drinkin'. I try not to drink on the job. Well, just a little nip now and then. But today, my seventy-fourth birthday, I'm nippin'. It's makin' me talk. Don't mean nothin' by it. Ain't normally this friendly. But I got enough hooch in me, and it's my birthday, so, I'm friendly. You savvy that?"

"Yes, sir."

"While ago"—he pulled a metal flask from inside his lunch sack as he talked—"I added me some of this to my RC. So I'm goin' at it steady. I don't know why I'm tellin' this. You ain't gonna tell your old man are you? He'd fire me. And maybe he ought to."

"No, sir. I mean, I don't plan to."

Buster nodded, said, "Gonna be dark in about half hour. They be comin' in here in droves see this John Wayne cowboy movie. I'm looking forward to it myself and I watch it every night. You don't got no better seat than right here in the projection booth. You at the source here, son. Come on in. I ain't gonna bite."

Buster got up from the lawn chair and went inside the booth. I didn't really want to go inside with him, drinking like he was, but I didn't want to hurt his feelings either. I crutched after him, Nub bringing up my heels.

Buster snapped open a round box, took out a reel, rolled it in his hands, flicked it onto the projector, smooth as a soldier loading a machine gun.

"When I ain't been drinkin', I can't do that so smooth," he said. "Stay here with me, I show you how to run the machine. I could keel over anyday. Then your daddy would need someone to do this. Hell, I don't even think he knows how. I just do what I was doin' before he bought this here picture show. You know, used to be a fine house right back of here, all this was a big front lawn. Wasn't no drive-in picture show and no highway either."

"Yes, sir, I knew that."

"Say you did?"

I told him about the pieces of the house up in the trees behind us.

"That was a fine house. Burned down with that little Stilwind gal in it."

"Did you know the Stilwinds?"

"Well, me and them didn't exactly attend the same parties. Know what I'm sayin'? But I knew who they were. Was always somethin' odd about that house burnin', that girl in there. There was all kind of talk, but most of it was just that. Talk."

There were a couple of chairs inside the projection booth, and we took to them.

"What was odd about it?" I asked.

"Heard tell from Jukes—he's called that 'cause he plays the blues in juke joints sometimes. He's a cousin and the night janitor over to the police station, high school, and newspaper. He picks up bits and pieces of story from all them places. White people don't notice a colored much. Jukes said that little girl got burned up, cops found wire around her wrists and ankles."

"Wire?"

"Someone tied her to the bed, boy."

"You're sure?"

"No, I ain't sure. Jukes overheard that when he's cleanin'. If'n there was somethin' to it, no one ever did nothin' about it, said anything about it, 'cause that come down on the Stilwinds, and ain't nobody wantin' to come down on rich folk."

"They think a Stilwind tied her to the bed, set the house on fire with her in it?"

"With everyone in it. Only all the others got out. 'Cept that little girl. She burned up 'cause the fire started in her room and she couldn't get out. Those are the facts accordin' to Jukes. I don't know he heard right or told it right. But, they say you could hear her screamin' while the house burned down. Sounded like an old wounded panther. Her mama tried to go in there after her. Flames was too high. Folks held her back, or she'd have run right through that fire and been burned up herself."

"If the police thought one of the Stilwinds did it, why didn't they arrest them?"

"Don't get ahead of the facts. Just maybe one of the Stilwinds could have done it. Had they arrested a Stilwind, police force would have changed overnight. Back then Stilwinds was even more powerful than they are now, 'cause town wasn't so big and they was all the big money that was in it."

"How come the Stilwinds didn't stay on the hill after they moved up there? Why did they move away?"

"Place supposed to be haunted by the ghost of that little girl burned up. Say she followed them up there to that house. Didn't rebuild here 'cause they didn't want bad memories, so they built up there on the hill. What I think, is memories followed them up that hill, not ghosts. They didn't get far enough away. Maybe they can't get nowhere far enough. What ghost mostly is, son, is memories."

"Which Stilwind do you think set the fire?"

Buster laughed. "Boy, you is somethin'. I done told you no one got any proof any of them set a fire . . . 'Course, guess it don't hurt to play with ideas. You got to consider all the angles of a thing. Lots thought it was James, because he was younger and might have been playin' with fire. But, hell, he was a teenage fella, so he wasn't playin' if he done it. And if it was him, why did he tie his sister up? Was he just mean? Jealous? Had a grudge against her? Who knows? Families is like windows with curtains. Some folks keep the curtains pulled back. Most open and close them from time to time, and some don't ever pull them back and you don't never get no look inside. So, ain't none of us outsiders really know what goes on in a family.

"Let's see. There was an older sister, but she moved off before all this happened. Ain't nobody thinks the mother did it, 'cause she was so overcome with it all. Story was, when they moved up on the hill, she seen her daughter at night at the foot of her bed, burnin', holdin' out her arms for help. It was more than the old lady could take. She lost her mind to save herself.

"Then there's the father. The old man, though he ain't old as me. He moved out of the house when his wife went nuts, started livin' in the hotel downtown. The Griffith Hotel."

"Does the father still live in the hotel?"

"Reckon he does. You real snoopy 'bout these people, ain't you?"

"Did you know about a girl named Margret?"

"Margret? Who you talkin' about, boy?"

I told him about the box, the letters, the ghost, the whole cloth of it. Once I started, I couldn't shut up. You'd have thought I was drunk too.

"I remember 'bout that girl. I just didn't remember the name. Them two things happenin' in one night was big news.

Fire and murder. Margret, well, she the daughter of a woman liked to take in men, you know what I mean?"

Being a recent sophisticate, I did know what he meant.

"Yes, sir."

"I know that little girl's mama in more ways than one. Me and her did business. She's still living in the same house. She popular with the colored crowd, her being lighter. Mostly white and Mexican, I think. It's a sad thing, boy, when a dark man got to feel better by bein' with a light woman. Some kind of misery in all that somewhere."

"Was that why you were with her?"

"You too young to talk about that. But I will say I ain't seen her in years. And as to why I was with her, it was because she was cheap. That's the God's awful truth. I always did prefer me a woman black as midnight. But more than that, I like a good deal. Always get the best deal you can on somethin'. Don't just jump at the first offer on any business come along . . . Winnie Wood, that was her name. It just come back to me."

"Then her daughter was Margret Wood?"

"I think she used the Wood name. You a regular little investigator, ain't you, boy? That's good. You might be a policeman, you grow up."

"Never thought about it."

"You investigatin' on this, ain't you?"

"I'm curious."

"That's what it takes to be a law. And the good part is when a problem all comes together, click, click, click, like a tumbler in a safe . . . I used to be a law."

"Really? A Texas Ranger?"

"Not any colored Rangers, son. But I was law.

"My granddaddy was known as Deadwood Dick, like a number of men was. He claimed to be the real one, or so my daddy told me. Said he was the Deadwood Dick that was written about in the dime novels. You don't know what a dime novel is, do you? They was a kind of book or magazine. Adventure stories about Western folks. Daddy was a tracker for the U.S. Army. He helped track Geronimo down. My father was part Indian himself, Seminole. But he wasn't like me. He was black as old coaly and rode a big white horse with a black mane and tail. I remember that about him. He had him a white sombrero turned up in front and wore chaps and fine Mexican boots with spurs. He had a way about him. They said he'd been with not only colored and Indian women, but Mexican and whites. He was deadly and good with a gun. He took up with a young woman half Seminole and part African and Cajun, and she was my mother. So I got lots of Indian in me, well as colored and Cajun. I grew up under the trackin' business, ended up living with my mother in Indian Territory—Oklahoma. My father went off on a track oncet and no one ever heard of him again. Figure Indians got him. My mother used to say Indians got him, all right. A squaw.

"I became a Seminole Lighthorse when I was sixteen. Later, I added Lighthorse to my name. Lighthorse is a Seminole lawman in the small nation that was part of the Five Civilized Tribes. You heard of that, ain't you?"

"No, sir."

"Indians. Creeks. Cherokees. Choctaws. Seminoles. Chickasaws. They all made up what the white people called the Five Civilized Tribes. They had their own laws and run the nations when it come to Indian matters. I liked the life, but it come to an end and I come to East Texas. Been here ever since. Ain't nothin' ever been as good as them days. Wasn't nobody callin' me nigger then. Least not to my face."

"You say it."

"What?"

"Nigger. You say it. So does Rosy Mae."

"It's kind of got to be a habit. But let me tell you so you'll know, as my mama used to say. Coloreds don't like that said by no white people. Understand? I don't like it said by no colored if he says it mean-like."

"Did the Lighthorse arrest people?"

"Arrested 'em. Executed them if'n they needed it."

"Really?"

"That's right. I knowed a fella named Bob Johnston. He was mostly Seminole. He had some white blood in him, but a drop of Indian made you Seminole. Lot of coloreds with a drop preferred to be Seminoles. They was treated better. Some coloreds just joined up with the Seminole and became members of the tribe. Didn't have no drop of Indian blood in 'em.

"Anyway, Bob got in a tussle with a friend, another Seminole, and killed him in a drunk fight. He was sentenced to death by the tribal council. No one wanted to keep him in a jail, 'cause there wasn't none, so they turned him loose, told him what day to be back for his execution. He showed up on that day, which wasn't unusual. That was the way things were done with our people. They gave him a big lunch, laughed with him, gave him a smoke, a snort of whiskey, and if one had been available, they might have given him a woman. After he ate, they pinned a white paper heart on his chest where they felt it beatin', and he stretched out on the ground on a blanket, and me and another colored-mix fella was given the job to shoot him.

"One man covered Bob's nose and mouth so he couldn't breathe good, and Bob didn't fight a lick. Me and this other fella, Cumsey was his name, leaned over and shot him right through that paper heart with our rifles. I remember I had an old Henry rifle, and with him lyin' down there on the ground and me with that rifle barrel just an inch from his chest, I was still afraid I'd miss, I was shakin' so much.

"I liked Bob. He was a good fella. Like me, he loved his drink too much and it got him in trouble. Hell, I been in some trouble and ain't no one ever shot me for it. I think about that now and then. Think about old Bob lyin' there, his breath cut off, and me and Cumsey shootin' him through the chest."

"I wouldn't have come back if they had let me go," I said.

"But Bob did. He had his honor. Honor was important then . . . What's your name?"

"Stanley."

"You mind I just call you Stan?"

"No."

"A man gave his word, he stuck by it, even if it was gonna mean his death. Least it was that way amongst the Seminoles. I can't say I've been able to live up to that good as old Bob. Hell, I think I agree with you. I'd have run off."

"How could you shoot him if you liked him?"

"Bob broke the law. Law laid down the law, and it laid it down on him. It was my job to uphold tribal law, and I did. I can't say as I felt all that good about it, but he did murder a man, and there wasn't no reason on it 'cept too much fire-water . . . They're startin' to file in now."

I saw cars moving in through the soft darkness, parking next to speakers, turning off their lights.

"How's about I show you some more about this here projector?" he said.

8

THAT NIGHT, lying in bed, I dreamed I smelled smoke. The feeling was so intense, I tried to awake, see if a fire had started in my room.

But there was another feeling that was more frightening than the smoke. It was again that sensation of someone in the room. It was stronger this time than it had ever been, and it took every ounce of courage and energy for me to open my eyes.

When I sat up in my bed, the stench of smoke went away immediately. Still, I had the uncomfortable impression of someone moving in the shadows. I fumbled for the lamp beside my bed, turned it on, was greeted with nothing.

An empty room.

I tried to remember what Buster had told me about thinking something was one thing, but not letting yourself decide it was until I knew for certain.

But in the night, that didn't seem to be a line of thinking that was helping much.

I noted the closet door was slightly open.

I had pulled a fresh pillow from there before bedtime. Had I failed to close it completely?

I sat up in bed for a long time, then slowly eased the covers off, took hold of my crutches, made my way to the closet, fearing any moment the door would swing open to reveal . . .

I was uncertain.

I took hold of the doorknob, started to pull it wider, decided I was being silly. I pushed it shut. Inside, I heard a kind of shuffling. Perhaps some of my junk shifting.

Or something lying down.

Goose bumps roamed over every inch of my skin. I crutched back to bed, feeling a coldness at my back in a room that was anything but cold. The fan in the window was beating the hot air about, and the water-cooled straw at its back was making things more muggy than comfortable, but in that moment, I was cold as a body on a cooling board. I climbed back in bed, sat against the headboard, pulled the covers up to my neck, stared at the closet door. I didn't turn out the light.

I decided then and there something must have followed me home from the house on the hill and was roaming the shadows of my room as well as hiding in my closet, maybe under the bed.

Something not of this world.

In time, however, sleep was stronger than fear, and I fell asleep with the light on, slept late into the morning.

In the sober light of day, I finally had the courage to look in the closet.

Nub came out wagging his tail. I felt like an idiot. And I thought of Buster's wisdom, and never forgot it. To this day, I'm a skeptic.

———

NEXT DAY, a hot morning, nearly noon, I looked out through the crack between water fan and window frame, saw a large black man standing out by the highway, looking at our drive-in.

I had never seen him before. I eased up to the crack, got down on my knees, and looked out. He was big and tall and wore a wide-brimmed hat, work shirt, and overalls. He just stood there looking, smoking a cigarette. Perhaps he was taking in the mural, the cavalry and the Indians.

After a while, he tossed the butt of his cigarette and walked away. I didn't think much of it at the time.

———

DOWNSTAIRS, Rosy greeted me, waddled about the living room, slapping about with a duster. I went to the kitchen, poured myself a glass of milk.

Through the sliding glass door I saw Buster out back. He was carrying a paint can and brush. It was hours before he was supposed to be at work and it surprised me to see him.

As I went out, Nub eyeballed me like he might get up, but this time he held his place on the cool tile floor of the kitchen. Even a loyal dog needed a break now and then.

I made my way to the projection booth, tried to strike up a conversation, but he wasn't having any. It was as if a dark cloud full of thunder and lightning had fallen over him. He was in no mood to talk, and said so.

"This ain't my birthday, little boy, and I ain't been drinkin'. I got work to do. No offense, but I really don't want company."

"Sorry."

"Don't be sorry, just leave me alone."

I crutched back to the drive-in, went inside, and sat down at the table. Rosy Mae came over, said, "He hurt your feelin's, that old man did, didn't he?"

"No."

"Yes he did. I can tell way yo' face is hangin'. Don't pay that old buzzard no mind no how. He jes' a messed-up old man. He happy one day, mad the next."

"He was nice yesterday."

Rosy Mae sat down at the table. "Mr. Stanley . . . Stanley, he like that. Just as moody as an old milk cow, only worse. He thinks he's a high-falutin nigger. Heard tell he supposed to been some kind'a law in the Indi'n nations. Supposed to be part Indi'n or somethin'."

"He told me that."

"I don't even know it true. He could just be one of them red niggers from over Louisiana. He drinks, one time it make him friendly, next time it make him like a poison snake you done shook up and let go."

"He's not drinking today."

"Maybe it's when he's not drinking he is who he is. Or maybe it's the want of a drink that makes him like that. That's how them drinkers are, and it ain't never they fault if'n they tell it. Hear them say: 'Don't never trust no person don't drink,' and that's the silliest thing ever did hear. You better off not to trust them drinkers, 'cause drink is for the miserable. 'Course, that the truth, I ought to be swiggin' me a gallon jug."

"Thanks, Rosy. I feel better."

"Good. Yo' mama and daddy done went to town with Callie to buy her some school clothes. They say they gonna take you tomorrow. I'm gonna read me some of my magazines, you don't tell."

"You know I won't."

"All right then. I read the same ones over and over 'cause I ain't been nowhere to buy none. I got some words I run acrost though, and I don't know 'em. Marked them so you could help me."

"Let me see them."

She pulled a couple from her big bag of a purse, put them on the table, carefully opened them to dog-eared pages. She showed me the words that she had underlined with a pencil. They were words I knew. I told her how to say them and what they meant.

She darted to the living room, kicked off her shoes, lay on the couch, and began to read. Nub climbed up next to her feet, pressed himself to her. She wiggled her toes in his fur.

I looked out at the projection booth. Buster was painting it a fresh green color. It occurred to me he might be the one who painted the fence in the first place. If so, I wondered if he had been the artist who made the paintings of the aliens and such.

I watched him work. Unlike Rosy Mae, he seemed packed with endless energy and in need of a way to burn it off. I wanted to ask him about the paintings on the fence, but didn't dare. Not after the way he acted.

I crutched upstairs, got my Tarzan book, went outside, and sat on the long porch that faced the drive-in lot. Pretty soon I was lost in Tarzan's world.

I was near the end of the book when a shadow fell over me. I looked up. It was Buster.

"Stan, think you could get that ole fat gal to get me some lemonade or somethin'?"

"I heard that," Rosy Mae called from the living room. She

had the windows up to let in what wind there was, and the screens certainly didn't block voices.

"I don't care you heard it," Buster said. "I care I get some lemonade or somethin'."

Rosy Mae appeared at the screen door. "I ain't got no lemonade, nigger."

"Whatcha got that I'd want?"

"I got some ice tea, but you ain't gonna come in the house. Mr. Big Stanley wouldn't like that."

"Maybe there's other things you got I'd want. And they ain't any of Mr. Big Stanley's business."

"Well, you only gonna get ice tea."

Rosy Mae disappeared into the kitchen. She came back with a large fruit jar full of ice cubes and ice tea.

"This is what you drink out of," she said. "I don't want your lips on none of Miss Gal's dishes."

Buster took the tea, drank a long draught of it. "Ain't nothin' like ice tea for coolin' you, next to good spring or sweet well water that is. I do like good sweet water. You got any cookies, woman?"

"What makes you think I got cookies I'm gonna give you any?"

"You look like a gal wouldn't want a man to do without. Something sweet and dark . . . like this tea. Maybe somethin' sweeter . . . Like a cookie."

"Like a cookie?"

"You hear me."

Rosy Mae, still behind the screen, grinned. "It gonna be a cookie, on that you can be certain."

She went away, came back with a fistful of chocolate chips she had baked the day before. "Now you go on back to work, nigger."

Buster took the cookies, sat in the chair next to me, eating

them, drinking the tea. He said, "Let me tell you somethin',
boy. I kinda got my ways, and they ain't that good. But I want
you to know, I don't mean nothin' by 'em."

"Yes, sir."

"I'm what you call one moody nigger."

"Yes, sir."

"I don't much care someone gets mad at me, but I don't
want to hurt no one I didn't mean to, and that's all I'm gonna
say on the matter."

"Yes, sir."

"You want to talk now, I'll talk. I done painted most of my
buildin'."

"No, sir. I don't believe I have anything to say."

"Suit yourself."

He drank his tea, crunched his cookies. We sat in the shade
of the veranda and watched heat waves run across the drive-
in lot.

Finally, I said, "Did you do the artwork on the fence? The
space creatures?"

"I did. I oncet met a man told me he seen one of them
flyin' saucers."

He crunched another cookie.

"Really?"

"Said he seen a little man too. It was in a place called Aurora, Texas. About 1894. He and some other cowboys seen a
big flyin' thing crash. Now'days they call it a flyin' saucer. He
said he saw this little man that was knocked out of it. Told me
this when I was workin' on the 101 Ranch."

"Didn't Tom Mix work on that ranch?"

"How you know about an old movie cowboy like that?"

"My dad."

"He told you about him?"

"Yes, sir. Did you know Tom Mix?"

"No. I seen him oncet or twicet, but I didn't really know him. I liked that ranch. They pretty well treated a man same as any other if he could do his job. As for Tom Mix, he was a real cowboy, but one impressed me was Bill Pickett, and I did know him right well."

I looked blank.

"He was a colored man. Invented bull-doggin', like you see in the rodeo. But Bill done it with his teeth. He'd leap off a horse onto a bull, bite its lip, take it to the ground. Some folks called him the Dusky Demon."

It occurred to me we had lost sight of what Buster had originally started our conversation with.

"What about the flying saucer?"

"Well, this fella told me this little body he seen was buried in the graveyard there in Aurora. He described it to me, and I painted it on the fence there like he told it. But the green color, well, I did that 'cause later folks started callin' them little green men. Fella said he seen the critter, told me it was actually kinda gray-lookin'."

"You believe that man's story?"

"Naw, but it's a good story, ain't it?"

"How come you didn't paint more things on the fence?"

"Got tired and shy of paint. Just had the green stuff left."

"Do you paint at home?"

"Just the shack I live in. Painted it last week."

"You have a family?"

"Had a wife. Way back in the nations. Indian gal. Pretty thing, if a little stout. She come down with smallpox and died. I had another. A colored girl named Talley. We had a daughter. Talley run off with a lighter-skin nigger and took my daughter, Helen, with her. I gave up on marriage after that."

"Your wife and daughter live here?"

"Mineola. Helen's got her a husband and family. Man

she's married to treats her good. Works some kind of way for the railroad."

"You know a lot about her."

"I check on her. My grandbabies, they eight and four and two. All boys. I ain't never seen them but from a distance."

"Maybe you should introduce yourself."

"Helen be proud to meet me. She thinks I knocked up her mother and run off, but it was her mother who left, not me. But she ain't gonna believe that . . . Well, it ain't gettin' no earlier or any cooler, so I ought to see I can finish up."

———————

INSIDE THE HOUSE, I sat at the table, holding my book, but not reading it. I decided to fix myself some tea, but no sooner had I got my crutches under me, started for the refrigerator, than Rosy Mae was on her feet. Her magazines went into her bag faster than a frightened armadillo darting into a hole.

"What you want, little Stanley? Some tea? Let me get that for ya."

"You don't need to do that," I said.

"I know," she said, and winked. "But I hear yo daddy's car out there."

I grinned, sat at the table. She poured me ice tea, put the remaining cookies in front of me on a bright yellow plate.

"You won't tell I gave that nigger cookies and tea, will you?"

"I don't care."

"I ain't sure yo daddy would like it."

"I won't tell."

True to Rosy Mae's sharp hearing, I heard the door open, and Callie, Mom, and Daddy burst inside laughing. They had a number of sacks. They brought them into the living room, put them on the couch.

Mom, carrying a small brown bag with grease stains, greeted us, came into the kitchen, Callie and Daddy following. Mom said, "You won't believe the sale we got down at K-Woolens. We bought all kinds of things for school. I got you some things too. I know you don't like to shop, so I got you some jeans and shirts. We can go tomorrow and fit some shoes. I want you to get some tennies and some nice dress shoes. We might as well get you a winter coat too. They're on sale."

"We bought me a coat," Callie said, "but it's so hard to want to buy one, hot as it is right now. I did find a pretty one, flares at the bottom—I'll try it on for you later, and I got the cutest clothes. And Mom found some for herself. She made Daddy buy some nice pants, a shirt, and some shoes, and we went to lunch at the drugstore cafe."

Daddy grinned. He had that beleaguered look of a man who had shopped well beyond his wants. Which was pretty much like my wants. Little to none.

Glancing at the Tarzan book, Daddy said, "Monkeys carry Tarzan off in this one?"

"No, sir. This one's got dinosaurs in it."

"Dinosaurs? Guess I haven't got a clue what Tarzan's about."

"I brought you home somethin', dear," Mom said. "A nice hamburger and some fries from the cafe. There's one in there for you too, Rosy Mae."

"Thank you, ma'am."

Mom put the greasy sack on the table in front of me. I opened it, got out the hamburger and fries, put them on the plate next to my cookies. I pushed the sack over to Rosy Mae, who without hesitation sat at the table and began to eat.

Mom said to me, "You eat the hamburger before you have any more cookies, you hear, dear."

"Yes, ma'am."

Rosy Mae said, "You know, my cousin Ju William cooks there at the drugstore cafe."

"Well, it must run in the family," Callie said. "Our lunch was so good."

Daddy looked out the screen door, saw Buster painting the projection booth. "What in the hell is Buster doing here this time of day? I don't pay him overtime."

Daddy looked at me.

"He was here when I got up."

"Well, he better not expect more money, 'cause I don't have it . . . Though that old booth does need painting . . . I don't know. Maybe I can work something out with him. Least I won't have to paint it myself out in this horrid, hot sun. But good God, that green. I'd have bought him a better color paint. Blue maybe."

Daddy went out the screen door, walked toward the projection booth. He seemed to be pushing heat waves before him.

Buster looked up at Daddy, stopped painting, laid the paintbrush down gently on the edge of the paint can.

Daddy met him without shaking hands. I could hear Daddy talking, but couldn't understand him. Buster nodded as Daddy talked, and I thought, the man Daddy's talking to talked to Daddy's childhood hero, Tom Mix. I wondered what Daddy would think about that.

When Rosy Mae finished her hamburger, which didn't take long, Mom and her went into the living room and Mom showed her what they had bought.

Rosy Mae shrieked, said, "Oh, this so pretty, Miss Gal."

It was a big dress about the size of a campaign tent, and it was all the colors of the rainbow. It was called a muumuu, and Mom had gotten it for Rosy Mae.

"I thought this would be a nice surprise," Mom said. "A colorful house dress."

"Well, it's certainly colorful. Thank you, Miss Gal. You so sweet."

"You're more than welcome, Rosy Mae."

While this was going on, Callie came over and whispered in my ear. "Let's talk."

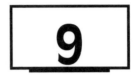

9

W E WENT OUT on the veranda, Callie holding the door for me as I crutched outside. We stood in the shade of the overhang, Callie next to a support post, me leaning on my crutches.

"I'm free. I don't have to stay at the house anymore."

"How did that happen?"

"You don't sound happy for me."

"I'm happy . . . It's good. Yeehaw."

Callie gave me the hairy eyeball. When she did that she was almost scary, way she slitted her eyes. She favored Daddy then.

After a moment of scrutinizing me, she said, "Mom was talking to some other mothers, and guess what, their daughters all came up with those nasty things in their bedrooms, and they were daughters who dated or at least knew Chester."

"So they were all doing it with him."

"No they weren't. And Stanley, don't try and talk like

someone who knows something. You had never even heard of such a thing just a few days ago. Several girls had those in their rooms, or in their houses. I don't know all the details. But they all believe they were planted, and we all think we know who did it. Jane Jersey. She has a grudge against any girl who's pretty and might attract someone she might want, even if she couldn't have them. She pretends it's about Chester, but believe me, not that many girls really want Chester."

"Who said you were pretty?"

"Well . . . I am. Mom says so."

"Like Mom's going to tell you the truth. She thinks Nub's cute."

"He is . . . Do you want to hear what I have to say or not?"

"Go on."

"So, I don't have to stay home now. Mom is going to talk to Jane's mother, see if she can put the brakes on what she's doing. Really, I don't care. Long as I'm not confined here."

"What's Daddy think?"

"He believes me now, he just doesn't know who's responsible. But who else could it be? Who would know us all, and want to do such a thing?"

"You got me."

"You're not being nice, Stanley Mitchel, Jr., and I was going to do something nice for you."

"What?"

"Are you going to be nice?"

I sighed. "I'll try."

"I'm going to take you shoe shopping tomorrow."

"That's it?"

"No. And while we're out, why don't we see if we can find something out about James Stilwind and the girl that was murdered. Did you know the cafe we were at today is the one he owns? And he owns the movie house next door. The Palace."

"Did you see him?"

"No. I don't think he actually stays there much. He hires people to run it for him. But we can go there tomorrow for lunch. Mom already said so, and while we're there, maybe we can find out something. Maybe we can find out something about that poor girl that was murdered over by the railroad tracks. And mainly, I get out of the house."

"I take back anything I said that might have hurt your feelings, Callie."

"Good for you."

———

EARLY THE NEXT MORNING Callie woke me up and I dressed quickly, pulling on blue jeans Mom had cut so that they would fit over my cast.

Callie drove the family car to JC Penney so I could look at shoes. I ended up with two pair. A black dress pair and a pair of black and white high-top tennis shoes. The way the cast fit, going over not only my leg, but part of my foot, I could try on only one shoe and hope its mate fit.

About eleven, we rode over to the drugstore cafe James Stilwind owned. While we drove, listening to rock and roll on the car radio, I told Callie everything I had learned from Buster.

I was hungry when we arrived, and had in fact been hungry for a couple of hours, having skipped breakfast.

The drugstore was clean and bright. Since we were early, it was not yet full. We ordered hamburgers and french fries and cherry Cokes, sat near the counter and ate.

The radio in the drugstore was playing "Rock and Roll Is Here to Stay" by Danny and the Juniors, and by the time we were halfway through our hamburgers, we heard "Book of

Love" by the Monotones, and "Splish Splash" by Bobby Darin.

I knew most of the songs by heart, having listened to them on my Hopalong Cassidy radio late at night in my room, just me, the moonlight, and Nub.

At that moment, I felt I could have sat there all day and listened to music, maybe had another Coke, and in time, another hamburger. The hamburger was good, and I remembered Rosy Mae said she had a relative who was the cook.

The guy behind the counter was only a little older-looking than Callie. He was wearing a soda jerk hat, and he pushed that up so Callie could see he had curly hair with one curl that fell down on his forehead. It looked like a trained curl to me.

He leaned over the counter, said, "The food good?"

"It's fine," Callie said.

"Good. We try to please."

Callie said, "You didn't cook it."

"No. Nigger cooked it."

"I wish you wouldn't say that word."

"Nigger?"

"Yes."

"For you, while you're here, I won't say it. I won't say coon or jungle bunny either."

He thought that was going to get a laugh from us, but it didn't. Callie said, "Thank you. Mr. Stilwind owns this place, doesn't he?"

"He does. Why?"

"Just curious."

"I know why you're curious. He has money."

"That's a terrible thing to say."

"That's how women are. They won't pay attention to a nice young man who has yet to put his prospects together, but they'll go all out for some older guy with a Corvette and lots of money."

Callie raised an eyebrow. "He has a Vette?"

"See," said the counter boy.

"I'm just joking," Callie said. "What's your name?"

"Timothy Shaw. They call me Tim."

"I'm Callie Mitchel. This is my brother, Stanley."

"Glad to meet you . . . Wasn't right at lunchtime, I'd give you a free soda. Come by early mornings, late afternoons, no one's looking, I'll make you one."

Since we were early for lunch, and no one else was in the drugstore, I assumed this was a lie Timothy was telling. I'm sure Callie thought the same, but she didn't let on. She stayed charming.

"That's nice of you, Tim. But I am curious about Mr. Stilwind."

"Figures. You know, he dyes his hair. He looks good for his age, but he dyes his hair."

"How old is he?"

"Thirties, I guess."

"That's not old."

"It's pretty old. And besides, he's got a girlfriend. And he was married once."

"Have children?"

"I don't think so, but his girlfriend is young as you."

"She pretty?"

"Not as pretty as you. But yes, she's pretty. What do you care about him for? I'm free, white, and twenty-one, and I got a pretty good jalopy, little spending money. Besides, you and me, all we need is the moon."

"You think?" Callie said.

"Sure."

"Doesn't Mr. Stilwind own not only this business, but the movie next door?"

"He owns lots of stuff. Hangs out over there a lot. His girl-friend used to work the concession counter. That's how he met her. She was a homecoming queen, cheerleader or something. Both. I don't know. Can you imagine a young girl like that with an old man like that?"

"If I stretch my imagination."

"Come on, baby, is there a chance for you and me?"

"There's a chance for just about anything, Timothy."

"I got prospects, honey. I'm going to go to college next year, if I save enough money."

"What do you want to be?"

"I want to get an associate's degree, start my own busi-ness."

"What kind of business, Tim?"

"I haven't figured that part out yet. But I can tell you this. It won't end up with me being no soda jerk."

———

AFTER LUNCH I looked through the drugstore magazine rack, bought Rosy Mae some new movie magazines, bought myself a couple of comic books.

We walked over to the theater James Stilwind owned, the Palace. Or rather Callie walked, and I crutched.

"Tim liked me, didn't he?" Callie said.

"I guess so."

"He's kinda cute."

"If you like soda jerks. Or in his case, just a jerk."

"I might get a free soda out of it, maybe an ice cream sun-dae. But you're right. He is kind of a jerk."

"Him and that curl."

"I thought the curl was cute," Callie said.

Chester White's jalopy appeared beside us. He pulled to the curb, parked, slid over to the passenger side and opened the door. The grease on his pompadour shone bright blue in the sunlight. "Callie. How you doin'?"

Callie didn't answer.

"Hey, sport," he said. "What happened to you?"

I didn't answer either.

"Your old man still mad at me, Callie?"

"Yes. And so am I. I've heard about all those other girls. And what you did with them, and Jane . . . Well, she got me in trouble. Or so I think."

"Yeah, I heard about that."

"You did?"

"Jane told me she did it to get you in trouble. She doesn't like you. She doesn't like the other girls either. Hell, she doesn't like anyone. Her dog won't play with her unless she's got a pork chop tied around her neck."

"You play with her. She have to tie a pork chop around her neck to get you?"

"Sometimes."

"Yeah, I bet."

"Hey, she got those things from her brother and put soap water in them. She thought it was funny."

"She did, did she?"

"I don't think it's funny," Chester said. "She's sayin' what's in it came from me. It didn't. I don't dispense soap."

"It could have been something other than soap. Couldn't it, Chester?"

"I'm not perfect. Yeah, it could have. It might have, a year ago. But me and her, we don't see each other now. She's just jealous I was seein' you."

"Since you're not seeing me now, she won't have to be

jealous anymore, will she, Chester? For that matter, you can go back to doing what you were doing with her. And if you can't do that, there's always Mrs. Palm and her five daughters. Good day, Chester."

"Aw, baby, don't be that way."

"Don't call me baby, Chester. Why don't you go check the oil in your hair. If you can find a deep-enough dip stick."

"That's a low blow, darlin'."

We started moving again. A moment later the jalopy screamed by us, made a curve almost on two wheels, and was out of sight.

"He still likes me," she said. "Fact is, I think he likes me more now."

"You love it, don't you?"

"I love seein' how silly men can be. Yes."

As we neared the theater a sharp red and white Thunderbird pulled up to the curb. The door opened. A tall man who looked like a movie star got out of the car. He had light brown hair and it was longish with a curl like Timothy's, only more natural-looking. His clothes were sporty and expensive. White coat, tan pants, tan and white shoes.

As he got out of the car, I saw his socks were light blue with dark blue clocks on them.

He went around, opened the passenger door on the Thunderbird, and a woman got out. She had shoulder-length, poofed-out, peroxide-blond hair. She was wearing tight gold pants that quit at the calf, a white shirt with a frilly collar, thick-heeled sandals that strapped high on the ankle. As she came around front of the car, stepped up on the curb, I realized she was quite young.

The man took hold of her arm and marched toward the theater, passing us. He looked at Callie as he did, gave her a smile

that was big enough and bright enough and wild enough to belong in a lion's mouth.

As he passed the ticket booth, he nodded at the lady inside,
went into the theater with the blonde on his arm, glanced back
over his shoulder at Callie.

"I bet that's him," Callie said.

"You mean Stilwind?"

"Uh huh. That's his girlfriend. The one Tim told us about.
Think I'm that cute, Stanley?"

"I think you're so ugly you'd have to sneak up on a glass
of lemonade."

"Funny, Stanley."

"I thought Tim said he drove a Vette."

"Maybe he thought the Thunderbird was a Vette. Maybe he
has both."

"Maybe that's not him."

Never having been around that kind of money, I found it
hard to imagine having so much you could own two fancy
sports cars, a nice plaid jacket, and a pretty blonde.

"I don't see how he could have done such a thing as you
think," Callie said.

"I don't think anything," I said, trying to echo what Buster
had taught me. "You're jumping to conclusions."

"I'm sure it crossed your mind."

"I think it's crossed your mind, and now that you see him,
you can't imagine it."

"What do you think?"

"He doesn't look very monstrous, does he?"

"No, he doesn't."

Callie walked over to the ticket booth. I stayed where I
was, but I could hear her. She said, "Was that Mr. Stilwind?"

The lady at the ticket booth said, "Yes. Do you need to
speak to him?"

"No. Thanks."

She came back. I said, "I heard."

"I just don't see how he could have done anything like that. He looks very nice."

"You mean you'd like to date him."

"I didn't say that."

"Maybe the jerk is right. Girls like nice cars and money. And you're not even eighteen. What do you think Daddy would say about that? You wanting to date a grown man."

"He'd say no," Callie said. "Or he'd beat him up. Let's forget it and go home, Stanley. I'm all tuckered out. I think this is one mystery that's just going to remain unsolved. But there is one good side. You heard what Chester said about the soap water and those awful things. This is just more support for me."

"Maybe you ought not push it."

"Oh, no. I want Daddy to believe me completely. And you, like it or not, are my witness."

I didn't like it, and that afternoon when we got home, Callie told Mom and Dad what happened with Chester, and I stood there to confirm it.

When she was finished, I saw Daddy let loose with a silent sigh. He patted Callie on the back and went outside.

"He believes me completely, then?" Callie asked Mom.

"He believes you," Mom said. "I think he's gone somewhere to cry."

———

His LOOKS don't mean a thing," Buster said. "You think all the peoples out there do bad things is ugly? Or look like monsters? Drag they knuckles on the grass? Huh, boy? You think that?"

It was night and we were in the drive-in booth and Buster was showing a picture, an Audie Murphy Western.

"I don't know. That Bubba Joe, they say he looks mean, and he is."

"You right about that. But that don't mean everyone looks mean is bad. Any more it means anyone looks sweet and kind as Howdy Doody is Howdy Doody. You hear me, boy?"

"Yes, sir."

"Consider that an important lesson. Looks is nice to look at, but underneath them . . . Well, you don't never know. Why you think so many men get in trouble with women? Them looks. Man goes for them looks, and underneath them looks you might find you a harpie. You know what that is?"

"No, sir."

"Evil winged women that torment people. Only difference in my experience with women in general, is they don't have the wings."

"You know a lot of stuff, Buster."

"I've forgot more than most people know. Listen here, you really interested in this murder business, ain't you?"

"I am."

"Now, kind of playin', what say I give you a little help on this. Just a little. I can't get big involved. White folks ain't keen on a nigger gettin' into their wood pile."

———

ALTHOUGH BUSTER OFFERED to help me, he wouldn't do it until I was off crutches. That took another couple of weeks, and even then I was afraid to put too much pressure on my leg. But after a day or two, I forgot all about it and even took to riding my bicycle that Dad had repaired.

The rules were I was not to go up the hill into the rich section, and if I was going to ride along the highway, it had to be on the grass, or the sidewalk when no one was coming.

One early morning I got up telling my parents I was going to ride my bike, and leaving Nub behind for a change, I rode into town, to the back of the newspaper office where I was to meet Buster.

The office was near the theater Stilwind owned. As I pedaled past it, I looked to see if James Stilwind or his Thunderbird were about. They weren't.

At the back of the newspaper office, in the brick alley, Buster was sitting on a wobbly bench up against the wall. He was sitting with a lean black man wearing a porkpie hat. The lean man was shaking a cigarette out of a pack of Lucky Strikes.

Between them was a cardboard box. As I rode up, the lean man lit the cigarette with a kitchen match he struck on the brick wall. He said, "They catch me on this, Buster, I'm gonna lose my job."

"They ain't gonna miss this stuff. And I'll bring it back."

"Well, you better go on with it, let me get back to my janitorin'."

"Thanks, Jukes," Buster said.

"Guess you welcome. You my cousin, Buster, but you pushin' it."

"Who pulled your ass out of the fire about half a dozen times?"

"Yeah, well, you right. But I still need this job."

"You got jobs all over the place," Buster said.

Jukes dropped his cigarette in the alley and stepped on it. "I'm gonna go inside now. You might ought to go on, case one of the newspaper gentlemen comes out the back door and sees two niggers with a white boy."

"You need to relax, Jukes."

"Yeah, right."

"Hey, Jukes, for the boy here, hit a note or two."

"Ah, now."

"Come on."

Jukes looked around. "Well, just a couple of notes."

He took a harmonica from his back pocket, hit a few notes, pulled it from his mouth, and sang:

> I got a two-timin' woman.
> I'm one-timin' man.
> She wants to get happy, but she don't understand.

The harmonica came up, a few notes, then:

> She a two-timin' woman—
> I'm one-timin' man.

He hit a few notes on the harmonica, sang:

> She tell Mr. Johnson, what he ought to do.
> Mr. Johnson don't listen.
> He don't care what she do.
> It don't matter darlin', what you say.
> Mr. Johnson, dadgumit, don't play that way.

The harmonica again. A couple of tap steps. Then:

> You say what you want.
> You say what you say.
> But I done told you darlin'
> Mr. Johnson don't play that way.

Jukes stopped, said, "That'll do for now. Y'all be careful, hear."

Jukes went inside.

Buster said, "How'd you like that?"

"Neat," I said. It would be several years later, thinking back on that song, that I'd truly understand it. I wondered if old Jukes made it up.

"We got to walk, kid."

He picked up the cardboard box, started off. I followed, pushing my bike.

I said, "Where are we going?"

"We gonna look at what I got in the box."

"What's that?"

"You gonna see. I had him puttin' this together for me for a week or so, waitin' on that leg of yours to get well. How is it?"

"It feels funny, but it doesn't hurt."

"That's the muscles in it. They hadn't got no workout till now. That bike ridin' is the best thing for it."

"I'm pushing it."

"Walkin' won't hurt you none neither. That's exercise, ain't it?"

"Where are we going?"

"The Section."

"What?"

"Well, you might know it better as Nigger Town. We gonna go to my house and study this stuff."

10

WE CAME TO a red-brick street where the oaks grew thick and close on either side. When the wind blew the limbs of one tree it tapped against its cousin across the street.

As we walked, on our right, we passed a fenced-in park and a statue of Robert E. Lee on which jet-black crows nested and relieved themselves, splattering it with white goo. I noted that one pile of it had fallen into and hardened over Robert E. Lee's right eye.

Behind the park was a cemetery containing the bodies of Civil War veterans. On some of the graves were little weather-faded Dixie flags and vases out of which poked the blackened and wilting stems of deceased flowers; on other graves were fresher blooms, among them roses bright as blood.

We hiked on until the street narrowed and there were bricks poking up willy-nilly where the weather had worked them loose and sometimes cracked them. Blades of grass had crept between many of the bricks, fallen over, and turned yellow.

Abruptly, the oaks changed. I realized for the first time the trees on Oak Street, as it was called, those closer into town, were pruned and preened and cared for. But as one went farther down Oak Street, into the Section, the oaks were twisted and some were diseased with blackened knots. All were as neglected as the old brick street.

It was the same tone for the colored graveyard that lay on the left side of the street behind the oaks, near where Dewmont Creek ran. There you could see stones leaning left and right. Many had fallen and some were busted. The grass was high and there were sprigs of trees growing, escaped from some stray acorn cast there by wind or a careless squirrel.

"It don't look as good as that cracker graveyard, do it?"

"Sir?"

"The colored field. Where the colored are buried, boy. It don't look as neat as that cracker yard where all them Dixie ducks is buried, does it?"

"No, sir."

"We don't keep it up. You know why?"

"No, sir."

"'Cause come Halloween, white boys come in and push the stones over and break 'em. We better off not doin' nothin'. Fixin' a stone, cuttin' down that grass, just attracts them fools. Ain't nothin' funnier or braver to them boys than pushin' over some colored's stone, or throwin' it in the creek, breakin' it up. They're cowards too, boy. Tell you why. They know ain't no colored gonna do anything to them out in the open, 'cause then you got the Kluxers, or some of their types. That ain't brave, now is it?"

"No, sir. I guess not."

"It ain't. That's what I'm tellin' you. Listen to me. I'm learnin' you somethin' here."

Along the street white faces began to disappear, replaced by colored faces. The cars at the curbs and up next to houses were for the most part older, the houses along the way less nice, some of them smaller than our living room back at the drive-in. They peeled paint, flapped porch boards, begged for shingles and window glass, leaned as if in desperate need of rest. There were outhouses out back of homes, no electric lines leading into most.

Sitting on porch steps, or porches, some settled in stuffed chairs from which the insides exploded in puffs of cotton like drooping nuclear clouds, were men, young and old. They wore their worn-out clothes with slouch hats like uniforms. Their faces looked as if they had survived a beating and expected another.

As we walked by one of the men called out.

"Did he follow you home, Buster?"

"He did," Buster said.

"You gonna keep 'im?"

"Ain't got no wife says I can't."

"I hear them little white boys is hard to train."

"Naw," Buster said. "Not if you whip 'em good with a sound piece of fishin' cane and put down newspapers."

"Whatcha gonna feed that boy?"

"Got it here in this cardboard box. Guts from the slaughterhouse. A hog's head."

"Hell, I want that hog's head," said one of the men. "Why don't you kill him, Buster, let me have that bicycle?"

"Your fat ass would flatten that bicycle," Buster said.

Laughter rose up, drifted away as we moved on.

I was, to put it mildly, becoming a bit nervous. What was I doing in the Section anyway? Had I lost my mind?

———

WE TOOK A SIDE STREET, passed some kids playing. One of them was a small boy with a snotty nose that had collected dust and made dirt roads from his nostrils to his lips. As we passed, he looked at us as if he might ask us for identification.

Alongside the railroad track we came to a small house the sick green color of our drive-in fence.

I pointed this out to Buster. He said, "It ought to look the same color. I took me some of the paint. It ain't pretty, but it keeps it from peelin' and it looks better than gray."

There was a large stone step that led up to the porch. The house was simple but looked clean and cared for. The screen in front of the door was a new one and the windows were clean with shutters drawn back. There was a metal lawn chair on the porch. It too was painted the same ugly green.

Behind the house, above all this, between railway and structure, rose an old billboard that had probably not been changed since World War Two. It was a happy white woman holding a Coke, a smile as bright and wide as an idiot's hopes.

At the corner of her smile was a rip. The wind and rain had caught the rip, torn it back a piece. Crows gathered atop the billboard, and just above the woman's head they had done what they had done to Robert E. Lee.

The crows looked down on us as if we might be something to eat. I leaned my bicycle against the porch. Buster took out a key, pulled back the screen, unlocked the door.

"Welcome to nigger heaven," he said.

Inside, the place was dark and smelled like stale paper. As Buster turned on the one weak overhead light, it became evident the smell was due to much of the walls being covered in shelves filled with books and magazines.

There was a closet and a little table near the wall that held a hot plate, dishes, and eating utensils. In the middle of the room was a large plank table with chairs. Against one wall, next to a bookshelf, was a narrow bed. Off center of the room was a heating stove made from an oil drum. A crooked pipe ran from it, exited through the ceiling. There was a pile of split wood lying beside it, ready for winter.

I said, "You read all these books?"

"What kind of question is that, boy? 'Course. Do you read?"

"Yes, sir."

"You got this many books?"

"No, sir."

"Well, you get you a collection of books. Read them, or at least try to read them. I'd offer you some cake but I don't have any."

"That's all right."

"I got coffee."

"I don't drink coffee much."

"Me neither. Except every morning, during the day, and in the afternoon. I think I got a warm RC though, you want it."

"Sure. Thanks."

Buster put the box on the plank table, gave me the RC, started coffee. He sat at the table, removed a number of folded newspapers and clippings from the box.

"Sit down, boy. Grab a chair."

I did, said, "What is this?"

"I told you Jukes was the janitor at the newspaper. Also the janitor at the police station and the high school. Just does the police station on the weekends. At the high school, he don't have to do anything in the summer. When school starts up, he's got a crew works for him. Old Jukes does all right."

"How do these clippings help us?"

"You aren't thinkin', boy . . . And quit lookin' out that back window. That girl on the billboard there, you ain't gonna see no titties fall out or nothin'. She's just paper."

I blushed. Buster said, "Now don't get upset or mad. I'm just kiddin' with you. A man's got to learn to joke and he's got to learn to laugh at his own self and know it's okay to think about titties. You don't do that, you ain't gonna be worth the powder it would take to blow your ass up. Thinkin' on titties too much is preoccupation, not thinkin' on them is sign of some kind of anemia. You listenin'?"

"Yes, sir."

"One of the things you better learn to laugh at is the women you can't have, 'cause they're gonna be plenty. Now, think. Why would we want clippin's that go back all these years?"

"I guess to read about the murder."

"All right. Now you're startin' to fan the fire. But we got clippin's here before that murder, and after it. Why is that?"

"I don't know."

"Things like this, sometimes they just happen. Man does the murder don't even know why he does it. When I was in Oklahoma, time I was tellin' you about, there was an Indian went off one morning and beat his wife to death with a stick of stove wood and set fire to the house, burned up their baby girl in her crib. He went out then and shot their dog and shot himself in the head. He wasn't as good a shot when it come to shootin' himself. He lived, but without his jaw. Asked why he done it. He didn't know. Said they hadn't been arguin', and in fact, she was quite lovin', and he really loved the baby, and the dog was second to none. But one mornin' he got up and seen his wife bent over the stove, tryin' to make his breakfast, and it just come on him. He took the stove wood and went to work. Said it seemed like a good idea at the time."

"Did they shoot him in the heart too?"

"Didn't execute him. Was considered made mad by the gods, or some kind of Indian evil. He was set free. Besides, he had to live with that face of his, and the bullet had punched a hole in his head and hit his brain and he wasn't good for nothin' after that. Limped, drank liquor, shit on himself when he wasn't falling down. Maybe he'd have been better with a shot through the heart.

"Just because he didn't have no pattern, rhyme, or reason, don't mean most of this murderin' business don't. It usually has. Money. Love. Or more often than not, just some kind of pride gone wild. Pride makes you want money, or lack of pride does, and it makes you want love and not want to take insults. Pride is at the bottom of everything, boy, except stone crazy."

"Does the murder of Margret and Jewel have a pattern?"

"Can't rightly say yet, but I figure it did. What we got to figure is are these two murders linked up, or did they happen separate-like. You know, a coincidence.

"If they're tied together, there was some reason behind it. You can figure that, you can kind of work backwards, or forwards, dependin' on the situation. You followin' me, boy?"

"Sort of . . . Well, not completely."

"You see, they got what they call a morgue at the newspaper, but not for dead folks. For dead papers. Things happened long ago. These start before the murder, and after the murder. This is just the first box. Juke's gonna get me others. But this one, it'll take some time to look through."

"What are we lookin' for?"

"There's some things we know we're lookin' for, and some things we don't know about yet."

"How will we know the things we don't know?"

"That depends on us."

"What do we know we're looking for?"

"We know we're lookin' for any mention of the Stilwind family and this Wood family that Margret belonged to. Don't care if it's just somethin' about them goin' some place, we want to study it."

"Goin' some place?"

"Stilwinds. They have money, boy. They did travelin'. Society section might have somethin' on that."

"Why do we care where they went?"

"Maybe we don't. But we're gonna look at it. Gonna look at anything has to do with them. We're gonna look for any kind of crime resembles the crimes we're interested in, before or after. Railway killin's, people burned up in fires, even if it's an accident. Then, we got maybe some police files to look at."

"Really?"

"I'm gonna trust you, Stanley. You got to be quiet about that. And you don't want to mention the papers either, hear?"

"Yes, sir."

"Find out I got Jukes takin' out old police files, well, he'll not only lose his job, he got a good chance of bein' hurt. Or worse. I'm askin' him a big thing just to figure on some dead white folks some years back just so you and me got somethin' to do."

"Why is Jukes doing it?"

"'Cause I once helped him out. In a big way."

"What kind of way?"

"That's between me and him."

"Why are you doing it?"

"I'm bored. I wanted to keep bein' a lawman, Stan. But after them old days, wasn't no place for me as a colored to do nothin' like that. I didn't want to move up North where I might do it, 'cause it's cold up there. Besides, they ain't no better than here. Just say they are."

"When do we get the police files?"

"When Jukes can nab 'em. They're old enough, I don't think they're gonna be missed. Least not right away. We'll put them back when we're finished."

"What if we do find out who did it?"

"Cross that bridge when we get to it."

———

THERE WERE ALL MANNER of things about the Stilwinds in the papers. There were buildings they bought, weddings they attended, travels abroad, an announcement the older daughter had moved away to England, general society stuff, the charities they gave to.

But nothing jumped out at me and said murder.

Buster read carefully and wrote from time to time on a yellow pad with a fat pencil. I said, "You finding anything?"

"Don't know. All has to come together like a puzzle. You get a piece here. You get one there. You find some things look like pieces and almost fit, but don't, so you toss 'em. But you don't toss 'em far. Sometimes you have to go back and get them. Most of the time, you solve business just by doin' business. You chip here, you chip there. You think about it. You want to make a statue, you start with a block of stone. You get through chippin' on it, you've cut away a lot of stone to make that statue."

"But we're not making a statue."

"Stan, it's what they call a comparison. It ain't supposed to mean just how it is. It's a metaphor."

"The way you talk, kind of words you use, changes a lot, Buster."

"It do, don't it?" He grinned at me. "Thing is, when it starts to come together, it's like tumblers in a safe. You know. Click, click, click. Now, tuck your head into them papers, boy, think about what you're reading."

———————

A COUPLE HOURS LATER, Buster said, "I'm gonna take me a little break, take some of my medicine. Might be a good idea if you run along home."

Buster went to the bookshelves, pulled back some paperback books, removed a small, flat bottle of liquor from behind them. "Keeps my heart pumpin'."

"Is it okay to go back by myself?"

"You scared colored gonna get you?"

"A little."

"At least you're honest. They won't bother you none. Just wave at them men on the porch. Besides, they're probably havin' their medicine 'bout now. Ain't much else for them to do. All the doctorin' jobs is filled up."

I got up to leave.

He said, "Take this home and read it. It'll get you thinkin' way you need to be thinkin'."

He handed me a paperback book with the title: *The Adventures of Sherlock Holmes.*

"Holmes, he had the mind for it, boy. He thought around corners and under rugs."

"How's that?"

"Read it. You'll figure what I mean."

I put the book in my back pocket, got my bicycle off the porch. The ride was rough along the busted brick streets. I came to the porch where the men had been, but they were gone.

I rode on until the trees spruced up and the bricks lay flat, on past the wrecked colored graveyard, on past the kept white graveyard, on into Dewmont, and from there I rode home.

11

NEXT FEW DAYS Buster brought the old newspapers to work. He arrived at least two hours before he needed to run the reels. Me and Nub spent time with him in the projection booth. We looked through the clippings. Well, Buster and I did. Nub lay on the floor on his back with his paws in the air. He was no help at all.

Buster and I catalogued anything interesting on yellow pads, put the catalogued papers aside for future reference.

Mornings, when Buster wasn't there, I read from the Sherlock Holmes stories or taught Rosy to read better. She had graduated from the movie magazines and comics, and was reading a few short stories out of Mom's magazines, like *The Saturday Evening Post*.

Sometimes Richard came by to visit, and we rode our bikes down to the wood-lined creek, hunted crawdads in the muddy shallow water.

We caught the crawdads by tying a piece of bacon to a

string, jerking the mud bugs out of the creek when they grabbed hold of it.

Richard would bring a bucket with him, and by noon of a good day, we had it half full of crawdads. Richard took them home to give to his mother, who boiled them until they were pink. Then she made rice and cooked vegetables and mixed them together.

I had eaten crawdads once or twice at their house and didn't like them much. They tasted muddy to me. And it was sad to see Richard's mother move about like a whipped dog, her eye blacked, her nose swollen, her lip pooched out like a patch on a bicycle tire. Just looking across the table at Richard's dad bent over his plate like a dark cloud about to rain on the world made the food in my mouth taste bad.

One day Richard came to our house on his bike and his eye was blacked.

"What happened?" I asked him.

"Daddy and Mama got into it," he said. "I tried to stop Daddy from kickin' her. He blacked my eye and she got kicked anyhow."

"Sorry."

"I reckon me and Mama had it comin'."

"No you didn't."

"Come on, let's go catch crawfish," he said.

Down at the creek fishing for mud bugs, Richard and I started talking about the ghost by the railroad tracks.

"Hey, want to sneak out tonight and go have a look? I can have you back before you're even missed."

"I don't know. Maybe."

"You can't be a sissy all your life."

"I'm no sissy."

"You do what you're told, don't you? I take chances."

"Well, my daddy doesn't beat the tar out of me over just anything either. He doesn't beat the tar out of me at all."

"My daddy says he's just tryin' to make me responsible."

"He's just tryin' to beat your ass. And he hits your mother too. My daddy doesn't ever hit my mother."

"She's sassy 'cause he don't."

"What if she is?"

"I don't mean nothin' by it, Stanley. But you want to fight, I'll fight you. I ain't afraid."

"And you might whip me, but don't talk about my mom or my family."

"You started it."

I was still squatting on the creek bank, holding a bacon-loaded string. I thought for a moment, said, "Guess I did. I didn't mean nothing."

"Me neither. I was just kiddin' when I called you a sissy. You ain't no sissy."

"Thanks."

"Sure. You want to slip off or not?"

"Why not," I said.

"I can come by tonight. About eleven or so. That work for you?"

"Better make it midnight."

"We can ride bikes to the sawmill, walk from there, since there ain't nothing but a rough trail."

We wrapped our lines on sticks, stuck them under the bridge for another time when we could get some bacon, then I walked home with Richard, him carrying the bucket with the crawdads in it.

We walked by the old abandoned sawmill. Most of it had rotted down and some of it had been torn away for lumber. One complete building remained. It was supported on posts and through a glassless window machinery could be seen. The roof was conical and had rusted and the rust made it look in the moonlight as if it were made of gold.

The structure was open in front and from it swung a long metal chute held up by rusted chains attached to rods on hinges. The chute dipped toward a damp, blackened sawdust pile which was flattened on top by wind and rain. Blue jays called out from the woods and one lit on the chute for a moment. Even its little weight made the long chute wobble on its chains. The bird took to the sky and made a dot that went away.

Dewmont was full of stories, and one of many I had heard from Richard was about a colored kid who had gone playing in the sawmill ruins and thought it would be fun to ride that old chute down into the sawdust pile. But when he got in the stuff, he went under, and was never found.

According to the story, somewhere beneath that huge mountain of sawdust were his bones, and maybe the bones of others as well.

I always wondered how people knew he was there if no one had seen it happen. And if he was there, surely someone would have dug his body out by now.

When I brought this up to Richard, he said, "That boy's mama had twelve other kids. She wasn't missin' one little nigger much."

When we got to his property, Richard's demeanor changed. He lost a step and his shoulders sagged.

He said, "I think me havin' these crawdads will calm Daddy's temper, since I been gone so long."

I didn't know what to say to that, so we just kept walking into his yard. According to Richard, their house had been handed down to them by his mother's parents. It was huge and once grand, but that grandness was gone.

The yard was lush with high weeds divided by a cracked concrete walk. The porch sagged and the front door hung crooked on its hinges. One side of the porch roof had a hole in it and the lumber was hanging down, black and wet-looking, soft, as if you could tear it apart with your bare hands.

Out back of the house I could hear their big black dog barking, running on its chain attached to the clothesline.

Richard paused, studied the dog as it ran back and forth.

"Daddy loves that dog," Richard said. "He's crazy about him."

Back and beyond the clothesline and the dog was the twenty acres or so Mr. Chapman farmed in potatoes and peas. There too were the crumbling outbuildings, the ill-fed plow mule contained within a rickety fence, and an anemic-looking hog in a mud hole surrounded by closely driven posts made of hoss apple wood. The hog lived on day-old toss-away cakes Mr. Chapman got from the bakery, scraps from the kitchen.

As we stepped on the porch, the door opened, and Mr. Chapman came out. He was a tall lean man who looked as if he had once been wet and wrung out too hard in a wash wringer. There didn't seem to be a drop of moisture in him or his hair, and his eyes were as dark and dry as pine nuts.

He looked at me, then at Richard.

"You got in that bucket, boy?"

"Crawdads," Richard said. "Enough for supper, I think."

"You think. Do you or don't you?"

"Yes, sir."

"You been gone all day, boy. I had some work for you to do."

"Sorry, sir."

"Get in the house, give 'em to your mama. Your friend can't stay."

"See you, Stanley," Richard said. The expression in his eyes was like a suicide note.

"Sure," I said.

Behind me, I heard the door slam, followed by a flat whapping sound. Richard cried out shrilly from behind the door and his father said something sharp. Then I was gone, on out to the road, walking fast, the sunlight warmer and cleaner out there, away from the weeds and the trees and the big rotting Chapman place.

———

I ARRIVED at the drive-in to find Mom in a state. She had been shopping with Callie and had had an adventure.

She was dressed in a black dress with a black hat with a red bow on it; it looked like something Robin Hood would wear if he were in mourning and was a sissy.

Mom removed the hat, which was somehow fastened with a couple of pins, put it on the drainboard by the sink. Her hands were shaking.

"He was pacing us, across the street," she told me and Rosy Mae.

"Shu it was him, Miss Gal?"

"Well, no. I've never seen him. But I think it was. He was big and very black. Had a fedora, pulled down just above his eyebrows. A longish coat. He looked strong."

"What kind of shoes was he wearin'?" Rosy Mae asked.

"I didn't think to look at his shoes," Mom said. "He could have been wearing ballet slippers for all I know. I have to sit down. Stanley, will you get me a glass of water?"

"He had on army style boots with red laces," Callie said. "I noticed it. I've never seen a man with red laces before."

I brought Mom a glass of water. She sat at the table, and after a few sips, she set the glass down and took a deep breath.

I hadn't noticed if the man out front of the drive-in the

other day, smoking a cigarette, was wearing army boots with red laces, but the rest of it, the clothes, the hat, fit.

Daddy, who had been out back, picking up trash from the drive-in yard, came in, said, "Stanley, I want you out here right now, picking up trash. You can't go off fishing when there's work to . . . What's going on here?"

"I'm not sure if anything is," Mom said. "I think it may be my imagination."

"Well," Daddy said, "am I going to have to imagine what happened?"

"No," Mom said. "I just don't know it was anything. You see, me and Callie, we were in town shopping. Going to Phillips's Grocery, but had to park down from the store a ways. It's coupon day for the store. They've started this thing with their own coupons—"

"Gal, for heaven's sake," Daddy said.

"Okay. Anyway. We were walking back to the car, and across the street was this big colored man wearing a brown fedora. He looked so scary. He . . . Well, I didn't like the way he was looking at us. As we walked back to the car, he paced us on the other side of the street. When we stopped, he stopped, and he glared at us. I didn't imagine that, did I, Callie?"

"No. He was watching us, Daddy."

"He followed us all the way to the car, and when we got inside, and I was starting to back out, he came next to the window and looked in. Didn't say anything. Didn't do anything. But he had the strangest look on his face. And his eyes, they were so . . ."

"Scary," Callie said. "Like something out of a monster movie."

"Yes. Something out of a monster movie. I froze with my foot on the brake."

"It was him, Miss Gal," Rosy Mae said. "He wear them red

laces all the time. I bought them for him. And he got that look. I seen that look many times, right before he hit me so hard my clothes changes colors."

Rosy Mae pulled up a chair, sat down.

"He done gone to followin' you, and it's all my fault."

"I invited you here," Mom said.

"Yes," Daddy said. "You did."

"I can get my stuff and be gone in jes' fifteen minutes," Rosy Mae said. "Ain't no one been nicer than you, Miss Gal. But I don't want to bring nothin' on your fambly."

"You hush up, Rosy," Mom said. "You aren't going anywhere."

"Maybe I should, Miss Gal."

"You go out there, roam those streets, he's going to hurt you," Mom said. "I guarantee it."

"And what about you?" Daddy said. "Sounds to me like he's going to hurt you. Or Callie."

Mom glared at him. "And what do you suggest?"

Daddy thought it over, said, "I suggest we leave things like they are. You're welcome here, Rosy. I don't want you roaming the streets. You really don't have anyplace to go . . . Do you?"

"No, sir, Mr. Stanley, I don't."

"Well, then, you got to stay. But this old dog ain't gonna hunt. Where did you see this nig . . . this fella?"

"On Main Street," Callie said. "But he'd be gone by now. You should have seen him, Daddy, lookin' in the car, scary-like."

"Where's he live, Rosy?" Daddy asked.

"Down in the Section."

"Where in the Section?"

She told him.

"I'll check by there," he said. "I don't find him, I'll call the police."

"No, Stanley," Mom said. "The man is dangerous. He might have a gun."

"He might not have no gun," Rosy said. "But he carry a knife or a razor all the time, and he cut you too, you can bet on that."

"Go to the police right away," Mom said.

"I'll be back," Daddy said. He went upstairs, put on a clean shirt, got his hat, went out.

I said, "You think he'll go to the police?"

Mom said, "I certainly hope so."

———

DADDY WAS GONE for some time. We were all nervous about his whereabouts. Mom and Callie went about household duties, and I picked up paper on the lot with the nail stick. When I finished, I read the last Sherlock Holmes story in the book Buster had loaned me, but my mind never really wrapped around it.

We were, to put it mildly, excited when Daddy finally came in the door, removing his hat.

"Did you tell the police?" Callie asked.

"I did," Daddy said. "I gave them the description you gave me. But first, I went by the shack where he lives . . . Where you lived, Rosy. He wasn't there. And neither was the shack."

"How's that, Mr. Stanley?"

"It was burned to the ground."

"He threatened to do that with me in it," Rosy Mae said. "I'm glad I wasn't in it."

"Police are out looking for him. They said they'd keep us posted."

"I want to keep all the doors locked," Mom said. "I'm scared for all of us."

"Not a bad idea," Daddy said, "but I doubt he'll come around here."

"I ain't puttin' nothin' past him," Rosy Mae said. "Not now. If'n he's big on the whiskey, they ain't no tellin'.'"

Suppose I should have mentioned seeing Bubba Joe, and I'm not exactly sure why I didn't. Sort of felt it really didn't matter. He wasn't out there now, and Mother and Callie were already upset enough, and if I told Daddy, he might charge off looking for him, might do something to him that need not be done. Or maybe, though it was hard to imagine, Bubba Joe might hurt Daddy.

I was a mess of emotions.

In the end, I was silent.

At least as far as my family went.

———

THE DAY WENT BY nervously. I found myself constantly looking to see if Bubba Joe was trying to storm the drive-in fence, or the locked gate where cars came in.

When Buster arrived that day, I went out to see him.

"You look skittish, boy."

"I am," and I told him why.

"He's a crazy nigger, Stanley. Always beatin' on women and such. I ain't never liked him, got no truck with him. But I don't think he'll come over here in the white section. He scared of whites. Not no individual white, but whites in general. Some coloreds I know think you get a cold from a white person it's twicet as bad as from a colored."

"I don't think Bubba Joe is the kind to worry about a cold."

"You got a point there."

"Think I saw him the other day. Out front of the drive-in, staring."

"Was he in the yard?"

"Out by the highway."

"Still don't think you need to shit yourself just yet. He ain't likely to come on a white man's property without an invitation . . . Well, he might. Ain't no tellin' what a crazy man will do."

I didn't exactly find that cheering, but I set about going through the newspaper clippings, primarily because Buster was enjoying it so much.

In the clippings I came across one about the murder and the fire written some days after they happened. It was a kind of sum-up of events so far. About how Margret's body had been found by a hunter, and that he had reported it. It said it was a tragedy, but you could tell from the article the main tragedy for the writer was the death of the Stilwind girl, the burning down of the house of a prominent family. The article listed all the school awards the Stilwind girl had won, said how pretty she was. Margret was just a murdered girl down by the railroad tracks.

I pointed this clipping out to Buster.

"So, this fella, whoever he is that's supposed to have done the killin' on Margret, you think he's running to make a killing back at the Stilwinds'?"

"I don't know. I guess."

"Think about it. He might have had time to get from the tracks to the Stilwind house, but then he got to get in, not get caught, and he got to tie the Stilwind girl up, gag her so she'll be quiet. He'd be busy, wouldn't he?"

"Yes, sir."

"He got to do all that, get the fire set, get out of the house without gettin' caught. Think on that."

I thought a moment, said, "Maybe he tied and gagged her, went and killed Margret, then came back and set the fire."

"Too much trouble."

"It's making my head hurt," I said.

"I hear that," Buster said. "I got a bit of an ache myself."

———

As NIGHT NEARED, I began to regret my plans with Richard. The idea of sneaking out frightened me. If my parents found out, I could be locked away at home for the rest of the summer.

There was also the fact I was scared because Bubba Joe was about. I had spent the day with a chill up my spine over Bubba Joe, and to think I might go out at night and wander about seemed crazy.

I could explain it to Richard, but it would sound like an excuse. I had made a deal and didn't want to disappoint him. Or to be more truthful, I didn't want to be perceived as a sissy, since he had already brought that possibility up.

As the sun set, my dread rose. After the family had gone to bed, and I presumably had gone to bed, I lay there with Nub, looking up at my ceiling, thinking about poor Margret, Jewel Ellen, the crazy woman in her abandoned house, the colored kid supposedly at the bottom of the heap of wood dust, and, of course, mean ole Bubba Joe and everything else that had crossed my mind in the last few weeks. Not to mention the memory of a braking semi-truck.

I thought about all those things until they jumbled together.

I considered listening to the radio for a while, but didn't. I just lay there with my hands crossed on my stomach, and waited. This proved too much for me, however. The tension was making me sweat. I decided to get up.

I had put on my pajamas for bed, but after I was certain the house was quiet, I dressed in blue jeans, tennis shoes, and an old blue shirt. I had a little wind-up clock, and I carried it over to the window and let the moonlight show me its face.

Eleven fifteen.

I pulled a chair next to the window, so while sitting I could see out the crack between window and window fan, watching for Richard. I put the clock on the floor next to me, and about every thirty seconds I checked it.

At eleven forty-five, Richard showed up. I could see him ride into the yard and stop, waiting for me.

I took my pocketknife off the top of the dresser, put it in my pocket. I put my clock on the nightstand. Nub was standing beside me, all ready to go on an adventure.

"Stay, Nub. Stay here."

Nub looked at me as if I had insulted him.

"Not this time, Nub. Stay."

Easing the door open, I glanced back at Nub, who was lying down, looking at me in that sad way only a dog can manage. I closed the door, stepped on the landing, went quietly downstairs.

When I entered the kitchen, Callie, wearing her pajamas, was standing at the refrigerator pouring milk into a glass. The light from inside it framed her and poured out on the floor.

"Stanley?"

"What are you doing up?"

"I'm pouring milk. What are you doing dressed?"

"Nothing."

"Bull. You were slipping out."

"Was not."

"Were too. You tell me what you're doing, or I'm going to wake up Mom and Daddy."

I hesitated. Lies slipped through my head like minnows through a big fish net, none of them big enough or good enough to catch and use.

"You're gonna wake up Rosy," I said.

Callie glanced toward the living room. We could hear Rosy snoring. It sounded like someone sawing logs with a dull crosscut.

"Let's step out back," she said.

She unlocked the back door and we went out on the veranda. "Now tell me," she said.

I gave her the background, briefly as I could.

"Ghosts?" she said. "You believe in ghosts?"

"I don't know. I wanted to find out."

Callie was quiet. She still had her glass of milk and she sipped it slowly.

"Richard's out front waiting on me."

"You know Bubba Joe could be out there."

"I know."

"Kind of exciting really."

Actually, I wasn't all that excited. I was just worried about being perceived as a sissy.

"I'm going with you."

"Do what?"

"I'm going with you. I want to see a ghost."

"You can't go with us."

"It's either I go, or I tell Mom and Daddy about you."

"I'll tell them you wanted to go too."

"They won't believe you."

"You could end up in trouble."

"So could you."

"You already been in trouble. Sure you want to chance it?"

"Want to chance yourself getting in trouble?"

"Oh, all right."

"I have to change."

"I'll tell Richard."

"If you know what's good for you, you won't try and slip off with him. You hear me, Stanley?"

"We're taking bikes as far as the sawmill."

"So, I'll bring my bike."

"Do you still remember how to ride?"

"I believe I can still figure it out. Now go out front and wait on me."

"I'll need the key to take my bike out."

Callie reached it off the key hook inside next to the door.

"All right. You unlock the gate, leave it open, hang the key on the latch, and I'll lock up when I get my bike out. I'll lock up the house as I come out."

————

I OPENED THE GATE, pushed my bicycle out to meet Richard. "I was beginning to think you were asleep," Richard said.

I thought: Now there was a lie I could have used. I could have told him I fell asleep. Why hadn't I thought of that?

It was too late, of course.

"My sister caught me. She's coming too."

"She can't."

"She can. Or she's going to tell on me."

"A girl."

"Yes, Richard. She is a girl. Sisters usually are."

He sighed. "All right. Where is she?"

"Getting dressed."

After about five minutes, Callie showed up pushing her bike, her hair tied back in a ponytail. She had on jeans rolled almost to the knee, pink tennis shoes, and a large pink shirt tied in front with the shirttails. In the moonlight I could see that she had put on lipstick.

"Who's the warpaint for?" I said. "The ghost?"

"You never know who you might meet." Callie straddled her bike, said, "I'm ready."

12

WE RODE SWIFTLY beneath the light of the partial moon.
The shadows of the pine trees fell silent across the road
in front of us in dark arrowhead shapes. The air was cool and
bats circled overhead diving at bugs. The only sound was the
whistling of bicycle tires on concrete, the grind of our chains
rolling on their sprockets as we pedaled.

When we came to the abandoned sawmill, we stopped and
looked at it. In the moonlight it seemed formidable. I half expected the machinery to start up. Every shadow I saw, was, for
an instant, a ghostly sawmill worker moving about his job.

"All the sawmill workers I ever knowed was missin' a finger," Richard said. "My daddy's worked sawmill some, and
he's missin' a finger on his left hand. Since he whips my ass
with the belt in his right, it ain't been a real hindrance to him.
'Sides, a missing piece of finger don't matter if you can make
a fist."

"I came to see a ghost," Callie said. "If there is such a thing. I don't want to hear about fingers cut off in sawmills."

"Place where it is is on the other side of the sawmill," Richard said. "Through the woods, down by the tracks. I can't guarantee you'll see anything. But that's where it's supposed to be."

"Through the woods?" Callie said.

"That's right." Richard looked at me. "That's why I didn't want you to bring a girl."

"What's that mean?" Callie asked.

"You sound all frighty. Ooooh, the woods. You might get a bramble in your hair."

"I didn't say I couldn't do it. Wouldn't do it. I merely asked where the ghost was. I'm here to see a ghost, aren't I? You think an old sawmill and some trees are going to stop me?"

"Did Stanley tell you this ghost hasn't got a head?"

"If you're trying to scare me, save it. I assume if I'm frightened by this ghost, if there is a ghost, I'll be just as scared if it has a head or doesn't."

"We'll leave our bikes by the sawmill," Richard said.

We pushed our bikes into the brush by the mill, leaned them against the rotting posts that held up the back wall. Richard looked at Callie, said, "Stanley tell you there's a little dead nigger boy under all that sawdust?"

"Do what?"

Richard paused to tell her the story. I realized in his own damaged way, he was flirting with Callie, trying to impress her.

"I don't believe that story at all," she said. "And I'd rather you not use that word in my presence."

"What word?"

"What you call Negroes."

"Niggers?"

"That's the word."

"Nigger, nigger, nigger."

Callie gave Richard a look that made him move back slightly. In the dark I could feel that look, and I wasn't even the target.

"Let's just go see the ghost," Callie said.

Richard's mouth formed the beginnings of one more smart remark, but he saved it. I thought that a wise decision.

———

THE MOONLIGHT LAY only on the trail in front of us, the rest of it was sucked up by the darkness between the trees. A night bird called, and a possum, surprised by our presence as we rounded the trail, hissed loudly at us, then scampered away and blended into the woods.

"I almost dirtied my pants," Callie said.

"I even jumped a little," Richard said.

"You jumped a lot," Callie said. "I thought you were going to jump up in my arms."

Before Richard could argue, we heard a sound, like sobbing, then the crunch of something followed by a whacking noise, then more crunching. All of this overlaid with the sobbing.

Richard, who was in front of us, held up his hand, and we stopped. "Step off the path," he said. His voice gave little more sound than the beating of a butterfly's wings.

We hunkered down by a big tree.

"What is that?" Callie asked. "An animal?"

"If it is, it ain't no animal I know of," Richard said. "And I'm in these woods all the time."

"Maybe this animal hasn't been in the woods when you're in them," Callie said. "Until now."

We listened some more. Definitely sobbing. A crunching sound. Then a sound like something smacking at the dirt.

"It's off up in the woods to the right," Richard said. "It could be the ghost."

"I thought she was by the railroad tracks?" I said.

"Maybe she got tired of the railroad tracks."

"That sounds like a man crying," Callie said.

"There's a little trail over on that side of the path," Richard said. "If we're real quiet, we can come out close enough to see what's making the noise."

"Are we sure we want to?" I said.

"We came to see the ghost, didn't we?" Richard said.

"I don't believe it's a ghost," Callie said.

"If we ain't afraid of a ghost," Richard said, "then we ought not be afraid of someone cryin', should we?"

"I suppose not," Callie said.

We got back on the path, went up a ways. Richard led us onto a side trail that was overlapped with brush. We had to bend low to pass along it. It eventually widened, the brush disappeared, and there were just pines planted in a row, awaiting the saw.

Through them we could see something moving. We eased up, staying close to trees. When we finally stopped and squatted down, we saw it was a man. He had his back to us. He was wearing a hat, and he was digging in the dirt. Beside him, on the ground, lay something large wrapped in a blanket. The man was sobbing as he dug.

"It's my daddy," Richard said. "I can tell."

"Why's he crying?" I asked.

"How would I know . . . I ain't never known him to cry. About nothin'."

"You think he's burying money?"

"What money? I can't believe this. I ain't never seen him cry like that."

"Everybody cries," Callie said.

"I ain't never seen my daddy cry," Richard said.

"Now you have," Callie said.

We continued to squat there, whispering, then finally fell silent. Mr. Chapman ceased digging with his shovel, dropped it on the ground, picked up an axe and went to chopping. After a moment, he put the axe down, grabbed the shovel, went back to digging. Finally he tossed the shovel down and dragged the blanket-wrapped object into the hole and started covering it with dirt.

After a time, he patted the ground with the shovel, said a soft prayer, then, with tools in hand, went through the woods sobbing.

"I want to see what it is," Richard said.

"Maybe we ought not," I said.

"If my daddy is cryin' over it," Richard said, "I want to see what it is."

"What do you think, Callie?" I asked.

"It don't matter what neither of you think," Richard said. "I'm gonna have me a look."

We moved cautiously over to the fresh diggings. Richard got down on his knees, began raking back the dirt. We joined him. Obviously, the digging had been hard, marred by all the roots, and that's what the axe had been for; there were pieces of chopped root mixed with the dirt.

There was a wide place above us with no tree limbs and the moonlight came through and landed right on the hole. It showed us what Mr. Chapman had put there. A patchwork quilt.

"That's one of my mother's quilts," Richard said.

"It's very pretty," Callie said. Then looked at me, like: What am I saying?

Richard took hold of the quilt, tugged, but nothing happened. He pulled harder. The blanket moved. A head rolled free, and moonlight fell into its visible, dirt-specked eye.

————

IT WAS A LARGE DOG'S HEAD.

At first, I thought the head had been severed, but it was merely rolling loosely on the neck.

"It's Butch," Richard said.

"Why is he burying a dog?" Callie asked. "Besides it being dead, of course."

"It's his dog," I said.

"Daddy was cryin' over the dog," Richard said. "He loved Butch. Damn. I didn't know he was dead. He was pretty old. I guess he just keeled over . . . Damn, cryin'."

I noticed Richard was crying as well. His tears in the moonlight looked like balls of amber that had heated up and come loose. They rolled down his face and over his chin. I thought at the time he was crying for Butch. Later I thought different.

"I wouldn't have thought he would have cried for anything. But Butch . . . I'll be damned."

"Maybe we should cover him back up," Callie said.

Richard pulled the quilt around Butch. We shoved the dirt back into the hole, finished by scraping pine straw over the grave with our feet.

"Tomorrow, I'll bring some rocks out here, put them on top," Richard said. "It'll keep the varmints from diggin' him up."

"You want to just go on home?" I said.

Richard shook his head. "No. I guess if I go home Daddy will see me. He may already know I'm gone. If I'm gonna take a beatin', I ought to take it for somethin' I did completely. He wouldn't want to know I seen him cryin', and I darn sure don't want him to know."

A breeze made the pines sigh, as if standing tall made them tired. When we reached the trail the breeze picked up, tossed leaves about, hurtled them past and against us like blinded birds.

As we went, I had the uncanny feeling that someone was following us. That sensation you get of dagger points in the back of your head. When I turned there was nothing but the trees bending and flapping and leaves flying. I wondered if it could be Mr. Chapman out there, watching, or the ghost, or an animal. Or Bubba Joe. Or my imagination.

The trail emptied into a field scraped flat and pocked with gravel. There was a little railway shed there with a big padlock on the door. A little farther out were the rails, glowing like silver ribbons in the moonlight. Even before we were close, you could smell the creosote on the railroad ties. It was strong enough to make your eyes water.

"Where's the ghost?" Callie asked.

"I didn't say she'd be standin' here waitin' on us," Richard said. "'Sides, this ain't where they found her body. It's up a ways. There ain't no guarantee you'll see anything."

We walked to the tracks, crossed, sauntered up to where the woods crept close to the tracks and there was only a bit of a gravel path next to the rails.

"I can't believe I'm out here doing this," Callie said. "I must be crazy."

"I didn't make you come," I said.

"I couldn't let you go by yourself. Jeeze Louise, what was I thinking. I could end up never leaving the house again.

Daddy just set me free, and here I am again, acting like an idiot. Well, actually, I didn't really do anything the first time."

"You sure have this time," I said.

"Why don't you shut your holes," Richard said. "If we come on the ghost, y'all gonna scare it away."

"If we can scare it, it isn't much of a ghost," Callie said.

I don't know how far we went, but in the woods you could see swampy water and hear huge bullfrogs calling as if through megaphones. The way they splashed in the water, they sounded big as dogs.

"I knowed this colored woman once told me there's a King of Bullfrogs," Richard said.

"A king?" Callie said.

"A great big bullfrog. Said he was once this old nig— colored man, and he got this spell put on him, and he turned into this big black bullfrog. He rules over all the frogs and snakes and swimmin' things."

"Isn't he lucky," Callie said.

"Why'd he get turned into a frog?" I asked.

"He messed with women, and his wife was a witch and she done it 'cause he wouldn't do right."

"Good for her," Callie said.

"He's supposed to steal kids, take them back to the swamp for the frogs to eat."

"Frogs don't have teeth," Callie said.

"They still eat."

"Well, they aren't big enough to eat children," she said.

"Mostly the King Frog eats them. He's got a crown on his head. He looks like a big colored man that squats like a frog. He ain't exactly a man or a frog, but kinda both."

"Maybe Chester would make a nice white frog to complement the black one," Callie said. "He could be the Queen Frog . . . Think you could get me that frog recipe, Richard?"

"I thought you didn't like Chester," I said.

"I don't. I liked him, you think I'd want him to be a frog?"

"Colored man's wife turned him into a frog," Richard said. "Didn't she like him?"

"Not after she turned him into a frog," Callie said.

"Ssshhhhhh," Richard said. "That's her house."

"Whose house?" I asked.

"Hers. Margret's. The girl got her head run over. The one that's a ghost."

A chill went over me. It was strange to think that I was perhaps walking ground she had walked.

Visible through the trees, beyond a stand of slick, slimy water, we could see a small, white, clapboard house. The moonlight leaned on it like a thug and made it very bright.

In the distance were other small houses. It was what some called a clapboard community.

"Her mother still lives there. Daddy says she shacks up with a nigger . . . a colored man. She's a whore is what I hear."

"You hear a lot," Callie said.

"What's that mean?"

"It means you hear all kinds of things, but that doesn't mean all, or any of it, is true."

"I tell you, that's the house. That's where Margret lived. Her body with the head cut off was found right around here somewheres. She wasn't that far from home."

"What's that?" I said.

Down the tracks where they bent around the trees and the swamp land, I could see something bright. It didn't have a definite color. Sometimes it seemed green, sometimes gold. It moved toward us bobbing up and down, as if it were being dribbled. Then it moved from side to side. Disappeared. Popped back into view and started moving toward us again.

"Someone coming down the tracks," Callie said.

"Where's the someone?" Richard said. "It's the ghost. It's Margret's ghost."

"With a flashlight," Callie said.

The light nodded up and down, crossed over the tracks, floated up a bit, then veered into the woods, hung over the slimy water, came back to the edge of the tracks and moved toward us.

"If it's a flashlight," I said, "whoever is carrying it is very busy. And very acrobatic. And he can walk on water."

The hairs on my neck and arms crawled, and I could feel my scalp constrict.

The light danced along the tracks, went past us.

"What is that?" Callie asked.

"I told you," Richard said. "That's her. The headless ghost. She's out here with a light, looking for her head."

"Where do ghosts get lights?" Callie said. "They go to a store and ask for a light? They buy ghostly flashlights?"

I looked at Callie. She talked cool, but I knew her well enough to know she had been startled.

We watched the light move down the tracks, pop into the woods, dance among the trees and on top of the water. Then, suddenly, it was gone.

I realized I had been holding my breath.

"I don't know if that was a ghost," I said. "But whatever it was, I've had enough. Let's go home."

"Let's stay on this side of the tracks," Callie said. "Maybe we'll see it again."

"I don't want to see it again," Richard said.

"Me neither," I said.

"Oh, don't be such Nellies. Come on."

As we walked it became apparent that in the woods next to us, near the water, something was moving. We all heard it and we stopped to listen, and what was moving stopped as well. I looked at the trees and the glimmer of water between them, but I couldn't see anyone.

We looked at one another, and without so much as a word, started moving again. As we did, the stepping alongside us started up, and this time I saw someone amongst the trees, moving quickly and carefully, darting from tree to tree. If that wasn't enough, to my right, I heard a humming sound.

I turned, glanced. Nothing. But I knew what it was.

The rails. They were humming because a train was approaching.

Callie gave me a look that showed she was finally, and truly, frightened. "Walk faster," she said.

We did. Much faster. So did our companion in the woods. And he was moving close to the edge of the trees, nearer to us. The train's headlight flashed behind us, filled the night with a glow like a second moon. The whistle sounded and I nearly jumped out of my skin.

"Run," Callie said. We broke and ran all out. Whoever, or whatever, was in the woods beside us began running as well; the harder we ran, the harder it ran.

I peered over my shoulder, saw a man lurch out of the woods, start sprinting behind us. I knew in a glance it must be Bubba Joe. His bulk was framed in the light of the train. His hat brim blew back and his coat trailed behind him like the rags of a wraith.

The train was chugging and puffing, popping sparks, blowing its whistle, telling anyone up the way that might listen it was coming fast and would soon cross the trestle bridge.

When it was almost on us, Callie, who was breathing heavy, said, "We got to cross the tracks. We don't, he'll catch us."

She crossed, her long legs flying like those of a grasshopper. I went after her. Richard followed as the train passed and the wind of it blew up the back of my shirt and ruffled my hair. The train charged on, clanked and sparked the rails, filled our nostrils with the stench of charred oil and hot scraped metal.

Our pursuer was left on the other side of the track.

I looked down the track, observed it was a long train a winding. It would be coming for some time before it passed us. I bent over and gulped air and felt as if I were going to throw up. We had missed death by only a few feet. I wanted to grab Callie and start hitting her, and I wanted to grab her and kiss her, because if we hadn't crossed, Bubba Joe, or whoever that was, would have caught us. I don't know what he would have done with us, but he would have caught us.

I said, "I think that was Bubba Joe."

"Could have just been some hobo," Callie said, taking a deep breath.

"I don't care who it was," Richard said. "I'm goin' home, and I don't care if Daddy does catch me and give me a beatin'."

We started walking away, then started running, and pretty soon we were on the wooded trail and the wind and the blowing leaves followed us all the way back to the sawmill. We paused there to get our breath. I looked up at the hanging metal ladder that led up to the upper level of what was left of the mill, heard the chute shift and creak in the breeze.

We got our bikes. Richard rode home. Me and Callie did the same.

Quietly, we put our bikes away, snuck into the house, talked briefly in my room about what we had done and seen. Callie finally wore out and went to bed.

All night I lay awake to look out the crack between the window and water fan, watching to see if Bubba Joe was there. I never saw him, and as the sun crept up, I became too tired to watch and fell sleep.

It was an uneasy sleep, full of the tall dark mill and its

creaking sawdust chute. The dancing light that might have been Margret. The black Frog King who should have left other women alone. Bubba Joe. The dead dog in the patchwork quilt. Richard's daddy sobbing, saying a prayer.

Finally, there was the snaky black train, its bright light and shrill whistle, the chill wind from the engine and boxcars as they passed us by.

PART THREE

Click, Click, Click

13

NEXT DAY, having slept poorly, I awoke early, checked all the locks on the doors and windows. There were no signs of anyone trying to break in.

I was checking the sliding back door when Daddy came in, pushing his hair back, wiping sleep from his eyes with a forearm.

He noticed what I was doing, studied me for a moment, said, "Sit down, boy."

I sat down at the table across from him. Half expected him to ask me where I had been last night.

"Don't let this Bubba Joe thing get to you," he said. "He isn't going to do anything to us. I'll make sure he leaves us alone. Wouldn't surprise me if the police have already picked him up. I'll call them right after I have coffee and breakfast. Want to help me fix Mom and Callie and Rosy some breakfast?"

"Sure."

While we prepared breakfast, I thought about last night. Maybe Daddy was wrong about Bubba Joe not being able to hurt us. A man like that, he might just come to our house with a knife in his hand.

Fact was, he may have been near our house last night, followed us to the tracks. I thought on that awhile, decided, not likely. With us on bicycles, that wouldn't have been easy, so maybe he picked up on us at the sawmill road. He could have been there. Hiding in the sawmill after burning down the house where he and Rosy Mae stayed.

Or he hadn't followed us at all. It was possible when we reached the railroad tracks he was in the vicinity. The woods were thick near the tracks and he could have been hiding most anywhere.

Whatever the case, I felt certain he had known who Callie and I were, and that he came after us as a sort of revenge for housing Rosy.

Rosy said he carried a knife or a razor, and I had no reason to doubt her. If he had caught us last night . . . Well, I didn't want to dwell on that.

As I thought about all this, I took the bread from the toaster, buttered it and applied jelly on top of that. The actual cooking of sausage, boiling the coffee, I left to Daddy.

When it was ready, he said, "Go wake 'em up, tell 'em breakfast is ready."

As I was heading out, Daddy said, "We ought to enjoy these summer days. School starts soon, and we won't have these lazy times together. It's good we're all home at the same time."

"Yes, sir."

I started out again. Daddy said, "Son?"

"Yes, sir."

"I love you."

I smiled at him, said, "You too," and I went to get the women.

————

THAT AFTERNOON Buster didn't show. He had been coming in early, but when I expected him, no Buster. When it came time for him to actually be there, still no Buster.

Daddy said, "Where in hell is that sonofabitch?"

We were out on the veranda by the snack bar. I said, "He told me if he didn't come in today, he was sick."

Daddy studied me with those steely eyes, and for a moment, I thought I'd crack. He said, "Why didn't you tell me before?"

"I forgot. He said he wasn't feeling well, and he might not be here, but I thought he would, and I just forgot about it."

"That so?"

"Yes, sir . . . But I can run the reels."

"You can?"

"Buster taught me how."

"Good. Real good. You go set it up, son. Tonight, you're the projectionist."

As I started for the booth, I felt a sense of relief. Sure, there was a certain feeling of guilt, having lied for Buster, but I felt it was a good lie. What Mom called a white lie. Buster was my friend and deserved my support.

That night I ran a Randolph Scott Western, and it went well, with only a slight delay between changing reels. This was greeted with horn honking and yells, but I made the transition quick enough, and by the end of the movie I felt like a pro. Daddy even brought me out a hamburger, Coke, and french fries.

He set the meal on the little table by the reel machine, said, "How would you like to take Buster's job?"

I didn't feel so smart anymore, and I sure didn't feel good.

"Oh, no, Daddy. I had trouble with that reel. I wasn't too smooth."

"You did all right. It was quick enough. Practice will make you better."

"Daddy, I don't think so. It's Buster's job."

"You and that old nigger have gotten pretty tight, haven't you?"

"Yes, sir."

"Stanley, you can do this job, and if you do it, I can pay you, keep the money in the family. And, frankly, I can pay you less. Until you have experience."

"I don't want Buster's job . . . I wouldn't want to do that, Daddy."

"All right. I respect that. But I'll tell you this. It's only a matter of time anyway. He's getting old. He drinks quite a bit. He's surly. Kind of uppity, if you ask me. And you can run the projector."

"He taught me. I don't think he did it so I could take his job."

"He misses again, doesn't plan ahead by telling me, and I don't mean leaving some message about how he might get sick, you are the projectionist. Understand, son? We have to work together. We're family. I know you like Buster but we have to take care of us first. Way we're going, we'll have every starving, sad nigger in town working here at the drive-in. We can't afford that."

Daddy gave me a pat on the head and went away.

14

FOLLOWING DAY, I wanted to find Buster, but Daddy had chores for me to do. I spent the morning picking up paper cups, wrappers, and condoms with the nail-pointed stick.

I hadn't forgotten Bubba Joe, but as it is with kids, it wasn't on my mind as much now that I was out of danger and it was daylight and the sun was bright and hot.

Noon, I was trapped by Rosy Mae's lunch. Cheeseburgers that were so good they made you want to cry.

While we ate, Callie reminded Daddy she had been exonerated, that he had beat up on Chester, and that Chester had been innocent.

Daddy said, "Well, he took the beating anyway."

"But Daddy," Callie said. "He didn't do anything."

"Yeah, but I know his type. It's just a matter of time. You stay away from him."

"Any word on Bubba Joe?" Mom asked Daddy.

"Not yet. I'll go by the police station later today. I have

some errands to run in town. There have been a couple rumors he's been seen."

"How do you know?" Mom asked.

"Because I check, dear. I didn't see any reason to disturb you about it unless there was some finality to the situation."

Callie edged an eye in my direction. We exchanged looks.

I ate the cheeseburger, then found my chance to slip off. As I was heading out the door, Daddy said, "You pick up everything?"

"Yes, sir."

"Where are you going?"

"I thought I'd try to find Richard. Maybe we could go fishing or something."

"You be back here in time to run the projector, just in case."

"Yes, sir."

"It looks like rain, Stanley," Mother said. "Don't stay away too long. It could really storm and you'd be caught out in it."

"I'll go in a store or something," I said. "I can take care of myself."

"I suppose so," Mother said, but she didn't sound all that confident. She said, "I'm just being a ninny, but I worry about Bubba Joe too. You want to stay away from anywhere he might be."

"And where would that be, Gal?" Daddy asked.

"I guess most anywhere."

"That's right," Daddy said. "Maybe you ought to stay here."

"He hasn't anything against me," I said.

Callie gave me a look. She said, "Maybe you ought not go."

"He can be a mean man," Rosy Mae said.

"I'll have Nub with me."

"That'll scare him off, all twenty-five pounds," Mom said.

I looked at Nub sitting on the floor. He was sleepy-looking, panting. He didn't look particularly scary.

"May I go?" I asked.

"Hell," Daddy said. "He's right. We're making a booger bear out of this Bubba Joe. He's not going to bother whites. I'll bet you on that. Be careful, son. And come home early. And Nub, you watch after him."

Nub beat his tail on the ground, ran over to Daddy and licked his hand. Daddy gave him a pet, then I called to Nub and we went outside.

I had certainly thought about the Bubba Joe situation, and, of course, had Daddy known about the other night, no way he would have let me go.

As it was, Daddy thought it was just a problem between coloreds, and that Bubba Joe was just trying to intimidate Mom and Callie that day as they were an opportune target. I think Daddy thought because we were white we had a kind of immunity as long as we were within our community.

I knew better. I also knew if it was true, I was about to leave our community. But I had to see Buster.

I intended to ride my bike, but when I got on it, the chain slipped off and I couldn't get it back on. I thought about trying to get Daddy to help, but decided against it. I didn't want to stall any longer, and didn't want Daddy to start asking questions or find some chore for me to do. Maybe decide it wasn't safe for me to go. I started off toward town walking, Nub trotting at my side.

————

WHEN I REACHED town the sky darkened and I had that uncomfortable feeling of being followed. Just like the other night when Bubba Joe had shown up. Or whoever it was. I had the same feeling now, but when I looked around I didn't see anyone. There was just Main Street and buildings and lots of cars parked along the street.

I took a deep breath and kept stepping. Above, the sky continued to darken; it gave me the willies. I thought of turning around, but didn't. Nub didn't seem to notice the change in the weather, or rather he didn't care. He was as happy as if he had good sense and a bone. But I did notice that from time to time he would stop, turn around and look back the way we had come, as if he too felt we were being followed.

That was not heartening.

I turned at Oak Street as it began to sprinkle, made my way toward where Buster lived. The sensation of being followed grew. But when I turned to look all I saw were the great oaks on either side of the street and the wind picking up leaves and blowing them about and two old cars rattling by with black faces behind the wheels.

I went past the men on the porch. They all waved at me, not bothering to torment me with comments. In fact, they looked friendly; it occurred to me their joking had been primarily designed for Buster.

We strolled until I saw the great billboard that hung over Buster's house, the bright woman's smile wet with rain and peeling as if everything she had been happy about was a lie. I went up on Buster's porch and knocked.

He didn't answer.

Me and Nub went around to the window at the back. I tried to look in, but didn't see anybody. All I could see was the table with boxes of newspapers on it.

Back on the front porch, I knocked again. Still he didn't answer.

I called Buster's name a few times, but I got the same lack of results.

I took hold of the doorknob, turned it, found it was unlocked.

I told Nub to stay, slipped inside.

Except for light coming through the back window, falling in a rectangle across the table, showing dust motes floating in it like gnats, the house was dark.

I called Buster's name again, then went looking. There were few places to look and I found him lying on the narrow bed pushed up against the wall.

He was lying with one hand under his head, the other thrown across his hip with the palm up. I touched him and called his name, but he didn't move. I listened for snoring, but didn't hear any. I didn't hear any breathing either. I noted a foul smell. I thought maybe the worst had happened.

Suddenly, he snorted, and began to snore. From that snoring came more of the foul odor, and though I had had little experience with it, I knew what the smell was.

Liquor.

Buster was stone dead drunk.

I shook him several times, but he didn't rise. I decided to give him time and try later. I went over to the table, turned on the light, began looking at what Buster had been reading.

More newspapers.

He had a pad on the table, and written on it were notes. One of the notes said: "Girl's mother."

I looked at it without understanding anything, went over and tried to wake him again. Still, no luck.

The room grew darker and the little slice of light from the window went away and left only the lantern light. The rain began to pound on the tin roof of Buster's shack like someone beating it with a chain. There was a lightning flash visible through the window, followed by darkness, roaring wind and pounding rain. I looked out the window, up at the billboard. It was nothing more than a sheet of rain.

I opened the door and checked on Nub. He was lying on the front porch close to the wall. He looked up at me, but seemed content enough. I went back inside.

I sat in a chair and listened to the rain beating Buster's home, waited for Buster to wake up.

I don't know how long I waited, but finally Buster did awake. I heard him snort like a hog, then make a kind of grumble noise. When I looked, he was throwing his feet over the side of the bed, sitting up. He had both hands holding his head, as if he wanted to keep it from falling off. When he looked up and saw me, he paused for a moment. "What in hell are you doing here?" he said.

"I come to check on you."

"Check on me? You think I need someone checkin' on me. Some little white boy to lead me around by the hand."

"I didn't mean anything by it, Buster."

"Didn't mean anything by it," he said, his voice a singsong mock of mine. "Just thought you'd come check on your nigger, didn't you?"

"No. I mean. We're friends, and I . . ."

"Friends? Who you kiddin', white boy? You and me ain't never been friends, and ain't never gonna be."

"I thought . . ."

"You thought too damn much, you little skeeter. Get on out of my house now."

"It's just Daddy said if you miss work again, you're fired. I lied for you. I told him you were sick—"

"Did I ask you to lie for me?"

"No. I—"

"I don't need nobody lying for me. Not to no white man or

any man. I don't show for work, that's my own business. And all this detective shit, forget it. You and me are through with this."

"I don't understand, Buster. What did I do—"

"Just go."

"Buster—"

He snatched up a book lying beside the bed and tossed it at me. It struck the far wall, fell to the floor in a flutter of pages.

I jerked open the door and went out. Rain was blasting hard against the porch and it was as dark as a night without moonlight. Nub was still lying where I had left him. He beat his tail on the porch when I called his name.

I closed the door, stood looking into the wet, wind-swept darkness. I could see the road, but not well. Too much rain, too many tears.

I waited until there was a lightning flash, and in that flash I saw where the road was. And I saw something else. Nub stiffened by my side and growled.

What I saw was someone standing on the other side of the road. In that flash I couldn't tell if who I saw was black or white, only that they wore a hat and the hat was washed down from the pressure of the rain, fell over their face and drained water from the brim.

I was caught between a hammer and an anvil. I couldn't stay with Buster, and I didn't want to find out who it was on the other side of the road. Someone willing to stand in the storm and wait.

When the lightning lit up the world again, there was no one there. All right, I thought. He's moved on. Maybe he thinks I'm going to go back inside the house. Maybe he doesn't think anything. Maybe it isn't Bubba Joe, just some passerby.

That was a good thing for me to think. The idea gave me a moment of courage.

When the flash was gone and darkness settled over everything like a hood, I took a deep breath, steeled myself, stepped off the porch, into the wind and rain. The wind was hard to walk against. The rain was cold and ran down my collar. Instantly my clothes were sticking to me as if they had been coated on the inside with Elmer's Glue-All. I could feel Nub pushed up against my leg.

I managed to stick to the side road and make it to the main brick street, then I turned toward town. About all I had to guide me then was an occasional flash of lightning and the feel of those bricks beneath my feet.

I knew if I could reach the white part of town, Mr. Phillips would let Nub and me into his store. Nub was allowed because he had good manners.

I hadn't gone far, thinking this, when I realized to my horror that the bricks that were my guide were no longer under me. I was on the grass that led alongside the street on the creek side. I knew it was the creek side because the rain was causing the water to run fast and I could hear it as loud as if it were running and splashing inside my brain.

I got under a big oak tree, or rather I walked into one and stopped, put my back against it, and shivered in the cold rain. I thought about what I had been taught about trees and storms. Worst place to be was under a tree, as lightning tended to seek the tallest object. But the oak was big and thick. The leaves were large and close together and blocked out some of the rain, and because of that, I could see around me. Not very far, but farther than with it coming down in sheets against my face.

I thought maybe I might be better off to chance the protection of the tree, wait until the storm slacked or passed, but when the lightning flashed again, I had to change my mind.

Standing no less than a dozen feet away, a hat slouched

over his face, was a huge colored man, his hands hanging limp at his sides like hams on twisted strands of thick dark rope.

In that flash, he lifted his head and his eyes latched on me. I have never seen such hatred in a face; those eyes were as black as peepholes into hell. Nub growled, pressed up against me. Then the mean face was gone and I was inside my little umbrella of vision. The rain beyond the thick, leafy boughs of the oak was as compact as the black curtains on a hearse.

I thought: What kind of man is he?

How could he see to follow me?

The brim of his hat? Did that give him an edge?

Or was he just a man of the outdoors? Maybe he had adjusted his eyes longer and better to the rain-swept darkness?

It didn't matter.

It was a mystery beyond me, and not one I was going to solve. The final answer was simple. He could get around and see out here better than I could because he was not afraid of the forces of nature; he was one of them.

I rushed around the oak, to the other side, leaned there, trying to consider what to do. Any moment I expected to see his head nod around to my side of the tree. Then he would grab me.

It was too much to think about.

I started running, all true planning out the window.

I ran hard until I hit a tree and was knocked back, dazed. I tried to get a knee under me, but I kept falling down, partly because the grass was slick, and partly because I was addled.

Nub was leaping up against me in encouragement, and he had begun to bark.

I was almost to my feet when I was grabbed by the shirt collar and spun around. There was a shape close to me, and I could feel heavy breathing against my face and smell tobacco and whiskey. Then there was a voice, like something coming up to me from the depths of a cave, carried on the wings of a bat. The hand gripped and twisted my collar so tight it was cutting off the blood flow to the side of my neck. I was starting to get woozy.

"You peckerwoods took away my Rosy Mae. Now I'm gonna take you away, all your little goddamn white ass family."

Any doubt that Bubba Joe might not hold a grudge against us for Rosy Mae leaving, or that he wouldn't hurt white people, was tossed out the window of the world in that moment.

Then I heard a growl and a snap. Bubba Joe let out a yell, and I knew Nub had him by the leg.

The lightning flashed again, and I could see Bubba Joe clearly. His face was covered in scars and his nose was slightly off center from some old break, his mouth was wide open and he was letting forth a stream of profanity.

Nub was clamped down, going for the bone.

Bubba Joe shook his leg, yelled, cursed, tried to kick Nub free and not let go of me. But it wasn't working. Bubba Joe shot a hand under his coat, brought out a knife big enough to use in the Trojan War, and at the same time let go of my shirt.

"You little bastard," Bubba Joe said, and I realized he was talking to Nub, not me.

I screamed, "Run away, Nub. Run."

But Nub didn't run. He kept biting.

I heard Nub yip and I tried to lash out with my hands, hoping to take Bubba Joe down. But it was like striking a bag full of sand. I could feel my hands being scratched on his thick stubble of beard. Bubba Joe clutched my shirt again.

I waited for the plunge of the knife, but it didn't come.

There was a jerk. Bubba Joe's hand came loose of my shirt, and the next thing I knew, two dark figures were wrestling in the rain. One of them the stout and wide Bubba Joe. The other tall and lanky. I couldn't really see him, but I knew that one was Buster Abbot Lighthorse Smith.

My eyes were better adjusted to the darkness now. I could make out Buster sliding up against Bubba Joe. Bubba Joe's feet went up in the air, and over went Bubba Joe, Nub still hanging on to his leg. Bubba Joe smacked the ground hard. Nub came loose and went spiraling.

The lightning flashed again and I saw Buster better. He had a clasp knife in his hand, one knee on Bubba Joe's left arm, his other leg stretched out, holding Bubba Joe's right wrist with his foot. I could see Bubba Joe's big knife in that hand, but of course, being held down like that, he couldn't use it.

Nub had lost his grip on Bubba Joe's leg, but now he had Bubba Joe by the ear and was biting and pulling for all he was worth, growling so loud it sounded like a car engine running. Bubba Joe, pinned or not, had not stopped his string of profanity.

I saw Buster's hand and clasp knife move. I heard a yell. Then a gurgle. Some moans. I stood there for what seemed like the turning of the century.

Slowly my eyes adjusted. Buster was still in the position I had last seen him, holding his clasp knife, but his head was turned toward me. Nub was sitting by Bubba Joe's head, panting, looking as contented as if he had just caught a rabbit.

Bubba Joe lay still. I went over, loomed above them, and when the lightning came again, I saw clearly that Bubba Joe's throat was cut. The wound looked like the mouth I had cut in last year's Halloween pumpkin, only bloody; the blood ran along his throat, mixed with the rain and was carried away. Bubba Joe's head was turned toward me. His eyes were open. He was shivering.

Then his eyes changed. They were no longer peepholes

into hell. Those holes had been boarded up, and that left him down there in the pit, no way out.

Buster grabbed me, pulled me over to a tree, pushed me up against it. "Damn you, boy. Damn you . . . Are you okay, boy? You cut anywhere?"

"No . . . no, sir."

"Damn you, don't you listen to me I get like that. I got the moods. It's the whiskey. It gives me the moods. Shit, boy. You okay? You ought not have run off like that."

"I thought it was better than being hit with a book."

"Ah, Jesus. Damn, boy."

"What about Bubba Joe?"

"Strong sonofabitch."

"Not for you."

"Jujitsu, boy."

"What?"

"Don't worry about it, son. He's dead . . . Goddamn, that is some dog you got there. He's not big enough to climb up on a step without a grunt, and did you see the way he took after that Bubba Joe? You see that?"

"Yes, sir."

"Some dog, he is. Keep that dog."

"I was going to."

"That there is a dog, boy. Ain't big, but he's got the fight in him. Balls like a brass elephant . . . Damn. Let me think. Right now we got to get rid of Bubba Joe. Creek there is good enough. Ain't no one gonna miss this fella. He turns up, ain't no one gonna be sad. Tell you what. You stay where you are."

Buster took hold of Bubba Joe, dragged him off. In the distance I heard a splash. Buster came back.

"Water will carry him along, I reckon," Buster said. "It's runnin' good and hard . . . You can't say nothin'. Nothin' at all.

Maybe I'm wrong and someone will miss him. You understand me? Don't say nothin'."

"No, sir. I won't."

Buster bent over and threw up. He did this for several minutes. I was glad for the pounding rain, or the smell would have been overwhelming.

"You sick?" I asked.

"Drunk," he said. "Come on. Let's get back to the house and get you dry. And make me some coffee. Damn, boy. I didn't mean to send you out in the rain."

"Yes you did."

"It's the moods. You understand, don't you? I knew what I had done and shouldn't have done right after I done it. You'd already gone out then. Can't blame you. Decided to come get you . . . See the way that dog lit into him? Some dog you got there, boy. You know about moods, don't you? Understand, don't you?"

My sister certainly had them, and so did my father, but nothing like this. Looking back now, I know that Buster's mood swings were probably due to some chemical deficiency mixed with the alcohol, but as of that moment in time, I could only think what so many Southerners thought back then about an odd friend or relative: "It was just his way."

When we got back to Buster's, he let Nub inside with us, had me strip off my clothes. He wrapped a blanket around me and I sat in a chair while he stoked up that old stove of his with chunks of wood and scraps of paper. When the fire was burning hot enough to melt silver, he had me sit by the open door of the stove, next to my clothes, which he shook out and racked on the back of a chair. I thought about what had almost happened to me, and had happened to Bubba Joe. I shook not only with cold, but with fear. I felt vulnerable and embarrassed sitting there in wet underwear.

"You sure he's dead?" I said.

"Oh, yeah, Stan, he's dead. I know dead when I see it. I've seen it a few times."

"Shouldn't we tell the law? It's self-defense."

"No tellin' how them law will act when it's a colored done the killin'. Even if it's colored killing colored. No tellin', so we ain't gonna tell. Are we?"

"No, sir. You saved my life, Buster."

"Wouldn't have needed to had I not acted like a jackass."

"He must have been following me from home. He's been watching our house, 'cause of Rosy Mae. I saw him the other night. Me and my sister and a friend sneaked out of the house to go down and look for Margret's ghost, and we saw it, a kind of light, and then we saw Bubba Joe. He chased us. But we lost him by running in front of a train, leaving him on the other side."

"You knew he was out there?"

"Yes, sir."

"But you came here to tell me about my job?"

"Yes, sir."

"You little fool."

I hung my head. A few moments went by, then Buster, almost bright, said: "The railway light. I've seen that. That ain't no ghost, boy."

"What is it then?"

"I don't know. I seen similar lights out at Marfa, Texas, once. But whatever it is, it ain't no ghost. It's some kind of gas or somethin'. Hell, I don't know. But it ain't no ghost."

"You killed him, Buster. He's dead."

"Yep. He's dead all right. In time he'd have got Rosy or one of you, 'cept maybe your daddy. That's a hell of a man, your daddy."

"I've never heard you say anything good about him before."

"You haven't really heard me say anything bad about him."

"No."

"Listen. I recognize him for what he is. A good father. I wasn't never that. He cares for you. He's tough, and everyone in town knows it. White town, and here on the colored side. Your daddy is known, boy."

"How?"

"Men know. I can't tell you how. Way he carries himself. 'Course, I don't think he likes colored all that much."

"I don't know. He helped Rosy Mae. He's still helpin' her. He says some things that sound bad, but he does pretty good."

"I suppose you're right. You didn't get cut nowhere, did you?"

"No. It was like he was studying on me. Like he was looking to make it last."

"That would have been his way. He got in a knife fight up the old sawmill once, took his time on that nigger. Cut him maybe fifty times, near killed him, got cut a lot himself, but he didn't mind it. Figured he could finish a knife fight at any time."

"He didn't finish you."

"I took him by surprise, and I had a couple of Jap tricks up my sleeve. I learned them from folks picked it up in the army. And I wasn't gonna give him a chance. I threw him, pinned him, finished him. He'd have killed me otherwise. I had to do what I did. You understand that, boy?"

"Yes, sir."

Buster looked down at his shirt. It was covered in blood and the rain had washed it down and into his trousers.

"You're hurt," I said.

"His blood. It sprayed. I'll change shirts."

He took off the bloody shirt and put it in the stove. It burst into flames. His skinny body was covered with scars. Across his back there were welts that made it look as if barbed wire were under his skin.

He got a folded shirt from a box under his bed, slipped it on.

"Someone will find him, won't they?" I said.

"Starts to smell . . . Yeah, they'll find him. And you and me, we ain't gonna say a word. Are we?"

"No, sir."

"I don't mean that as a threat, boy. I'm askin' as a friend."

"You did save my life."

"Suppose I did. Your dog took a little cut."

"What?"

"It ain't nothin'. I'm gonna pour some stuff on it. He'll be good as new. Hell, tough dog like this, he don't even know he's been cut."

Nub may not have minded the cut, but he sure minded that alcohol. He bit Buster.

———

WHILE MY CLOTHES finished drying, we moved to the table, me with a blanket draped over me, Buster drinking coffee, trying to get "the mood out of him," he said.

He got a record player and put a record on it and let it play. "Need to get my mind off this," he said. "Got to not think on it too hard."

The record was of a kind I had never heard before. It wasn't rock and roll, but it reminded me of it.

"That's the blues," Buster said. "Big Joe Turner."

We listened. While we did, I looked at his notes. I said: "What does this mean, Buster?"

It was what I had seen earlier: "Girl's mother."

"That means we got maybe a wedge into this. A way of pushing open the case and seein' what's inside. You find the roots of somethin', then you can better understand the flower of the thing. The flower bein' the murders and the murderers."

"So what do you know?"

"Well, what I know is the mother of that little white girl killed down by the tracks is still alive and maybe she knows something. You remember, I told you how I knew her."

"Yes, sir."

"I talked to some folks I know would know if she's still alive, and she is. She ain't that old actually. She's still in the same house."

"I know," I said. "Down by the tracks near the swamp, not far from the trestle bridge. That's where we went to see the ghost. It's near where Margret was killed."

"You gettin' to be a first-class snoop, Stan. The momma, Winnie, she might know somethin'. I think we can talk to her. Normally I wouldn't bother to talk to no white woman 'cause it could get me lynched. But I know who Winnie is, and she lives with a black man down there by the slough. He's an ornery sort named Chance. Besides, she's not all white. She's dark-skinned 'cause she's got that Mexican, or Puerto Rican, or whatever in her. But I told you that."

"We're going to see her now?"

"Of course not. Not in this weather. And though she's used to seein' men with little or no clothes on, I don't think you'd be all that anxious to go over there in your drawers. Now am I right?"

"Yes, sir."

"What we need to do now is get you dressed and home."

"You'll be at work tonight?"

"If I can stay away from the liquor."

"Daddy told me you don't come to work . . . he's gonna make me the projectionist. I don't want that."

"I know you don't. You're a true friend. And I ain't much of one."

"It doesn't get any truer than what you did for me."

"You go on home and don't think about this no more. You ain't at fault no kind of way. And Bubba Joe, he's about as important to the world as a flea. Another thing. I don't do what I'm supposed to do, you ain't doin' me no shame takin' my job. A man's responsible for what he does or doesn't do. Hear what I'm sayin'?"

"Yes, sir . . . But, Buster . . . Please be there."

"I will. I really do try to keep my word, but that old alcohol gets on me sometimes. You ever been coon huntin', boy?"

"No, sir."

"Well, you get dogs runnin' a coon, and you get down in the bottoms, and that ole coon, when he's bein' chased, he'll lead those dogs out into the wetlands, deep water if he can, then he'll jump on a dog's head and try and drown him. I ain't a lyin'. That's what he'll do. And that dog, he's done committed himself to that deep water, and he's got this coon on him with teeth and claws, and a coon's strong for its size, and it's pushin' down on him, and it's all that dog can do to swim and fight and keep his head above water. Sometimes he does. Sometimes he don't. Alcohol is like that. It's like I'm out in deep water, and that stuff is jumpin' on my head, tryin' to hold me under. I keep fightin'. One day, I don't shake it, that ole coon is gonna win. Gonna push me under for good . . . Good thing, though, is, I'm out of whiskey and ain't got money for more."

———

THE RAIN HAD DIED, but it was still misty. I decided I had to go home anyway. I got dressed. My clothes felt strange, toasty in spots, damp in others.

"You get home. You pet that dog good, you hear?"

"I will," I said.

As I tentatively stepped off the steps, started away, Buster, who had followed me as far as the porch, said, "You ain't got no worry about him anymore. Trust me on that. But that storm ain't through yet. You just got a lull. You get on. Hear?"

I nodded at him, and kept walking.

With the wind gone and the sky less black, it was no longer cold and the summer heat began to make things steam and soon I was sweating like a staked goat at a Fourth of July picnic.

I walked by where Bubba Joe had bought the farm. I saw his knife lying there. Buster had forgotten to pick it up.

I looked around. No one was in sight. I went over and kicked the knife against a tree, used the toe of my shoe to knock dirt over it.

As I did this, a tremble went through me. I thought of Bubba Joe chasing us the other night, earlier today when he had his hand twisted in my shirt, his breath beating me with tobacco and liquor. I thought about the way Buster had drawn his own knife across Bubba Joe's throat, quick and simple like a teacher drawing a chalk line. I thought too of the creek where Buster had tossed Bubba Joe like so much rotten wood.

I could hear the creek water rushing, full of the power of the rain. I thought of Bubba Joe lying down there, the crawdads working at him like they work at bacon on a string. I had the urge to go over for a look. But didn't.

ARRIVED HOME in the late afternoon. When I stepped inside the house, I tried my best to act as if nothing had happened. At first, somehow, I thought my family knew. They were as excited to see me as Lazarus's family was to see him step from the tomb.

Rosy Mae started in with, "We been worried 'bout you, Mr. Stanley. We thought you'd have enough sense to come home right away, way that storm was goin'."

Callie laughed. "But you didn't."

"I got stranded in town," I said. "I sat it out in the drugstore."

I felt sick to my stomach lying like that, but didn't know what else to do. Telling them I had gone to Buster's and that Buster was stone drunk, and Bubba Joe had tried to kill me, and Buster had cut his throat, just didn't seem like the kind of information they needed to hear right then. In fact, it was information I wasn't supposed to tell anyone. Ever.

"We should never have let you go out with that storm brewing," Mom said. "I get so mad at myself when I allow my common sense to be overridden by my desire to make you happy."

"I bet there won't be any use opening the drive-in tonight," Dad said, standing at the front door, looking out. "I got a feeling the rain will start up again."

Mom hustled me through the kitchen, into their bathroom, pulled a big towel out of the cabinet and gave it to me. I was still damp, and so were my clothes, but compared to how wet I had been, I thought of myself as comfortable.

"Go upstairs and put on some dry clothes," Mom said. "Come down and I'll have you some cocoa warmed up . . . Is Nub bleeding?"

She had eyeballed a streak of blood running down his fur, and she bent down to examine him.

"Yeah," I said. "He sort of run off for a while. I guess he got in a fight."

Now I was compounding my lie.

Daddy came into the kitchen, bent over Nub, examined the wound. "Looks like a knife cut. Must have been a cat he got into it with. I'll put some alcohol on it."

"He won't like that," I said.

"He won't even notice."

Since Buster had poured alcohol on Nub, and Nub had yelped, I knew he minded.

Upstairs, I put on some dry clothes, combed my hair in front of the mirror. I looked at my face, thinking somehow it looked different. Older. Scared. Confused maybe.

I sat for a moment, just breathing. Trying to get my strength and courage back. I felt as if something living inside of me had been stolen, taken away and mistreated, then returned without all of its legs.

Downstairs, I found Nub dried off and doctored. He was lying on the floor on a thick towel Mom had laid down.

"How did he like the alcohol?" I asked.

"You were right," Daddy said. "He didn't like it."

I had the cocoa while Mom clucked over me.

Callie had said very little. She sat at the far end of the table with her own cup of cocoa, looking at me with those wood-burner eyes of hers.

Finally, everyone but myself moved into the living room. They planned to watch television, but the storm had come back and was so fierce, they knew that was pointless. With only three channels, and one of them brought in only by judicious turning of the outside antenna, it would have been nothing but a crackling noise and a screenful of electric snow.

I sat in the kitchen and sipped my cocoa. Rosy Mae came in from the living room to start dinner. She said, "You look like you done seen a ghost, Mr. Stanley."

"Just Stanley. Remember?"

"You ain't been in no kind of trouble, have you, Stanley?"

I shook my head. Rosy Mae didn't push it. She got a cup, went to the stove, poured the remaining hot milk from the pan into her cup, then stirred in cocoa.

"It works better you put the cocoa in first," I said.

"I didn't know that, and me bein' a cook. But I don't drink me no cocoa much."

She sat down at the table and studied me. "You sure you're all right? I read one of them Sherlock Holmes stories from that book. He sure smart, ain't he?"

"He is."

Dad came into the kitchen, opened the refrigerator, got out a pitcher of tea and poured it into a tall glass with flower designs. He mixed sugar into it, sat at the table and stirred his tea with a spoon. He said, "Weather stays this bad, I'm just gonna close her down tonight. I thought the family could go see the minstrel show at the school."

I knew the word family would exclude Rosy Mae. Rosy, taking the cue, left the room.

"What's a minstrel show?" I asked.

"Well, this one is some white folks just having a little fun. They put on blackface makeup, big white lips, and play music. Tell a few jokes. I've been to a few of them. They're entertaining."

After what I had gone through, the idea of staying home alone with the wind howling around the house was more than I wanted to deal with.

"That sounds fine to me."

"We'll have to wait, see if it clears," Daddy said. "It does, we got to open up. Tell you the truth, I hope it does stay this way. We could all use a night out."

———

IT WAS ABOUT SIX when Buster showed up for work. It was still raining and he came through the back like he always did, where the cars drove out. He was wearing a rain slicker with the hood pulled over his head. He was carrying a metal container with a handle and had a thermos under his arm. He went out to the projection booth.

Daddy was standing at the back door, watching Buster go into the booth. He said, "Now he shows up. He couldn't show when we're going to be open, he has to show now. Get on your slicker, go out there and tell him we're closing tonight. And I hope he doesn't expect to get paid just for showing up. He gets paid when we all get paid, and tonight no one gets paid. Except maybe the farmers. And that minstrel show."

I got my rain slicker, slipped it on, went out to the projection booth. Buster had removed his rain gear, turned on his little light, and was sitting there plucking items from the metal container.

"I brought some newspaper accounts to read," he said. "And plenty of black coffee."

"There isn't going to be any movie tonight," I said, pulling my hood back.

"Figured as much, but I thought I ought to show for work. Stan, I may not always seem like a friend, but I appreciate you bein' one."

"You saved my life."

"Matter of time for Bubba Joe. Just happened to be me did him in. Could have been anyone. Would have eventually been someone."

"You talked about Margret's mother. That she was . . . well . . ."

"A prostitute."

"That means lots of men would come there . . . to Margret's house. Right?"

"Yeah."

"It could have been any of them, couldn't it?"

"It could have."

About that time, Daddy called from the house. "Come on, Stanley. You need to get ready."

"We're going to see the minstrel show," I said.

"That'll be a treat. Seein' a bunch of peckerwoods in blackface . . . You go on. We'll talk later. Hey, I was gonna stay here and read. Think your daddy would mind?"

"Not if you don't mention it."

"Maybe that dog of yours—"

"Nub?"

"Yeah. Nub. Maybe he could come out and keep me company."

"I'll tell Rosy Mae to let him out after we leave."

"Good. And Stan, them letters from Margret? Could I see them?"

"I'll try and slip them out. I can't promise, but I'll try."

"Good enough."

I pulled my hood up and went out into the rain.

———————

THE MINSTREL SHOW was at our school, which back then housed all grades except kindergarten. Kindergarten was operated out of a teacher's house.

The show was in our school auditorium, and you paid fifty cents to get in. There were signs on the wall outside of the auditorium. They read: "NIGGER MINSTREL SHOW. Clean humor for the family. Music. Jokes. Hijinks. Fifty cents."

Inside we took our seats, which were about a third of the way from the front. In the back an old colored janitor stood ready with his rolling garbage can to pick up messes when it was over. The messes would be cups and wrappers for food and drinks being sold to raise money for the band and baseball team to buy equipment.

The PTA had put a table alongside the wall. They had soft drinks in a couple of coolers and they made hot dogs on the spot, pulling the dogs from an electric stew pot with long tongs, slapping them on mustard- and relish-coated buns.

It took about fifteen minutes for the auditorium to fill, and fill it did. There were even a few people standing in the back.

When the lights went down, two white men dressed in blackface with white lips came out, one played a banjo, and they both sang. The songs were what many think of as slave classics, like "Way Down Upon the Swanee River," "Jimmy

Crack Corn," and later on a few religious numbers, like "The Great Speckled Bird" and "I'll Fly Away."

There were jokes, all of them with Negroes as the butt. The jokes had to do with fishing, eating watermelon and fried chicken, being lazy and happy as birds; just funny colored people who loved to laugh, sing, and dance, and make white folks smile.

I was getting into the spirit of things, laughing along with everyone else, when I heard a loud coarse laugh from the back of the auditorium. I turned to look. It was the old colored janitor standing by his rolling trash can, a broom sticking out of it. He was laughing so hard I thought maybe he might have to be knocked unconscious to shut him up.

In that moment something switched on inside of me. And I thought, here's a colored man who thinks this is funny. That making fun of him and his people is humor.

I didn't laugh another time. And it wasn't due to resistance. Nothing they did on stage the rest of the night struck me as funny.

On the way home I was so silent, Daddy asked me if I was okay, if I had had fun.

I told him I had. I didn't know what else to say.

Callie said, "Well, I laughed a few times, and I liked the music, but I don't know any colored people like that. I don't think Rosy Mae would have liked it."

"It's not for Rosy Mae," Dad said.

"My point exactly," Callie said.

I looked at her, sitting across from me on the back seat, and I truly loved her for the very first time in my life. I had come to like her in the last few days, but now I loved her.

Mother said, "I think you're right, Callie. Actually, me going to see that makes me a little ashamed. And did you see that sign? Nigger Minstrel. Not even Colored or Negro. But Nigger."

"No harm's meant in it," Daddy said.

"It hurt my feelings," Mom said.

We drove to the Dairy Queen, parked out front, under the canopy, and with the windows rolled down we could hear the rain pounding on it.

A young blond girl in blue jeans and a man's shirt, her hair in a ponytail, came out to the car. Water was splashing up and under the canopy and hitting her on the shoes and blue jeans and you could tell from the look on her face she didn't like it.

When she saw Callie she shrieked, and Callie shrieked. This seems to be the teenage girl greeting. Obviously they knew each other. Callie seemed to know everyone. They exchanged greetings, said we have to talk, then the girl, whose name was Nancy, took a pencil out from behind her ear, a pad from her back blue jeans pocket, and asked what we'd have.

We ordered and Nancy went away. Daddy said, "You girls sound like wounded birds."

"Oh, Daddy," Callie said.

When the food came, it was on a tray that fastened to Daddy's window. He sorted out who had what, and we sat there and ate. Daddy tried to bring up the minstrel show, to talk about a funny moment here and there, and though we had all laughed at times, none of us were proud of it, except maybe Daddy, who couldn't see any wrong in it.

We ate, gave up our tray, and drove away from there, the rain pummeling us harder than ever.

16

SUMMER VACATION was winding down. I was nervous about the prospect of starting a new school, and I had Bubba Joe on my mind. At night, when I tried to lie down, I no longer thought of something ghostly. I thought of Bubba Joe. The way he had looked at me just before the light went out of his eyes and his soul fell down that long tunnel to hell.

Bubba Joe had deserved it. Buster had saved my life. But it wasn't that easy. Someone cleared their throat, the water gurgled down the sink, it sounded like that gurgle Bubba Joe had made before he let go and went away.

Even some of the movies we showed bothered me. The way people died on film was not the way Bubba Joe died. No last words, dramatic moments. Just bloody and dead.

I tried to stay busy, and one thing I stayed busy with was mine and Buster's mystery. I guess it was Callie's mystery too. I kept her informed but she didn't show much interest.

She started dating Drew Cleves. He seemed nice enough. He had treated me well enough that day on the hill.

Mama liked him.

Daddy didn't. Then again, he wasn't crazy about any boy who dated or even wanted to date Callie.

Because of Drew, Callie was out on dates a lot, driving away the summer, going downtown to the indoor movie, hanging out at the drugstore over hamburgers and malts.

The family still thought about Bubba Joe now and then, but not much. It was assumed he had moved on since the cops hadn't heard of nor seen hide nor hair of him.

I, of course, knew he was dead, and every day I woke up as if waiting for the other shoe to drop. A big shoe. Bubba Joe's body found somewhere along the creek. In time, though, even I thought less about him.

Daddy had gotten used to me going out to the projection booth to spend time with Buster, and I think, in the back of his mind, he thought I was learning better how to run the projector. It was a practical consideration for him. For me it was fun.

We had still not talked to Winnie.

I asked Buster about that.

"I'm holdin' back," he said. "This is a game to us, but that was her daughter got killed."

"I really do care who killed her. I'd like to see the police nab him."

"That may be, Stan, but this woman, she don't understand that."

"What is there to understand?"

"She gonna believe some boy and a nigger gonna get her daughter justice? That's hard to buy, even if we are sincere . . . And you know, I don't think there's a chance in hell we'll solve anything. I'm doing it to keep from thinkin' about whiskey and what I ought'a have done and didn't and won't never and can't never do. You understand what I'm sayin', boy?"

"Yes, sir."

"I ain't sayin' your heart ain't in the right place, I'm just tellin' you life ain't fair. Just 'cause you want somethin', don't mean you'll get it. It ain't like them Sherlock Holmes stories. They help you to think. Why I gave the book to you— You keep it. I don't want it back. Anything happens to me, all them books are yours—"

"Nothing is going to happen—"

"Just listen. Life ain't fair, and it don't always have everything fit together like a puzzle. Some things just are and there ain't no explainin' them. You can come up with maybes, and sometimes you'll find the real reason. But a lot of what happens don't never make sense and don't never jibe together. Hear me?"

"Yes, sir . . . But, isn't there some way we can talk to her?"

Buster grinned at me. "You ain't no quitter. I give you that. Maybe there is. I been thinkin' on it. If I do talk to her, it ain't gonna be we. It's gonna be me."

"But you said—"

"Don't remember what I said, but I ain't gonna drag no little white boy off to a whore's house to chat about her dead daughter. Now how you think your daddy feel about that? You think that's gonna do my job any good?"

I was disappointed. I thought I was going to be in on it. Not only the investigation, but meeting Margret's mother, and a live whore. I sat there for a while and listened to the reel clatter in the projector. I knew pouting would get me nowhere with Buster. Finally, I said, "Well, when are you going to do it?"

Buster pursed his lips. "Tonight, when I finish here."

"Won't that be late?"

"Not for her. I'll report to you tomorrow mornin', if you'll come over to the street alongside the grocery. We can sit on the curb and visit. Let's say nine in the mornin'."

"If I'm not there, Daddy or Mom hung me up. Okay?"

"I understand."

———

NEXT MORNING I was up early. I left a note saying I was going to buy comic books at the drugstore with my allowance.

Rosy caught me on the way out.

"Where you runnin' off to this mornin' without yo' dog?" She was sitting up on the couch, scratching her head.

"I'm going to buy comics. I thought I might be in town for a while, so I left Nub in my room. Will you let him out later?"

"Them comics won't be there after breakfast?"

"I don't want breakfast."

"Don't need to go without yo' breakfast. Let me fix you toast and eggs."

I started to beg off, but didn't want to seem too hasty.

Rosy made eggs and toast, prepared some for herself, along with coffee. She had gotten a lot more sure of herself around the house, and had even taken to giving Daddy orders. Which he took.

While I ate, Rosy said, "I can read gooder now. Gonna start workin' on the way I talk next. Don't want to sound like no field hand all my life. You can help me on that."

"I don't have perfect diction either."

"You don't sound ignern't, though."

"Well, you might say 'I can read better' instead of 'gooder.' There really isn't a word called gooder."

"Gotta be. Been sayin' it all my life."

"Yes, ma'am."

"I ain't so sure you ought to be goin' out there with Bubba Joe around. I ain't like yo' daddy. I ain't so sure he's not gonna bother no white boy."

"I think I'm all right, Rosy. Really."

"Yeah, well, I ain't one to tell you nothin', but you watch yo'self, hear?"

———

I RODE MY BICYCLE to the place Buster asked me to meet him. It was Saturday, and the town was jumping. I saw Buster standing at the far end of the street. He had a pop bottle and was sipping from it.

As I got closer, I noticed just how old he was. He had quit putting shoe polish on his hair, and it was white at the roots. He was tall, but slouched, as if the world were on his shoulders and it had grown too heavy.

I leaned my bike against the curb and sat beside him. A white lady carrying a shopping bag of groceries came by and saw us sitting there. She gave us a kind of smirk and kept walking.

"What she got to sneer about," Buster said. "She was any uglier they'd have to hire someone to guide her around while she wore a sack over her head."

I laughed. He grinned, reached inside his shirt pocket and took out a PayDay candy bar. "Thought you might like one. I got myself a plain Hershey's. My teeth don't like them peanuts in a PayDay."

"Did you see Margret's mother?"

"I did. It was kinda interestin', Stan. And we got to rethink a few things."

I had unwrapped the candy bar and, in spite of Rosy's breakfast, dove into it.

"Now, I couldn't just go out there and say howdy, I want to talk about your daughter got her head run over by a train, or whatever the hell happened to it. Took some of them letters you had, Stan, and I gave them back to her."

"You did?"

"Uh huh. May see them as your letters, but really they belonged to her daughter, so I thought the mother should have them. Some of them anyway. I wanted to keep a few around for the flavor, case we needed to look back over them and make sure of somethin'. Just picked out ones didn't matter much, repeated what had already been said.

"Told her I found them workin' out back the drive-in fence, buried in a jar. I don't know why I said a jar, but I did."

"What did she say?"

"Let me set this up. Went out there late last night. Her husband—he's common-law, which means they just live together—he invited me in, gave me a cup of coffee, 'cause she was busy, if you know what I mean, in the back room."

"Her husband knows?"

"He's her pimp, Stan."

"Pimp?"

He explained what a pimp was, added: "He gets a big share of the money. Likes money so much, I had to pay him some to sit and talk for a half hour. He didn't care I had letters from Winnie's daughter, felt I was burnin' work time. So, I had to pay. Expensive coffee that way."

"He isn't Margret's father, right?"

"I told you. Some Puerto Rican, or Mexican. Winnie is mixed herself. This here was a colored gent."

"What did Miss . . . Miss Winnie think?"

"Hate to report, but she feel same as her husband. Least,

she had to act like she did around her old man, 'cause he'll beat her she don't do right the way he sees right. I didn't see him whup her, but I know how it works with pimps and whores, even if they live together as husband and wife."

"That's terrible."

"Well, Stan, they ain't the PTA. Know what I'm sayin'? She looked the letters over a little, gave 'em back to me. Said toss 'em, whatever."

"She didn't cry?"

"She didn't even tear up. She said, 'You got money on the clock, boy, why don't you use it for somethin' matters.'

"Now, I was tempted. She don't look too bad, and I did put down ten dollars . . . I told her, sure, and we went in the back room, and when she closed the door, she said, 'You're gonna have to be kinda quiet so we can talk.' We sat on the bed and she took the letters again and looked them over. This time she cried a little."

"So she was sad?"

"In her own way. You see . . . Well, let me go through it. I showed her the letters again, and she said, Margret always treated her good, but she didn't believe the girl got pregnant."

"But Margret says she is in the letters."

"No. No she doesn't, Stan. What I noticed right off was she talked about pregnancy, didn't say she was with baby. There's never one line in them letters says she's pregnant. Says she and J can deal with pregnancy, but she ain't talkin' about herself."

"Who could she have been talking about? James can't get pregnant."

"No," Buster said. "No, he can't. But I'll come back to that. Asked Margret's mama about James Stilwind, and she said she didn't know him, but that Margret was friends with the little Stilwind girl."

"Jewel Ellen."

"That's right. Said they together all the time. That she knew the Stilwinds didn't approve. Margret couldn't go over to her place, for instance. She said the Stilwinds didn't approve of her profession, and they didn't approve that she had turned Margret out."

"Turned her out?"

"Made a whore of her."

"Her own daughter? She did that?"

"Winnie thought she was passin' on the family trade, Stan."

"Margret was just a girl!"

"Lot of men like that. Little girls, I mean. They sick sonsabitches in the world, Stan. Margret was a real moneymaker, her mother said. But she didn't like the life and wanted to do more with herself. Thought she could run off to Hollywood and be an actress, 'cause she was so pretty. Winnie said she tried to tell Margret she wasn't good for nothin' else but what she was doin'."

"That's horrible."

"It is. But she's tellin' all this to me with tears in her eyes. She loved her daughter in her fashion, but she just doesn't have any bottom to her, Stan. She couldn't see her daughter doin' any better than her, makin' anything of herself. Said how irritated she'd been that the girl wanted to go to school, and she didn't want her to. This what a person does when they really love themselves better than they own child. Don't want them to improve.

"Finally Margret did quit, started picking up jobs here and there. Savin' for goin' to Hollywood. Mother called it pissant labor and sneered, like what she was doin' herself was some kind of scientist work."

"This is hard to understand," I said.

"Come from a family like yours, it is. But Winnie was worried Margret wouldn't take to whorin'. Then she found out Margret was different. Said at first it made her mad, then she thought it might be a way to make some unexpected money. But then Margret got killed."

"What does she mean different, Buster?"

"When Winnie said that, things in the letters clicked. J ain't James. It's Jewel."

"But she's a girl."

"Uh huh. Sometimes it goes that way."

"You mean . . ."

"Yep. That's different."

"A girl can make a girl pregnant?"

"No, son. That requires a man. Or a boy. Like I said, don't think it was Margret that was pregnant. Mother might not know for sure, of course, but from them letters, and what I learned, I think Jewel Ellen was pregnant, and Margret was talkin' about the two of them raisin' the child after it was born."

Buster looked at me, saw I was bewildered.

"Growin' up, just full of confusion, ain't it, Stan?"

"I'll say."

"Question is this: Who is the father of Jewel Ellen's baby? We start from that idea, even if it's just an idea, and we see where that leads us. Thing I'm thinkin' is this: If Jewel was funny for Margret, then maybe she's not wantin' a man. Or maybe she wants both. It happens. That ain't it, it means some man could have raped her? If that's the case, who done it? So, that's where we are."

"Wow."

"One thing I didn't mention, Stan, was I did end up buyin' me a little bootleg liquor from Jukes before I went out there. Took it with me, and in the bedroom, me and Winnie shared it. So she talked a lot. About all manner of things. But wasn't all that much of it about her daughter. She gave me the letters back a second time, said for me to do what I wanted with them.

"She was gettin' a little tipsy, so I said, 'You sure you don't know this James Stilwind?' She said she'd never met him, but her old man—meanin' her husband, pimp—had taken some money from James's daddy. I asked her why, and she said, 'cause he wanted them to be quiet."

"About what?"

"About her daughter knowin' Jewel. Said it was a lot of money Old Man Stilwind gave 'em and she hadn't said a word about it until now, because she didn't think it mattered. She figured they didn't want Jewel Ellen's memory sullied by her sayin' she was queer. Bottom line is, Winnie misses her daughter in her own way, but she was willin' to take money, be quiet, not talk to the police, even if it meant not solvin' her daughter's death. Money was more important to her."

Buster settled back and sipped the last of the pop he was drinking.

"That's all?" I said.

"I had ten minutes left on my ten dollars, and I used them."

"Oh."

"One thing I've learned over the years. Don't waste your money."

———————

BUSTER SAID he was going home to sleep for a while. I decided to actually buy comic books. I walked along as if in a dream. The world was certainly turning out to be a peculiar place, and I was becoming one perplexed little boy.

Jewel and Margret? Girlfriends? Real girlfriends?

I went over to Greene's and looked at the comics. They had three long shelves and they were full of comics and other kinds of magazines. I found several that looked good, checked to see how many dimes were in my pocket. I had a dollar's worth.

I bought an *Adventure Comics, Challengers of the Unknown,* and a thing called *Strange Worlds.* I even broke down and bought *Superman's Girlfriend Lois Lane.*

I checked the back of the store where the five-cent comics were. The ones with half the cover cut off. Some of them were fairly recent, but many were old. Maybe as much as two or three years. I guessed everyone but me and Richard Chapman were picky about the state of our comics.

I picked out three or four, including a dust-covered one called *Captain Flash.* Like all those on the back table, the top half of the cover had been cut off, and the cutting had decapitated a dinosaur. It left a fellow in a red and blue suit with a big rock in his hand. A masked companion in yellow lay knocked down at his feet. The bottom logo read: "The Beasts From 1,000,000 B.C."

I bought the comics, and an RC, went out to sit on the curb and read.

It was warm out, but not uncomfortable. A light wind was blowing and there was the smell of honeysuckle with it.

After a while, the comics did the trick. They took me out of the world I lived in, which had within a matter of weeks become more baffling than I could have ever imagined. At that moment, I preferred the world with bright color panels and superheroes.

By the time I read two of the comics, the real world had drifted back in. I thought of Margret and Jewel.

I had been flustered enough about male and female relations, and now this. I'd have to ask Callie about it. She seemed to be a fountain of information. So was Buster, but sometimes his fountain gushed a little too powerfully for me.

I heard a car horn honk. Looked up. Near the curb was a fine-looking blue Cadillac. It had fins like a spacecraft. The window on the passenger's side was rolled down, and Callie, in her ponytailed exuberance, was leaning out of the window yelling at me.

I thought: Think of the devil.

Drew Cleves was at the wheel.

"Come ride with us, Stanley," Callie said.

I gathered up my comic books and pop bottle, went over to the car.

"You got to watch that pop," Cleves said. "My father's car. He'd kill me if I got anything on the seats."

"Sure," I said. "One minute."

I drained the RC, took the bottle into Greene's store, traded it for two cents.

Outside, in the Cadillac, Callie said, "Isn't this divine?"

"Daddy says it's like driving your living room," Drew said.

It was the biggest, most luxurious car I had ever been in. The seats were soft leather. I was tempted to stretch out and go to sleep.

Callie said, "We're driving out to the lake."

"You don't have to go if you don't want to," Drew said. "I could drive you around the block or so and let you out back here."

"He can't get a feel for it just around the block," Callie said. "Come on, Stanley."

"I don't know how long we're going to be out there," Drew said. "It could be a while."

"That's okay," I said.

"It's pretty hot," he said.

"Oh, not with this nice wind blowing," Callie said. "And the lake will be even nicer."

"I suppose," Drew said, but he didn't look very happy. He leaned over the seat and looked at me as if pleading. "You're sure you want to go?"

"Sure," I said.

"Well, all right," he said, and drove us away.

———

NEAR THE LAKE the trees were thinner because the bulldozers that had made the lake had knocked them down. Where they had done their scraping, red clay sloped into the water. There was no sand on the shore, just clay. I mentioned this.

"They have to haul it in," Drew said, as we got out of the car.

"It would have been a lot nicer," Callie said, "if they had left more trees. Maybe the shore wouldn't be falling off into the water if they had."

"My father owns the company that made the lake," Drew said.

"He could have still left more trees," Callie said, never one to waffle on an opinion if she sincerely held it.

Drew didn't really care, however. He was holding Callie's hand as they walked. He moved like his feet weren't touching the ground.

It was awfully mushy to me at the time, and I hated seeing it, Callie holding hands and cooing, Drew falling all over himself. It was hard to believe he had the grace to run with a football.

The cool wind blew for a time, and we walked, and talked.

None of it was about murder and whores and girls liking girls or headless bodies on railroad tracks.

We went along the edge of the lake for some distance, but it was too muddy to get up close, and though we had had plenty of rain, it had been compensated for by the heat, which had sucked away a lot of the water. You could see a couple of little islands out in the center of the lake, maybe thirty or forty feet apart, and the vegetation on them had died flat-out and turned the islands to mounds of dirt. There was a smell in the air of dead fish, and the kind of smell that makes the skin crawl, the kind associated with water moccasins who have lain in slick, smelly river mud gone sour and stale.

After an hour or so, we started back. Partly because the wind had stopped blowing and it was now hot as a baker's oven. We stopped at a log near the car and sat and scraped our shoes free of mud with sticks.

"Daddy says they're going to put in some tables and benches, cooking areas, boat ramps. Maybe plant some trees."

"Like the ones that were here?" Callie said.

"Fast-growing trees. There's going to be a colored section too. On the other side of the lake."

"How convenient," Callie said.

"I haven't a thing against coloreds," Drew said. "Really."

He sounded like he meant it.

"Why don't we go back to town," Drew said, "get a burger and soda?"

By this time, I was actually starting to get hungry. That's the way kids are. Bottomless pits.

"Callie, you got any money?" I asked.

"I'll take care of you," Drew said.

"You can take care of me," Callie said, "but I have Stanley's money. He's not your responsibility. You're not dating both of us."

"Well," Drew said, "that's true. But I don't mind."

"You're sweet," Callie said, in that syrupy voice she uses when she wants something from Daddy, "but it's not a problem."

We tooled back into town in the Cadillac, and I must admit I felt pretty special when we stopped in front of the drugstore and climbed out of that fine machine, stood on the hot sidewalk like three gods descended from heaven.

———

WE HAD HAMBURGERS and malts at the drugstore, and I might add Drew paid for all of it. Timothy was working again, and he looked less than happy to see Callie with Drew. He put our food on the table like he was delivering bubonic plague. He had his soda hat pulled down close to his eyes, and his mouth was held so tight the thin line it made could have been used to thread a needle.

"What's with him?" Drew said.

"Don't pay him any mind," Callie said.

"He wants to date her," I said.

"Stanley!" Callie said, as if this revelation shocked her.

"You want me to take care of him?" Drew said.

"What? Hit him because he wants to date me?"

"Tell him to leave you alone."

"No, Drew. I want to eat, then maybe we can go to the movie. It starts at one. I've already checked."

"You have a theater," he said. "Don't you get tired of movies?"

"No," she said. "And that's our theater. I think of it, I mostly think of work. Besides, I want to see the movie at the Palace."

"It's a love story," I said.

"Well," Drew said. "If you want to."

I almost felt sorry for Drew, way Callie had him tied around her little finger. She could have asked him to take her to a ballet recital and have him watch while wearing a tutu and a beret, and he would have done it.

We went to the picture, and it bored me. I slept through most of it because the theater was air-conditioned. Back then, any place that was air-conditioned in the summer was a treat.

As we were going out, we saw James Stilwind at the candy and popcorn counter, leaning over it, talking to a young girl raking popcorn out of the popper into a bag.

"There's James Stilwind," Callie said.

"That's him?" Drew said. I thought he sounded a little sour about the recognition. I had a feeling he had come up in their private conversations. For all I knew, Callie had blabbed about all the things I had told her.

'Course, I was kind of a blabbermouth myself.

Stilwind turned his head, saw Callie. He had a bright white smile that looked as if it belonged in a Pepsodent commercial. "Y'all enjoy the picture?"

"It was good," Callie said.

"It was all right," Drew said.

I remained silent.

James came over to us, leaving the girl behind the counter looking pouty, raking popcorn, shoving it into bags, stacking it at the back of the popper.

"Haven't I seen you before?" James asked Callie.

"I believe so," she said. "We were coming out of the drug-store, and I saw you with your wife."

"Wife? No. You saw me with a date. I forget who it was, but she isn't my wife."

"You forget?" Callie said.

"Well, if it were you, I wouldn't forget."

"We have to go," Drew said.

"Sure," James said.

"And what's your name?" he asked Callie.

She told him.

He asked ours. We told him. I don't think he was listening.

"And you're James Stilwind?" Callie said.

"You know my name?"

"I know you own the theater, so I suppose it must be you."

"Come around anytime. Here . . ." He went back behind the candy counter, reached into a drawer, came back with three tickets. He gave us each one.

"Free passes," he said. "On me. I own the place. If I'm here, I'll see you get a free bag of corn and a soft drink."

"Thanks," Callie said.

"We got to go," Drew said, and he took Callie by the arm.

Outside, Callie said, "Drew, you're hurting my arm."

"Sorry. I didn't mean to."

"That's all right," she said, rubbing it.

"What a creep," Drew said.

"He seemed all right to me," Callie said.

Drew sighed. Even his daddy's Cadillac couldn't trump a handsome grown-up with his own theater and a Thunderbird that didn't belong to anyone's daddy.

I thought: James Stilwind is someone who should be talked to if I'm going to truly investigate this murder. Buster couldn't do it. Even the idea that a colored man might be quizzing a white man on something as sensitive as a sister's death could get him beat or worse.

Problem was, I didn't know how to do it either.

Drew drove us home. Except for Callie commenting on how much she liked what some girl walking along the sidewalk was wearing, it was a silent trip, the air thick enough to carve into shapes.

Drew let us out at the Dew Drop. Callie slid over and kissed him on the cheek. "See you soon, Drewsy?"

That kiss broke the ice. Drew smiled. "Sure. Real soon, I hope."

"You can bet on it," Callie said.

"See you, Drewsy," I said.

Drew gave me a stony look.

We got out of the car and started inside. I said, "You sure know how to work them, don't you, Callie?"

"Comes natural," she said.

17

WHEN WE CAME into the house Rosy and Mom were sitting on the couch. Mom had her arm around Rosy, and Rosy was crying. Daddy was leaning against the corner of the wall where the living room led into the kitchen.

Callie said, "Rosy, are you okay?"

"Let her be for a moment," Daddy said. "Y'all come in here."

We went into the kitchen. There was no door between the kitchen and living room, just an opening, so when we sat at the table he spoke softly.

"Bubba Joe," Daddy said. "They found him."

"Where?" Callie asked.

"Dead," Daddy said. "Washed up out of Dewmont Creek. They found him on the edge of a pasture. Creek had swollen during the rain, receded during the dry spell. He'd been dead awhile. Man owned the land where they found him didn't go back there often. When he did, to check on a cow, he found

Bubba Joe. He was so blowed up he thought he was a calf at first."

"Yuck," Callie said.

"But that's good, isn't it?" I said. "Not that he was blowed up, but that he's dead."

"Rosy still loves him," Callie said. "That's so sad."

"He tried to kill her," I said, and started to say he tried to kill me, but caught myself. "He might have tried to kill someone else. He might have killed someone else."

"That's true," Daddy said. "I don't miss him any."

"Did he drown?" Callie asked.

"Throat was cut. They think he might have been in the water awhile, but mostly he's been laid up in that pasture, going ripe."

"How did you find out about it?" Callie asked.

"Barbershop."

"It could just be a rumor," she said.

"Man told me was the man who found him," Daddy said. "And the police called to tell me too. I told Gal and Rosy."

"Sorry as I am for Rosy," Callie said, "it's a relief."

"True enough," Daddy said.

Daddy went back into the living room.

Callie said, "You think that was him that chased us that night?"

"Sure of it," I said.

"Then I guess it's good he's dead, huh?"

"Oh yeah," I said. "It's good."

———

LATER THAT DAY I went out on the veranda where Rosy had retreated. She sat there looking out at the projection booth. I sat down in a chair beside her. I said, "Rosy, I'm sorry."

"Ain't no need to be, Mr. Stanley. He wasn't no good man. He had it comin'. I don't know why I feel like I do."

"I'm sorry you and him didn't work out better. That he wasn't a better man."

"Me too, Mr. Stanley."

"Just Stanley," I said.

"You know what your daddy done say?"

"No," I said.

"He told me now Bubba Joe dead, it don't matter none about stayin' here. I don't got to go nowhere. He gonna fix that top floor up and get me a fan, and cut me out a window right there above them cowboys and Indians."

"That's good, Rosy."

"He say I can stay on and work and he gonna give me a wage and I gonna have weekends off if I want 'em. Gal didn't say that, and she didn't put him up to it. He tell me that, and he pat me on the back."

There were tears in my eyes. I looked away from her, out toward the projection booth.

Rosy reached over, took my hand. I gently squeezed it. She bent her head and cried more deeply than before. I pulled my chair closer to hers. She put her head on my shoulder and kept crying. We sat that way until she was out of tears.

———

On Monday, near dark, me and Nub went out to greet Buster as he came to work. In the projection booth I told him about Bubba Joe being found.

"I know," Buster said. "I heard it through the grapevine. Ain't nothin' happens in this town, or the Section, gets by them birds on that porch over by my house. Word gets to them fast

as if it come by telephone . . . It was just a matter of time . . .
You didn't say nothin', did you?"

"No, sir. 'Course not."

We had a new picture to run. *The Fly,* starring Vincent
Price. A year ago it would have frightened me to death, and
that part where the fly with the little human head says "Help
me!" would have given me a nightmare.

Not now. Not after seeing the ghost light, being chased at
night by Bubba Joe, nearly being hit by a train, and then seeing Buster cut Bubba's throat and throw him in the creek.

This night I wasn't watching the movie. Buster and I were
sitting in the projection booth with the little light on, sitting at
the small table on which were spread a number of newspaper
clippings and a manila folder.

"Yeah, I know you'll be quiet about it, Stan. Ain't that I'm
ashamed of killin' him, you want to know true. I ain't lost one
minute's sleep. He had it comin'. But I don't need no police."

"You sure we shouldn't tell them?"

"I'm sure. They might just let it go. Not give a damn. But
they could decide to make sure I went upriver. That ain't exactly what I had in mind for an old-age pension. Prison stripes
and workin' on a chain gang in the hot sun. I wouldn't last six
months at my age."

"Don't worry," I said. "These clippings, the folder? You
have something to show me?"

"The folder's got police reports in it. Told you Jukes would
come through. Let me lay some of this on you, Stan. Now just
listen. Put it together with what you know, but don't hold to
anything you know. Understand?"

"I think so."

"Think around corners. Figure out what it could be, but
don't hold to that bein' it till there's nothing else to hold to but
that."

"All right."

"These clippings, we got news that the oldest girl, she left town. You remember me telling you that before?"

"Yes, sir."

"She went off to London, England. It's right here in the society section. Ones that make up this town's society is about three families. Stilwinds is one of the families. This Stilwind girl goin' off was five years before the murder of either them other girls, Margret and Jewel. Now we got an old police report here. Jukes didn't give this one to me right off, but when I read this in the paper about Susan, that was her name, goin' off to London, it got me to thinkin'. She's fifteen it says, and it's a January when she goes. What's that say to you?"

"It's winter?"

"That ain't got a damn thing to do with it. Think, boy. How old are you?"

"Thirteen."

"Yeah. And what you got to do when the summer's over?"

"Go to school."

"Give the little boy a candy cigar. That's right. Go to school. Now, does what I told you come up different now?"

"She left during school . . . She had to leave."

"There you go. So I'm thinkin', she goes off during schooltime, and she's fifteen, and they send her to London, what's the reason? I figured she was pregnant. That's what them rich folks do if they got a girl gets knocked up. They send them away to have the baby or they send them away to get rid of it. I thought, well, maybe they just wanted her to be educated in England. It could be that way. Rich folks do that. But high school. All of a sudden, three years or so before she graduates . . . Didn't sound right.

"So, I say to Jukes. Jukes. Go back to when this gal left and get me the police reports for then."

"Wouldn't you want hospital reports? To see if she was pregnant?"

"Good thinkin', but can't get 'em. May not even exist now."

"But why police?"

"Nothin' says this has anything to do with the police, but I got to go on my gut sometimes. I get to thinkin', what if some event happened with Susan about then and they want to send her off."

"But why would the cops care if she's pregnant?"

"What if it isn't that she's pregnant?"

"I'm confused now."

"That was just my guess, but I had to guess another way too. Maybe somethin' happened with her that was in the police files. Anything. Like she got into some kind of robbin', and her daddy wanted to send her off. Delinquent stuff."

"I guess it could be that."

"But it wasn't. It's like both ideas I had come together. See, Stan, the old police chief, he kept all his records just like you're supposed to do. Figure I was him, I would too. Things can come back on you. My figure is the chief, Rowan was his name, his idea of justice was whatever he wanted to dole out. Colored usually got justice right then and there from him. Same with some cracker. It's the rich folks get judges, when that's even bothered with."

"What are you buildin' up to, Buster?"

Buster opened the folder, took out some pages.

"This here is written by the chief himself. Just his notes. Says: 'Susan Ann Stilwind came in tonight and said someone had been messing with her. I asked her who, and she said it was her family. She said she didn't want to say, but she wanted to be taken away from there. I said, who in your family, and she still didn't say. She hadn't been here more than a few minutes talking to me when her daddy, Mr. Stilwind, come in. He said she was going around spreading lies. What she was saying wasn't true. She was saying it because he had run off the boy that did it to her and now she was ashamed and so mad she wanted him to look bad by saying what she was saying. I didn't ask her any more. I told them it might be a good idea if she didn't stay home anymore. That she should go off somewhere for a time. Mr. Stilwind said he'd make arrangements. She broke down crying and wouldn't let him touch her, but she went off with him after cussing me.'

"Then you read the society pages, and she's goin' off to study in England. This was in the paper a week after this chief dated his entry. She was probably already gone when that word hit the paper."

"Her father did it?" I asked.

"Chief thought so. Says for her daddy not to have her at home anymore, and to send her off. What's that say to you? Chief's way of solvin' the problem. Send her off so the old man can't do it to her no more, and she's able to have the baby in privacy."

"I guess the chief wasn't all bad."

"How do you figure? He was protectin' the old man more than the girl. Sent her off so the old man doesn't get embarrassed, it doesn't hurt the town. He wanted to help that girl, he'd have looked into the matter and done somethin'. Only reason he wrote it down and kept it is if somethin' came back on him. That way he could show he tried to do something about the matter. Wouldn't be accused of sweeping it under the rug.

"Better yet, he could use that file to make sure Stilwind didn't push him around, money or no money, 'cause that's what Stilwind does. He pushes people around with his money. Other thing. Chief retired not long after Jewel Ellen was murdered."

"Susan leaving and Jewel Ellen dying are connected to the chief?"

"They're connected to the Stilwind family and the chief. Remember them letters? I believe Jewel Ellen was pregnant by him, like the other'n. The old man sent one off, but maybe this one was determined to talk."

"So he murdered her."

Buster nodded. "Could be. I know the chief bought a nice little house down by the river. Gets a new car every year or so. All this on a lawman's retirement. Jukes done told me all that."

"But if he was paid off, why would he leave the notes in the file for anyone to see?"

"'Cause he never actually went to Stilwind and said pay me off. Stilwind just did. Didn't want chief to say what he knew. Stilwind may not have known a report was written down and filed, but he might have feared it was. Chief was willing to take the money without argument and Stilwind was willin' to pay it 'cause that's how he solves his problems. With money.

"As for the notes. That's all they are, notes. They don't really say Stilwind did somethin' to her. But it sure makes it look that way. He left them there so if things come back on him, he wouldn't have taken them with him when he left, to maybe use as blackmail. He could say, 'They're right in the files. And you know, it does look like he might have done somethin' to that girl. Didn't pick up on that then. Should'a, but missed it.' Hear what I'm sayin'?"

"Yes, sir. I think so. But what about Margret?"

"Maybe Jewel Ellen told Margret, and Stilwind found out. Jewel got mad, blurted it out. Could'a told him she liked girls, not men. That would hurt his pride even more. Could have said she and Margret were gonna raise the baby. He wouldn't want that. Wouldn't want a granddaughter by his own daughter runnin' around. That's bad for business."

"Could he kill his own daughter?"

"There's people will do anything, Stan."

"What can we do about it?"

"Done told you, boy. Just a game. Who's gonna listen if we tell this? We back to the same old problem. A boy and an old nigger with a big tale. And there's this. Could be this is just part of the tale. Could be like the blind men and the elephant. Everyone's holding a different part of the elephant, and they all got the elephant all right, but they all describe the part they holdin' as the whole elephant. They're all right and they're all wrong. What it may come down to in the end, is we done our best and we figured some things, but we ain't got nothin' left but to let it go. I know that's all I got left. Lettin' it go."

"James Stilwind could know something."

"You're not letting it go, are you?"

"No, sir."

Buster sighed.

"He lived in the house with Jewel Ellen and his father," I said, "so he might know some answers."

"He ain't told them answers already, what makes you think he's gonna tell 'em now?"

"How would I talk to James about such a thing?"

"I ain't got no answers on that," Buster said, pushing the chief's notes back into the folder. "That's your problem. You figure on it."

"Do you have any advice?"

"No."

———

LATER, I went back to help Callie at the concession stand. After all of his explaining, and my not being ready to drop it all as a finished game, Buster grew morose, like one of his moods was coming down on him. I'd seen all of his moods I wanted to see.

I was sure he was on to the truth, but that there were more concrete answers out there, something we could take to the police. If James knew something, maybe he could be tricked into letting it go. It wasn't a very clever thought, but when I was that age clever thoughts were not my forte.

Me and Callie hadn't had a customer for an hour. We sat and tossed stale popcorn toward Coke cups, seeing who could get more popcorn in. Callie was winning.

"What did you think of James Stilwind?" I asked.

"He gave us tickets, didn't he?"

"But what did you think of him?"

"Oh, he's cute. He's arrogant. A little full of himself and show-offy. And he looks very young for his age. He must be in his late thirties at least. Right?"

"That means he was fifteen or so when his sister was burned up in that fire."

"I suppose . . . Are you still thinking he did that horrible thing?"

"I thought that was your idea."

"Surely not."

"Well, one of us had that idea. Maybe it was me."

She looked at me and smiled. It was that special way of hers that let you know she thought you were an idiot, but she was going to pretend you were precious, even if you knew she was pretending and she knew you knew.

"Drop it, Stanley. Quit snooping."

"Tell me you're not interested."

"Okay, I'm a little interested. James intrigues me. Some."

"And it makes Drew crazy."

"Yes. It makes Drew crazy."

"Why do you do that, Callie?"

"Because I can, I guess. It's harmless."

"Do you think you could talk to James?"

"Talk. About what?"

"About the murder case."

"There is no murder case. You're not a detective, Stanley."

"It's still fun. You could talk to him about it. You know, use your charms."

"I don't know, Stanley. It's one thing to flirt. But to pry . . . I don't know."

"Guess you're right," I said. "No one would talk about something like that. Not even if they thought you were pretty."

"Oh, they might. But I wouldn't do that."

"Sure. I understand."

"If I wanted, I could make him talk."

"I bet you could."

"You don't sound convinced."

"What's it matter to you? You're right. It's silly. I'm sure you could do it if you wanted."

"I don't believe you think I can, Stanley."

"I didn't say that."

"Yeah, but I can tell the way you act you don't think I can . . . All right. You're on. Give me a few days."

I kept myself cool, calm, and collected, so as not to blow it. By golly, for once I had outsmarted my sister.

18

A S SUMMER WOUND DOWN and school loomed on the horizon, I tried to stuff myself as full as I could of the time left.

In those remaining dog days of summer vacation I still thought of Margret and Jewel Ellen. Thoughts of them would flare from time to time, like a fire fanned by the wind, then would die down as quickly as they had jumped up.

I rode my bike all over, except to the top of the great hill that led to the house I now called the Witch House. I bought lots of comics and read them while sitting out on the veranda, their bright images and two-dimensional heroes burning themselves into the back of my brain.

I read Tarzan, Hardy Boys, and Nancy Drew books, and when I wore out with comics and books and riding my bike, me and Nub wandered the woods and creeks.

I had also come to really miss Richard, who in that last week of summer I had not seen at all. It was as if he had been sucked up by a windstorm and carried off to Oz. I went by his house once, but when I knocked, no one answered.

Another thing me and Nub did with our summer days was spend time looking up at those pieces of house in the trees. In my imagination I thought at night the house came together up there, like a puzzle snapped in place by the gods. All except the metal stairway, which remained outside and wound its way to an open window, and I would climb that metal ladder and enter the house through it.

It was always dark in my daydreams, and when I clambered through the window, I would see Jewel, on the bed, bound in sheets and blankets, ropes wrapped around her, stinking of gasoline. I would sit on the windowsill and look at her. She would turn her head, and out of her mouth would come flames.

I would sit in the window frame and watch her burn.

Sometimes I daydreamed of Margret, wandering the tracks headless, that little light we had seen jumping up and down before her.

These moments moved farther and farther apart.

On one of the last days of summer, about midday, the sun so hot leaves and limbs sagged and the birds were silent with heat exhaustion, me and Nub were out beneath the trees back of the drive-in, loving the shade.

Nub had found his squirrel tormentor, or one just like it, and was soon once more up the oak tree, on a limb, telling that squirrel what he thought of him. Way he scurried up that tree, you would have thought Nub was part cat. I was sure if I could translate dog language I wouldn't want to repeat what Nub was saying to that squirrel. What the squirrel was chattering back was probably no less flammable.

I laughed at them awhile, then found myself looking up at the rotting fragments in the trees again. Since last time I had been there, a piece or two had disintegrated and fallen to the ground, shattered into blackened slivers.

The metal staircase still hung in place, however, and I knew I had to climb it. The idea had been with me all summer, and I couldn't let the summer end without trying it.

It was a foolish thing to consider, but it's one of the faults of being a boy.

I climbed about halfway up and felt the stairs sway. But only sway. They seemed to be caught up good in pine boughs and vines that had twisted up the trunk of the tree closest to the stairwell.

The stairway had survived the fire in place, the rest of the house burning down around it. Vines, a tree, and time, had lifted it out of the ground and held it just above its former position like a twisty metal worm captured in a giant spiderweb.

Halfway up, the stairs wobbled and I had a vision of some rusted spot giving way. I decided to go back down. When I turned, I saw Mr. Chapman coming through the woods. He was walking, carrying a large walking stick. He saw me on the stairway, came over, looked up, put his hands on one of the rails. The stairway shook and moved much more than my weight had moved it.

"Please don't do that, Mr. Chapman," I said.

"That scare you?"

"Yes."

"Seen that boy of mine?"

"No, sir."

"You ain't lyin' to me, are you?"

"No, sir."

"I don't like being lied to."

"I haven't seen him."

Chapman looked around, then looked back up at me and grinned. He shook the stairway. "Tell me the truth now, boy."

"Don't. I'm going to fall."

Nub, who had been occupied with his squirrel, realized I was being threatened. He leaped from his limb, hit the ground, rolled to his feet, darted straight for Chapman.

"Hey, hey," Chapman said.

Nub bit at Chapman's ankle. "Stop it!" Chapman said, and he swatted at Nub, struck him with the stick, knocked him rolling.

"He thinks you're hurting me," I yelled, starting down. "Leave him be. I'll get him."

"Don't care what he thinks."

Nub was up again, growling. You would have thought he was a German shepherd. And maybe, in his mind, he was. Nub shot at Chapman like an arrow. The stick swung, missed. Nub caught Chapman by the ankle. Chapman let out a scream.

"Stop it," I said. "Leave him alone."

"I'll kill him."

"No you won't." It was Callie. She was inside the drive-in, standing on something next to the fence, her shoulders and head poking up over the top of it. She had a handful of rocks from the gravel drive.

"I'll beat him to death," Chapman said, and he struck at Nub, hitting him, knocking him down and out.

"Now, bury the little bastard."

It went through my head like a shot that this was the same man we had seen in the woods crying over a dog. It wasn't a thought I considered long. I started climbing down. I didn't know what I was going to do, but my eyes were filled with tears and I was crazy mad.

Callie whistled a rock through the air. It hit Chapman on the shoulder. He let out a scream. "You hell-spawn. You Jezebel."

Another rock whistled, caught him on the side of the head. He jerked a hand to the spot and yelled.

Callie started whistling one rock after another. Chapman broke and ran back a ways. I was on the ground now, and he turned, glared at me. "Don't you never come around no more, you hear? You see that boy of mine, tell him he's gonna take a hell of a beatin'. And one for you too."

Callie threw another rock. Chapman thought he was out of distance of her throwing arm, but the rock hit him in the leg. Another went whistling, struck the tree next to him.

"You better quit, missy. I'll get you too."

That was when I saw Daddy on the outside of the fence, coming around on the side closest to Chapman. Chapman didn't see him. He was too busy taunting me and Callie.

I went over to pick up Nub. He was still breathing. He opened his eyes and looked at me as if trying to focus. He had the same look Buster had when he was coming off his drunk.

Chapman was in the middle of a diatribe when he looked up and saw Daddy. "Now you ought to go on and leave me be. I'm just tryin' to help these youngin's get some manners."

As Daddy neared Chapman, Chapman swung the walking stick. Daddy swatted at it, sucked it into him, moved slightly, and now he had the stick.

Chapman tried to run, but Daddy was on him. The stick swung, caught Chapman on the leg, knocked him down. Daddy tossed the stick away and kicked Chapman in the throat. Chapman went to the ground gagging. I heard Callie yelling at Daddy to stop.

When I looked up he had Chapman pulled to his knees and was slapping him the way he had slapped Chester, but with greater enthusiasm.

"You weasel. You do all right hitting kids and women and little dogs, don't you, you greasy sleazeball bastard. I get through with you, you won't know on which side of your face to pick your nose."

"Daddy!" Callie had climbed over the fence and was running toward him. Me, I didn't move.

I picked up Nub, held him close to me. He wiggled.

Callie had hold of Daddy's slapping hand. Dad shoved Chapman to the ground. Chapman, bleeding from mouth, nose, and ears, said, "A Chapman don't forget."

"Good," Daddy said. "Think I wanted this to slip your mind?"

"And that damn girl. Woman ain't supposed to raise their hand to a man."

Daddy kicked Chapman in the ribs. "Who says you're a man."

"Daddy," Callie said, grabbing him. "That's enough."

"I'll get you, missy," Chapman said, tonguing a tooth out of his bloody mouth.

Callie let go of Daddy and kicked Chapman under the chin, like she was trying to make a field goal. Chapman, who had been trying to rise, was knocked back flat. Callie said, "No you won't, you sleazy little turd."

"What did you say?" Daddy said.

"You said *bastard*," Callie said.

"Suppose I did," Daddy said. "Chapman. The Mitchels don't forget either. Your boy is welcome anytime. But don't let me see you. Even in town."

Chapman wobbled to his feet. Daddy bent quickly, picked up Chapman's stick. Chapman flinched. Daddy tossed it to him. "Don't forget this. You might want to beat a wounded animal to death on the way home."

Chapman took the walking stick, wheeled, started through the woods as quickly as a man with a limp could go.

Back at the house, I sat at the table holding Nub in my lap, happy the worst he had gotten was a lump on the head. I felt as if I was living some kind of curse that started by my opening that Pandora's box of letters.

More had happened to my family in one summer than had happened in my entire life. Perhaps more than had happened in my parents' lives, even if they were unaware of much of it. I couldn't help but think by finding and opening that box I had insulted the dark gods, brought them scuttling and scratching across that fine dark line between black mystery and reality; brought them here mad and devilish and full of harm. They were even picking on the family dog.

Mom was leaning against the counter listening to Callie tell what had happened. The rest of us, including Rosy, were sitting around the table.

"I hit him with a rock good," Callie said.

"That's not good, Callie," Mom said. "That's nothing to be proud of."

"Oh, I don't know," Dad said. "It says something for her hand-to-eye coordination, the fine function of young muscles. And a goddamn good aim."

"That's right," Rosy said. "Miss Callie, she can toss a rock. I seen her hit a blue jay the other day."

"Rosy," Callie said. "I didn't mean to. I mean, I threw it, but I didn't think it would hit it."

"Killed it deader than a stump," Rosy said.

Mom and Dad looked at Callie in that manner only parents can manage.

"Really," Callie said. "I didn't mean to kill it. I was just playing around."

"Still," I said, trying to manage a save, "she has a good arm."

"Flings like Whitey Ford," Daddy said.

"Stanley," Mom said. "That's no way to talk. Bragging on

her for something like that. Killing a poor bird. Hitting Mr. Chapman."

"Several times," Dad said.

"Several times?" Mom said.

"He was shaking Stan out of a tree," Callie said.

"Off a stairway actually," I said.

"A stairway?" Mom asked.

I explained. Mom said, "I didn't know that was back there. You didn't tell me that was back there. I'll have to see that."

I probably hadn't mentioned it because in my mind it was connected to finding the letters, which even now I didn't mention. And neither did Callie.

"What was wrong with Mr. Chapman, Daddy?" I said. "He's always cranky, but . . ."

"Was he drinking, Stanley?" Mom asked Dad.

"I don't think so," Dad said. "I didn't smell it on his breath. Then again, I wasn't trying to."

"Daddy was too busy slapping him to smell his breath," Callie said.

"That drinkin' turn a man bad," Rosy said. "I ought to know. I bet he was drinkin'. He used to work right there where them trees is now. In that old Stilwind house. He such a good-looking man then."

"I remember you saying that before," I said. "It's hard to imagine."

"You sure, Rosy?" Callie said. "He looks like something out of a monster movie to me."

"After that fire happened, it was like he turn ugly," Rosy said. "Like it done burned him bad as it burned that little Stilwind girl."

"I believe I'm behind on all this," Mom said.

"Me too," Daddy said.

Me, Callie, and Rosy filled in the blanks. Well, Rosy told

what she knew and me and Callie told what we thought we ought to tell. I still didn't mention what me and Buster had been doing, all the stuff I had found out. I sure didn't tell them about Winnie Wood, Margret's mother, or about how Buster had not only interrogated her, but had helped her practice her profession. And I didn't even know how to begin about Jewel and Margret and what they were doing. Then, of course, there was the pregnancy. So far, concerning my experiences of the summer, all that was missing were flying saucers and the Loch Ness Monster.

"How come you and Callie know all about this?" Mom asked me.

"Heard it around," I said.

"They say that Margret's ghost out at the railroad tracks," Rosy said. "Heard theys one of them ghosts in that house on the hill. Jewel Ellen's ghost."

"Ghosts all over," Daddy said.

"No one lives in the house on the hill anymore," I said.

"How do you know?" Daddy said.

"I've heard that," I said.

Daddy thought for a moment, pursed his lips, said, "I think that's why you rode up the hill that day you had the wreck. To see if you could see a ghost. Comes together now. Is that it?"

It was close enough, so I said, "Yes, sir."

Daddy shook his head.

"There isn't a ghost though," I said. "It's Mrs. Stilwind. She leaves the old folks home sometimes and goes there and people see her."

"How do you know that?" Mom asked.

I decided I had to tell the truth on this one. "Buster told me."

"He did, did he?" Daddy said.

"Boy," Callie said, chuckling, changing the subject back to

where we had started. "Daddy sure gave Mr. Chapman a butt whipping."

"That's enough of that talk," Mom said.

"Well," Callie said, "he did."

"I did," Daddy said.

"He slapped him the way he slapped Chester, only harder," I said.

"Chester, by the way," Mom said, "was innocent."

"I've said it before," Daddy said. "Chester was bound to do something eventually, and he probably did something before, so he had it coming."

"That's a silly way to think," Mom said.

"I suppose it is," Daddy said. "But it's my only excuse."

"Mr. Chapman had it coming," Callie said. "Whap, whap, whap. And Daddy hit him with a stick too. And he cussed."

"Stanley, what kind of talk is that around the children?"

"Pretty foul, I suppose," Daddy said. "It was a strained moment."

Daddy said this as if it were the only time he had ever let go of a string of colorful expletives.

"I can't imagine what that poor little Richard goes through," Mom said. "It has to be horrible. Where's his mother during all this? What's she doing about it?"

"Mr. Chapman beats her," I said. "He slaps Richard around too. I've seen them with knots and fat lips and black eyes."

"What a man," Daddy said.

"This time he got slapped around," Callie said. "Did you see him try to melt into the ground? He was looking for some kind of hole to go into."

"Weasels like holes," Daddy said. "Any place where they can't see the light of day."

"I can't imagine why Mrs. Chapman puts up with such,"

Mom said. "Your daddy ever did that, I'd be gone. After I killed him."

"I only slap guys around," Daddy said. "When they have it coming, of course."

"Nub bit him," I said. "He tried to protect me."

"Poor Nub got hit with a stick," Callie said.

"He's all right," Daddy said. "He'll have a knot and a headache, but he's all right. Good ole Nub."

"I'll give our brave hero dog a can of dog food, right now," Mom said.

"What about the rest of us heroes?" Callie said.

"Nub first," Mom said. "Besides, I haven't enough dog food to go around."

"That's funny," Daddy said.

"I'll bake some cookies for the rest of you. No. This is a real celebration. Rosy will bake the cookies and I'll help."

This was a special moment, I thought. Mom had accepted that Rosy was the better cook, and that was the end of it.

"It gettin' right around dinnertime, Miss Gal," Rosy said. "Why don't I fix some dinner. Some fried chicken and greens, corn bread and mashed taters. Then I'll fix some oatmeal cookies make your stomach wish it was twice its own size."

"I won't fight that idea," Daddy said.

19

THREE DAYS BEFORE SCHOOL, a Saturday, Mom sent me and Callie to town to buy some school supplies. Callie, who had been learning to drive, took the car. Back then, though you had to have a license, the cops didn't check them much. Fewer people, looser rules. You could drive around when you were thirteen, no problem.

Daddy wasn't quite that loose with the rules, but he had started to let Callie drive at sixteen. With him in the car at first, and finally, now and then, alone.

We shopped, got the few things we needed. Mostly pens and pencils. They had a new kind of fountain pen you put little plastic cartridges full of ink into, and when those wore out, you replaced them. We bought a couple of those and lots of replacement cartridges. We bought Big Chief tablets, colored map pencils, two small dictionaries, and lots of writing paper and composition notebooks.

I loved all of that stuff. It was exciting. It was a great way to end a summer and prepare for a school year. I was actually starting to look forward to school.

Of course, within a month to six weeks I'd be sick of all of it and anxious for Thanksgiving, and then the Christmas holidays.

We finished around noon, put our booty in the car, then walked to the drugstore for a hamburger. Tim was working. He was still brooding over Callie's last appearance there with Drew. We sat at the counter and he took our order, trying not to show any interest. But Callie's green eyes and that glossy mane of a ponytail melted him.

"So," he said, after writing down our order on a pad. "Where's your boyfriend?"

"I'm not sure," Callie said.

"He like a permanent thing? I mean, are you going steady?"

"No," she said.

"You dating other people?"

"Not just now."

"I see. But you might."

"Sure. I might."

"What about Stilwind? You still interested in him? He's too old for you, you know."

"I'm not interested in him."

Hope had returned to Tim's breast. He said, "I'll get this stuff going."

He took the order back to the cook, shoved the slip through the service window.

We ate our hamburgers, Tim checking on us inordinately. Callie was very nice, smiled a lot. Tim looked as if he might break down and cry. He felt he had a chance now. We got extra Cokes with our meal.

When we finished, started outside, I said, "You like him too?"

"Not really. But I didn't want him to spit in our food. And we got extra Cokes."

"I think you just like messing with him."

"You know I do."

Callie walked over to the theater's pay booth, examined the times posted there for the double feature. She came back and looked at her watch. "Movie starts in about fifteen minutes. Want to go? At least see the first feature?"

"Tim reminded you of James Stilwind. Well, I'm not interested in James Stilwind anymore."

This wasn't entirely true, but the nearness and excitement of starting school, the events of the other day, the whipping Daddy had given Chapman, had sucked some of the curiosity out of me.

"You were just nuts about finding out more about him the other day," Callie said.

"I know," I said. "Not now . . . You don't want to see a movie that bad, Callie. I know you. You want to mess with Stilwind."

"Just a little," she said. "By the way. I got the time, but I forgot to see what's showing."

What was showing was *Frankenstein—1970,* starring one of my favorites, Boris Karloff. The main show was *Touch of Evil,* starring Charlton Heston and Orson Welles. Looking back, it was a strange mixture, but the Palace hadn't quite gotten down the art of arranging double features. *Frankenstein—1970* would have been better served at the drive-in.

We used the free passes James gave us, and once inside, Callie immediately tried to spot James, but he was nowhere to be seen.

I could tell she was disappointed, but the idea of seeing a new movie for free was exciting enough to make her forget about it. The air-conditioning was welcome. The day had already started to swelter.

We sat in our seats waiting for the lights to go down and the movie to come up. I said, "Did you really kill a blue jay?"

"I did," Callie said. "I really didn't think I would hit it. I wanted to try. I love baseball, and I wanted to see if I could throw. I don't know why they don't have girls' baseball. Mom said during the war they had women's baseball. She said she saw a game. Another thing, Drew said girls didn't play baseball because it was hardball and girls could get hurt. That doesn't make any sense. Boys get hurt."

"Girls are weaker than boys," I said.

"You're weaker than me."

She was right on this matter. I decided to be silent.

The lights went down. A newsreel was shown as part of the Saturday morning kid show. It was an old reel from the war, well dated. I have no idea why it was shown. All I remember about it was the announcer saying ". . . Japs come out of their holes on Iwo Jima . . ."

Next came cartoons. Road Runner and Coyote. We laughed our way through that one. Then came the kids' show, *Frankenstein—1970.*

Then came *Touch of Evil.* Unlike today, the price of one ticket took care of it all. You could sit through the kids' show, the main feature, usually a double feature (not this time since *Touch of Evil* was lengthy), and when it played again, you could sit through that, watch whatever was shown until the show closed up. That way you could see the kids' feature, a double feature, and another cartoon twice. It was a great way to spend a day and thirty-five cents.

When the movie was over, I stopped by the rest room. When I came out, there was James talking to Callie. James was grinning so wide his teeth looked like a piano row.

"Jim says he'll show me how the projector works," Callie said.

"We have one at home," I said. "I can show you."

"This one's a little different," James said. "It'll only take a minute. Why don't you go over to the concession, get whatever you want, tell them I said so. You want anything, hon?"

"No, I'm fine."

Hon? That was quick. He was already talking to her like she was a steady date.

"Just be a minute," Callie said.

"All right," I said.

I went over to the concession, realized I wasn't really in the mood for anything. I was still full and there was plenty of this stuff back at the drive-in. I stood near the wall next to the door and looked outside.

It was bright out there, and after the darkness of the theater, it was like a white-hot slap. I blinked until I could see again.

A light drizzle had come while we were watching the movie. It was long gone, but the streets steamed with condensation. Cars rode over it as if they were floating on cotton or clouds.

Bored of watching, I finally went over to the concession for something to do. I asked the girl working there if I could have a Coke. I told her James had sent me and that he said it was okay.

She went about drawing the Coke quickly, as if it was the foulest thing she had ever done. When she set it on the counter for me to take, I realized she was the girl who had been behind the counter before.

"He with your sister?" she said, smacking gum.

"He's showing her how the projector works."

She snorted. "That's not all he's showing her."

"What does that mean?"

She snorted again. "You're too young."

I wasn't as young as I was supposed to be. Not anymore. Not after this summer. I had a feeling go through me like red-hot needles. I left the Coke where it was and started walking to the door that led into the projection area.

The girl called, "You want this Coke, or not?"

I opened the door and found myself in a short dark hall with stairs in front of me. There was one little light there, and it was just enough you could see the stairs.

I went up the stairs. On the right was a wall, on the left a little runway and the booth. From the runway I could look down and see people in the balcony. Even in the shadows, I could see they were all colored people. I could see beyond the balcony and the front of the white customer rows. I could see the screen and I could hear the projector hum. Inside the projection room I could hear a muffled sound and something banging against the wall.

I stood there not knowing exactly what to do, but I finally made an executive decision. I went over to the booth and tried to open the door, but it was locked.

I said, "Callie."

"Go away," James said. "We'll be out."

His voice was barely audible, sounded as if it were muffled by pillows. The booth was near soundproof.

I kicked the door, kicked it hard.

"Get Daddy," Callie said. "Get—" and then her voice was muffled.

I banged my shoulder against the door, and I started to yell Callie's name.

I did this two or three times, then the door opened quickly, and James grabbed me and pulled me in and shut the door.

"Shut up. You'll disturb everyone. I ought to knock the shit out of you."

I looked and saw the projector clicking away, its little light glowing blue in there, and in the blueness of it I saw Callie against the wall. The front of her blouse had two buttons snapped off. I saw then that James had marks down his face. They ran from just below his eye to the bottom of his chin.

"What are you doing?" I said.

"You're too young to know," he said.

Callie hustled toward me. When she got to the door, she said to him, "Don't ever come near me. You hear? My daddy finds this out. And he will. He'll break every bone in your body."

James moved closer, laughed a little. "It probably wouldn't have been any good anyway. Some cross-the-tracks stuff. Drive-in trash. You little tramp. You're nothing but a tease."

Callie slapped him and stomped on his foot. He bent down and tried to say "bitch," but it didn't come out right.

Callie grabbed my arm and we went out and down and into the lobby, her holding the top of her blouse against her.

As we went by the concession, the girl there said, "Hey, girlie. He likes it rough, don't he? And let me tell you something. He gets it once, he doesn't want it twice. I know."

The Coke was still on the counter. Callie picked it up, flung it in the girl's face. "It doesn't surprise me you know," Callie said, and we went out into the sunshine.

We walked to the car, and when she was behind the steering wheel, she put her head on it and began to cry and shake.

"Did he hurt you, Callie?"

"He put his hand inside my blouse, the bastard. I scratched his face and I kicked him in his things. What hurts, Stan, is he thought I would let him. He always thought that, from the first time he saw me. I guess I did lead him on, teasing like that. But I didn't tease about . . . Well, you know. I just flirted. I . . . Oh, Stan. I don't know what I did."

"Whatever it was," I said, touching her arm, "he didn't have cause to do that."

She sat up and wiped her face with the back of her hand and drove home.

———

Back at the house, in the drive, Callie collected herself.

"Are you going to tell Daddy?" I said.

"I don't think I should. I don't want him to know I was—"

"You weren't doing anything. He offered to show you how the projector worked."

"I don't care how a projector works. I wanted to be with him . . . Not that way . . . He's older and cute, and I thought, well . . . I don't know what I thought. Oh, Drew isn't going to like this either. I like Drew. I shouldn't have been playing around like that. I wanted to prove to you I could get the information you wanted. But I don't know I really meant to do that. I was . . . I feel so . . . cheap."

"You're not cheap. You fought him, didn't you?"

"I did."

"Did it surprise him when you fought back?"

"Sure did. He tried to kiss me and I didn't let him. Lots of guys try to kiss me, so that was nothing, and I wasn't mean about it. I just said something like, 'Uh uh.' Then he put his hands on me and I slapped him. He didn't like that. He slapped me and I clawed his face. He grabbed my shirt, tore the buttons, said he'd do what he wanted. But I kicked him, and he went to his knees. He just got up when you came. I was ready to fight some more, but I'm glad you came and I didn't have to. It was near soundproof up there. That's why he took me up there. That way if I yelled, wasn't a thing anyone could do about it. They wouldn't hear me unless they were standing right outside the door. I'm glad you came, Stanley. I'm really glad."

"Me too."

Callie took a tissue from the glove box and worked on the makeup that had run from her eyes. She wiped her smudged lipstick off. She put on fresh makeup and pulled her blouse together where the buttons had come loose.

"I never knew things were like this," she said.

"Me neither."

"I look okay?"

"Except for the blouse . . . And you look a little hangdog. I was you, I'd go straight for my room."

"That's what I plan."

INSIDE, Rosy was on the couch reading a magazine. She stood up when we came in, realized she was caught not working. She smiled, then her smile went downhill. She studied Callie.

"What happened to you, Miss Callie?"

"Happened?" Callie said. "Oh, nothing. You mean my blouse? I caught it myself. With my hand. Stupid thing. I—"

"Miss Callie, you lyin' to me."

"Rosy. How dare you."

"Some man done had his hands on you."

"What are you talking about, Rosy? I can't believe—"

"I know, 'cause I been there enough I can tell. I can tell jes' the way you hold yo'self. You ain't at yourself, and I can tell."

"Rosy, you're being foolish."

Rosy stepped forward and lightly slapped Callie on the side of her face.

Callie looked up in astonishment, put her hand to her cheek.

"I don't mean to do more of what's already done, but I'm doin' it for your own good. You don't be keepin' this to yo'self. Don't do what I done. Man don't need to be puttin' his hands on you. You ask yo' mama. Yo' daddy don't treat her that way. Was it that Drew?"

Callie suddenly burst into tears. "No," she said.

"He hit you?" Rosy said, taking Callie in her arms.

"It wasn't him," I said. "It was James Stilwind."

Rosy nodded, guided Callie to the couch. Daddy came into the room, looked at me standing by the door, Callie on the couch with Rosy. Rosy was holding Callie, rocking her, saying, "It gonna be all right, girl."

"What in hell happened?" Daddy said.

No one answered.

Mom came into the room. "Why is Callie crying? Callie?"

Mom went over and sat on the couch so that Callie was between her and Rosy. Callie came loose of Rosy and hugged Mom.

Mom said, "Tell me, Callie."

"Listen to your mother," Daddy said. "Tell her . . . Who ripped your shirt? Callie?"

"Leave her alone, Mr. Stanley," Rosy said. "She got to take her time."

Daddy looked at me. "What happened, Stanley? You damn well better tell me. One of you better."

"Mr. Stanley, you go on and leave the room," Rosy said.

"What?" Daddy said. "Are you talkin' to me?"

"I'm lookin' at you, ain't I?" Rosy said.

"Now, Rosy—"

"Now, you listen to me. I'm grateful for all you done for me. But am I part of this family, or ain't I?"

Daddy groped for words, didn't find any.

Callie said between tears, "You are, Rosy. You are."

"She is," Mom said.

"Well . . . yeah," Daddy said.

"Then I got a say that matters, don't I?" Rosy said.

"Sure," Daddy said, "but—"

"No buts. You don't need to be in this business yet. This is for the women. Then, we'll tell you when you need to know."

"If someone has hurt my little girl, I need to know," Daddy said.

"You gonna find out soon enough," Rosy said. "Now go on and leave."

Daddy looked at me, said, "What about him?"

"He knows already," Rosy said. "Now go on."

Daddy, perplexed, turned and left the room. I heard him go outside on the veranda.

"Callie?" Mom said. "Can we have the story now? What could be the matter?"

Callie told her.

When she finished, Mom said, "If we tell your father, and we must, you know what's going to happen."

"He'll beat James up," Callie said.

"Kill him maybe," Mom said. "That's what worries me. You weren't raped. But you were mistreated."

"I flirted."

"Women flirt," Mom said. "That's what we do. A young girl like you, that's all you do. It comes with being sixteen, and it doesn't stop there. It goes on until your charms are rusty."

"Or they just run off and leave you," Rosy said.

"I am so sorry," Callie said.

"You ain't done nothin', honey," Rosy said, and patted Callie on the back.

"No, you haven't," Mom said. "But your daddy might. I don't know exactly how to handle this. Tell you what. Go upstairs, clean up, and when you come down, I'll have thought of something."

"And I'll fix you some cookies," Rosy said.

In our family, food was always thought of as medicine.

Callie went upstairs. Mom said to Rosy: "I'm tempted to tell Stanley right now, and have him get that man."

"You know Mr. Stanley kill that man, don't you?"

"I said as much."

Mom turned to me. "You were very brave, Stanley. I'm proud of you. Your daddy will be proud of you."

"Callie fought him off," I said. "Looked to me like James was glad I broke the door down. I think I saved him."

Rosy and Mom laughed.

Mom said, "I have to break this to Stanley in such a way he doesn't take a stick and go find Stilwind. I've got to come up with something."

"You could lie," Rosy said.

Mom looked at Rosy and laughed. They hugged one another.

"Don't think that hasn't crossed my mind," Mom said. "Lying has its place. And this may just be the place. Way I see it, it's over with. James Stilwind got his comeuppance, and Callie is okay."

"Does it once, he'll do it again," Rosy Mae said.

Mom, who was holding Rosy's hand, said, "You're right, of course. Nothing says this was his first time, for that matter."

"Oh yeah. He old enough he probably done done it befo'," Rosy said.

"I guess lying is out," Mom said.

"You could sugarcoat it some," Rosy said.

"How do you mix sugar in this?" Mom said.

"I can't say, Miss Gal."

Mom laughed. "Did you see Stanley's face when you told

him this wasn't any of his business and he had to leave the room?"

Rosy giggled. "I sho did. He didn't like it none, now did he?"

"No," Mom said, "but I sure got a kick out of it."

20

No ONE TOLD DADDY anything right away, and it was a long time before Callie came down from upstairs. She had bathed and was dressed in jeans and a man's shirt that fit her in a very loose fashion. She wasn't wearing any makeup.

When Daddy, who was sitting at the table drinking coffee, saw her, he said, "Young lady. Maybe now you should tell me what went on?"

Callie nodded. She sat down at the table. Mom and Rosy were fussing over a bowl of cake mix. Rosy poured the mix into a pan and quietly shoved it into the oven.

Mom said, "She can tell you, Stanley. But you have to hold your peace some. It's important that you do. We can talk about what we should do when she finishes. But you can't jump up and run off mad."

"Someone did something to you, didn't they?" Daddy said. He was already halfway out of his chair.

"That's exactly what I mean," Mom said. "Sit down, Stanley."

"I'm all right," Callie said.

"Someone didn't . . . They didn't . . ."

"No, Daddy. I'm fine."

Daddy eased back into his chair. Callie was just about to start her story when there was a knock on the door.

Rosy answered it. I heard her say, "Yes, sir. Can I help you?"

I heard a voice outside, but couldn't make it out.

Rosy said, "Yes, sir. This is the Mitchel residence . . . Oh. You wait here jes' one moment."

Rosy came back into the kitchen. "Mr. Stilwind. The older man. The daddy. He at the do'."

"Invite him in," Mom said.

Poor Daddy just looked perplexed.

Mr. Stilwind seemed so much older than I would have thought, and as Buster warned me, not all monsters look the part. He had a pleasantly wrinkled face with slightly red cheeks and a touch of sweat above his eyes. He was tall and well dressed, wearing a suit with vest, tie, and hat, which he removed as he entered the door. His shoes were buffed and I noticed the reflection of his hand in the shine of one of his fine leather shoes as he extended it for my father to shake.

"Irving Stilwind," he said. "I suppose you know why I'm here?"

"No," Daddy said.

"Yes," Mom said. "You're here to talk about what your son did to my daughter."

"What?" Daddy said.

"He hasn't heard yet," Mom said. "We were just about to discuss it."

"I see," said Mr. Stilwind. "Might we sit down?"

"Your son is a dead sonofabitch," Daddy said.

"Now you hold it," Mr. Stilwind said.

"Stanley," Mom said. "Just wait . . . Come sit down, Mr. Stilwind."

"I'll po' up some coffee," Rosy said.

They seated themselves around the table, except for Rosy, who made fresh coffee, and myself. I sat on the counter and let my feet hang.

"My son told me he had a misunderstanding," Mr. Stilwind said.

"It was no misunderstanding," Callie said. "A misunderstanding didn't tear my blouse."

"I think it's best the adults discuss this," Mr. Stilwind said.

"It happened to me," Callie said. "I think that makes my opinion worth something."

"A young girl. A young man. Things can go a little too fast."

"A little too fast," Callie said. "He had his motor running from the start, had his foot on the gas."

"Then," Mr. Stilwind said, "you must admit, you should not have gone with him. Should not have encouraged it."

"She didn't encourage nothin'," Rosy said. "That boy of yours ain't no boy. He a man. He know what he's doin'."

"I'm not accustomed to the hired help speaking to me in this manner. My help. Anyone's help."

"I'm beginning to have an idea what's going on here," Daddy said. "And what I'll tell you is this. If this boy is your only son, your name will not be spread. If you get my meaning."

"Are you threatening my son?" Mr. Stilwind said.

"If what I think is being said here is being said, then I wouldn't dare let you think I'm threatening. I'm making you a promise, and him one too."

"It may not be what you think, Daddy," Callie said. "I wasn't . . . Well, you know. Nothing like that."

Callie took time to tell her story. When she finished I told mine.

Stilwind said: "Girls tease. Boys don't always know when it's a tease. Perhaps you encouraged him."

"I don't care if she flirted with him or not," Daddy said. "He went too far, teased or not."

"He ain't got no right to lay hands on Miss Callie," Rosy said.

"I don't believe you have a dog in this fight," Stilwind said.

Callie barked sharply.

Stilwind turned red.

"Mr. Stilwind," Daddy said. "You and me, we're already on weak scaffolding. You speak one more time to Rosy like that, say one more disparaging thing about my daughter, suggest it, I'm going to forget you're twenty years older than me, and you may not wake up."

"Threaten me, and the police will know about it."

"I'll bury your ass in the suit you're wearin' out back of my place and I'll plant a goddamn row of cactus on top of it."

I laughed.

Daddy looked at me sharply, and I went silent.

Mr. Stilwind, red-faced, sat for a moment sucking air. Finally he calmed. "All right," he said. "Let me cut to the chase. My son told me what he did. He was ashamed of it. Let's say it was his fault—"

"It was," Daddy said.

"Very well. I'm prepared to apologize for him, and present you with some compensation for the anguish and so the story will not get spread."

"Compensation?" Daddy said.

"Money."

"You want to pay Callie off to not say anything?"

"The police will not get involved in this matter," Stilwind said. "I can assure you of that. I know them quite well. The chief, the old chief, and the young man who will most likely take over the job, are all good friends of mine. I've always had good relations with the police."

"You give them money, they're your friends," Daddy said. "That what you're saying?"

"You could say that. But the money I'm offering is substantial." Stilwind looked around. "You could do a lot with this place with that money."

"There's nothing wrong with this place that a good fumigation won't cure when you leave," Daddy said.

"I need not pay you a dime, sir. The police hardly see the flirtations of one little girl worth the trouble of bothering my son. I'm sure of this. But I don't need the word spread. It's not good for me. It's not good for my son. It certainly wouldn't be good for your daughter."

"Why isn't he here to speak for himself?" Mom asked.

"I felt this was the better way to go about it."

"Come in, pay us off, go to the house, forget it," Daddy said.

"If you want to break it down to a crude summation, I suppose you are right. It doesn't do us any good to do otherwise. Your family or mine."

"I think your son is a coward," Daddy said. "Uh uh, don't speak, Stilwind. You listen to me. I think *you* are a coward. I think you think your money gets you out of everything. You're fortunate the worst that happened was he tore my daughter's blouse. Otherwise, I'd kill him."

"You'd go to prison for the rest of your life," Stilwind said. "I'd see to that."

"That could be. Let me tell you this, and I'll deny it if

asked. I'm not going to bother your son. My daughter is all right. She took up for herself quite well. But, someday, he'll get his. I can promise you that."

"Don't lay a hand on him," Stilwind said. "Never. I promise you. I'm going to make things rough for you in this town. Ordinances may not be being obeyed here. Police might need to pull you over from time to time, just to check and see if you're driving right."

"You know," Daddy said. "I don't think you care about James at all. I think you care about you. How this hurts you, or your name. I bet this boy has been in plenty of trouble, that you've bought him out of all manner of it. He doesn't feel he has to be responsible. Just like I bet you've never been responsible."

"I earned all that I have," Stilwind said. "All of it."

"So have I. It may be less than you have, but I earned it. I think it gave me character. I think it gave you money and a shoeshine."

"Very well," Stilwind said, picking his hat from his knee and rising. "You had your chance. It was not meant as a bribe. Just a token of apology."

"Your apology is nothing to me. And I wouldn't give me too much trouble about ordinances either. I'm a fighter."

"Good day, sir," Stilwind said.

"I won't wish you that," Daddy said. "I wouldn't give a damn if you flipped your car and it killed you."

"Stanley," Mom said.

"You tell your son to stay away from my daughter. Forever."

Stilwind put on his hat and made his own way to the door. I went to the window and looked out. There was a colored man in a black suit with a black cap waiting beside a long black car. The colored man smiled and opened the back door for Stilwind. Stilwind got in without saying a word. The colored man drove the car away.

Rosy picked up Stilwind's coffee cup and dumped his coffee in the sink. "He didn't even drink a drop," she said. "And me goin' to all that trouble."

Callie took hold of Daddy's hand and squeezed it. "Thanks, Daddy."

Daddy squeezed her hand back.

"You did good," Mom said. "Except for that car wreck part."

"Meant it," Daddy said.

"Uh oh," Rosy said. "Think I smell our cake a burnin'."

He was here in your house?" Buster said, wiping the projector lens clean with a soft rag.

"Yes."

"Isn't that something? He old, ain't he?"

"Yes. Not real, real old. But older than Daddy."

"Old as me?"

"No, sir. I don't think so."

"Not many people are. And I'll tell you, I'm starting to feel it. That walk to work is catching up with me. I have to start about twenty minutes earlier these days, just so I can stop along the way and rest a little."

"Buster?"

"Yeah, Stan."

"What if it wasn't the father?"

"Do what?"

"What if it's James that did it? Not Mr. Stilwind?"

"You been thinking again, ain't you?"

"Remember what you showed me about Margret's letters?"

Buster put the rag in his back pocket and perched on the stool behind the projector.

"How do you mean?" he said.

"I assumed Margret was seeing James. I thought J was James and it was Jewel."

"That was a normal thing to think, Stan. More them that like the opposite than like the same."

"That report you read to me. The chief's report. Did the daughter actually say it was her father?"

"I said it could be other ways, didn't I, Stan?"

"You did."

Buster scratched his chin, stepped on a bug running across the floor. He said, "You're sayin' the report didn't say it was the father, so it could have been James . . . You know, it could. It could have been James knocked up the first sister, then the second. He was old enough. He maybe near forty now and still actin' like some kind of teenager, trickin' your sister like that . . . Older sister, Susan, she could have meant her brother. The old man just went down to the police station to smooth it over, way he tried to do today with your family. Sometimes a man thinks a son is more important than a daughter. It could be like that."

"Daddy thinks Stilwind doesn't really care for his James. Just didn't want to be embarrassed."

"Think your daddy's right on that one, Stan. So now you think it's James instead of the daddy?"

"Maybe."

"Ever think it might have been the daddy on one, the brother on the other? Lot of times, you learn how you act from how your family acts. You can't tell me Old Man Stilwind is all that good at how he acts. Evidence don't show that. James may have found out his father was havin' him a time with the older sister, and he done the same with the younger one. Now, mind you, I ain't sayin' it's that way. Just tryin' to teach you you can't think somethin' one way. That's why you supposed to have trials, not lynchin's. Most of the time things are just the way they look, but sometimes they ain't."

"What's a lynchin'?"

"Most people mean a hangin'. But we colored, we're talkin' about burnin', castratin', torturin'. Way the law likes to work is they can't find who done somethin', they just go out and get a nigger. Sometimes the nigger done it. Sometimes not. That's what I mean about a jury, and not just speculation. You see, you can think a thing all kinds of ways, even if you got bits of evidence. But evidence is in the way you look at it. 'Less you catch the sucker redhanded or they're tryin' to hurt you. Like Bubba Joe."

"Yes, sir."

"I seen a lynchin' once."

"Really?"

"Uh huh. Over in Nacogdoches. Nineteen and two it was. A nigger named Jim Buchannon. He was picked up for murderin' a man and his wife I think. Stole a rifle from them, they said. And he had the rifle, which he claimed he traded a white man for. And he might have done it too. Or he might have killed them white folks. Can't say.

"I was just passin' through, on my way to see a cousin, and I come to Nacogdoches on the day of the hangin'. It was an October and a nice cool day. They say there was a kind of trial, but the sheriff, John Spradley, he didn't think it was fair enough, and he done all he could to save the man for a trial. Hid him out on trains and such, took him from one spot or another. But they finally got him and told him he could be hung later or now, to make his choice. He chose to be hung. I was at the back of the crowd. They had a kind of tripod made of lumber and they put Buchannon on that box and kicked it out from under him, and he strangled to death. Slow-like. I told myself I wouldn't never purposely watch no hangin' again. It was like a picnic out there, Stan. All the men and women, mostly white, but there were colored too, way out back of it like me, and we was there to see that poor nigger hang, him swingin' with his toes just off the ground, that rope squeezin' the life out of him. It wasn't even tied right, and on purpose is my guess. That way they had a little more spectacle. No neck break, just slow and horrible, him kickin' and his tongue hangin' out of his mouth damn near six inches. There was a fellow out there sellin' peanuts, and people with wagons, with women and children in them, sittin' there havin' a picnic lunch.

"After it was all over I lost my lunch, and I left there and went on my way, avoidin' anyone and everyone that was white. I was afraid they might not be satisfied, and want 'em another nigger. There's a point in this story, Stan. What is it?"

"Don't jump to conclusions?"

"That's right. Just the other day, you was certain Old Man Stilwind had done it 'cause I laid out a little story for you. Now you done thought maybe James done it. And I thought maybe it was one of each . . . and the other thing is, outside of self-defense, the law is supposed to dish out justice, not you and me."

"But it doesn't always, does it?"

"Son, it ain't like Hopalong Cassidy. Sometimes the good guys lose."

————

I SAT OUT THERE with Buster and watched the movie, but went to my room after only one showing. I climbed into bed and thought about all that I had learned, and thought about Buster's story. The idea of a man swinging and strangling like that made me sick.

I lay in bed with my hands behind my head, Nub stretched out over my feet, kicking his foot from time to time as he chased an imaginary rabbit.

I felt pretty miserable about what had happened to Callie. I liked to think my arrival had helped stop what was going on. I should have never let her out of my sight. Not with a guy like James Stilwind. I had an idea what kind of person he was, and I had spent my time looking out the window of the theater.

It was so wild the way the world and Dewmont really were. Probably all towns were like this and most people never found out. I wished I were most people. It was like once the lid was off the world, everything that was ugly and secret came out.

Just a short time ago my biggest concern, my greatest disappointment, was discovering there was no Santa Claus.

I sighed and looked at the ceiling.

Things had to get better.

"They have to," I said aloud.

But fate wasn't through with me yet.

21

NEXT MORNING, after breakfast, I let Nub out. He ran to the projection booth and started barking. I thought maybe a coon or a possum had crawled in there. It had happened a couple of times when Buster left the door open, or so Daddy told me.

Daddy said he had to run the critters out with a broom, chase them until they climbed the fence and headed back into the woods.

I had yet to make such a discovery, and was about half excited to think I might have finally done so. I was a little scared too. A coon or a possum can turn nasty when cornered.

I picked up the poking stick we used for picking up trash, and went out there. The door was closed. Coons and possums didn't close doors behind them.

Buster?

If it was Buster, Nub wouldn't have barked.

Still, I called Buster's name.

He didn't answer.

"Nub," I said. "You sure?"

Nub scratched at the bottom of the door and growled. I said, "Whoever is in there, I got a gun. You better take it easy."

I started backing away, ready to get Daddy.

I heard a voice from inside. "It's okay, Stanley. It's me. Don't shoot."

"Richard?"

"Yeah. Don't get your daddy or mama."

The door cracked open, and Richard poked his head out. There was dirt crusted on one side of his face.

"Hey," he said.

"Hey," I said.

"You don't have a gun."

"No," I said. "What are you doing in the projection booth?"

"I climbed the fence when y'all closed down. Slept in here."

"Get back inside. I'm coming in."

Inside, Richard said, "I slept on the floor on that piece of carpet. Wasn't too bad. Best place I've slept in over a week."

Richard was wearing a pair of overalls, no shirt. The overalls looked as if they had been washed in mud and dried in sin. There were bumps on his face from mosquitoes and his nose had run and dirt was crusted on his upper lip like a Hitler mustache. One knee of his overalls was ripped and the kneecap that poked through it had a scab on it. He didn't have shoes on. His feet were caked with red clay and I could see scratches on top of them and along the ankles where he had outgrown his overalls.

"Your daddy was looking for you," I said.

"I know," he said.

"He and my daddy had words. They had more than words."

"When was this?"

I told him what happened and said I was really sorry.

"Don't be. I ain't been home since before that happened. It must have happened mornin' after the night I run off. He was lookin' for me 'cause I run away and he wasn't through whuppin' on me. He run me out in the middle of the night, and if I hadn't been sleepin' in my overalls I wouldn't be wearin' nothin'."

Richard turned. His back, bare except for the overall straps, showed long crusty red marks. "He got in some good licks, but I wouldn't gonna take no more, so I took off."

I noticed there were white scars next to the red marks. I knew his father whipped him more than I thought was right, but now I knew how bad he whipped him.

"Heavens," I said.

"He took a horsewhip to me. Belt's bad enough, but when I run, he grabbed up the whip, caught me out in the yard. It hadn't been dark, I don't know I'd have got away from him. He chased me a mile through the corn and then on out to the woods. Said he'd kill me if he caught me."

"What started it?"

"Comic books. He said all that readin' was makin' me think I was better'n him, and he wasn't gonna have that."

"That started it?"

"Yeah. Sort of. One thing led to another. I told him I thought maybe I ought to finish high school. He wanted me to quit. Said the law wouldn't do nothin'. Not around here. They didn't care."

Richard melted onto the carpet on the floor. I sat on the projection booth stool. I said, "Where have you been all this time?"

"Here and there. Out in them woods. Hid in a nigger's barn outside of town. Stole some food out of a house. Just enough to eat, mind you. Some old corn bread was left on the stove and

I got a piece a chicken out of the icebox. Left them a thank-you note, but I didn't put my name to it."

"Good grief, Richard."

"Just couldn't stay home no more. Daddy told me he was gonna kill me."

"Surely he didn't mean it."

Richard laughed, but he didn't sound all that amused. "You got it so good you don't know a thing about how it is. I didn't know it was any different till I met you. Just thought that's the way it was. Beatin's and all. Mamas havin' black eyes and a swollen lip all the time . . . Stanley, think maybe you could get me somethin' to eat?"

"I'll get you something."

"Maybe you can wrap me up a little somethin', some bread maybe. Let me have that old canteen of yours. You know, the army one? I'm gonna try and catch a boxcar out later."

"Where to?"

"Where my old man can't find me. I started to catch me one last night, but it wasn't slow enough. May need to walk up to the next town. I think they got a switchin' station there. Might go where I can get me a job of some kind. Workin' on a farm. I know how to work, and if they hire them little wetback kids, they're sure to hire me."

"What about your mother?"

"She don't care about me neither. Thought she did, but I finally come to think she don't. She lets him beat me."

"He beats her too," I said.

"I know. But . . ."

"What?"

"She kind of likes it."

"Likes a beating?"

"Uh huh. That's how come all this."

"I thought it was reading, wanting to go to school."

"That's what set him off finally, but it's because I run in on him beatin' her the other day, and I fought him. He whupped me good with his fists, and my mama told me to mind my own business. That it was the way they did things."

"She said that?"

"Yes."

"She could have been trying to help you. Keep you out of it."

"I wanted to think that, but way she looked . . . It was like she was havin' fun. Ain't nobody ought to like that, should they?"

"I wouldn't think so."

"I been stupid, Stanley. I been stayin' home for her, and she don't want me there." Richard started to cry. "I'm so tired."

"Come on, Richard, you don't need to stay out here."

"I don't want your parents to know. I don't want to tell nobody."

"It's all right, Richard. Really. Come on. Let's get Rosy to fix you a big breakfast. You know how she can cook."

I held out my hand and he took it, and I helped him up. He sniffed a few times and quit crying. We walked to the house. Richard walked with his head hung, and his poor wrecked feet lifted no more than they had to.

————

WHEN WE CAME IN through the back, Rosy saw Richard and looked at me. I said, "He needs something to eat, Rosy."

"Well, we gonna fix that," she said, and pans started clanging. Mom came into the kitchen a few moments later. She had slept late. She was still wearing her robe, and hair hung in her eyes.

"You sound like you're trying to tear down the house, Rosy . . . Oh, hi, Richard."

"Hi, Mrs. Mitchel."

"You look a mess, son. What have you been doing?"

Richard put his head on the table and started to cry again. Mom pulled a chair up next to him, put her arm around him. "I'm sorry. I didn't mean to hurt your feelings."

"It's not that," I said.

"What is it?" Mom asked.

"Let him eat now, Miss Gal," Rosy said. "That's what a growin' boy needs."

So Rosy cooked and Richard ate. When he was finished Mom didn't ask him any questions. She showed him where he could bathe and I went upstairs and got some of my clothes for him.

When Richard was finished, he dressed, except for shoes, and came back to the kitchen. Rosy and Mom were waiting on him. They had him perch on his knees on a chair in front of the sink, and they washed his hair, using strong soap and turpentine to kill lice. When they finished that, they rinsed his hair, dried it, combed it for him. Exhausted, he ended up on the living room couch.

Instantly, he was sound asleep.

Daddy came in for breakfast, and while Rosy cooked it, Mom guided him to the living room to see Richard sleeping on the couch.

"What's this about?" Daddy asked.

"Stanley?" Mom said.

In the kitchen, at the table, I explained.

I've heard of people like that," Daddy said. "They call them masochist, and the one does it to them a sadist."

"That's sick," Mom said.

"I suppose," Daddy said, "anyone wants to hurt someone and likes it, or someone likes or thinks they deserve being hurt, is, yeah, a little sick."

"You liked slapping Chester around," I said.

"I did. Liked slapping Chapman around, for that matter. Like it better now I know what he's done to that boy. But for me, not just anyone will do. James Stilwind would do. I'd like to slap him around."

"What are we going to do with Richard?" Mom asked.

"Nothing," Daddy said. "He can sleep in Stanley's room for now. By the way, where in the hell is Callie?"

"Still sleeping," Mom said.

"I hope she can get up when school starts," Dad said.

"We were late ourselves," Mom said.

"Yes," Daddy said, smiling at Mom, "but we weren't sleeping."

Mom reddened a little. "What if Mr. Chapman comes for him?"

"He won't," Daddy said. "He doesn't want to come around here. If he does, he gets another slapping."

"You can't solve everything by slapping someone around," Mom said.

"I know," Daddy said. "But some things you can. At least temporarily. Haven't seen Chester around here lately, have you?"

"We could call the police on Chapman," Mom said.

"They'd just take Richard back to him," Dad said. "Way the law works when kids run off, darn near no matter what the reason, law takes them back. There's folks believe kids belong to parents and they can do what they want with their own kids. Law wouldn't help, Gal."

"The law does that?" Mom asked. "Gives beat-up kids back?"

"Afraid so," Daddy said.

"What if Chapman calls the police?" I said. "He could call them on us."

"He could," Daddy said, "but he might be thinking we know more than he wants us to know. And we do. Law might give him Richard back, but Chapman wouldn't want us spreading his business. Town like this, his business would burn through it like a wildfire. Wouldn't be anyone didn't know it. When it comes right down to it, he and Stilwind aren't all that different."

"Do you think Stilwind will bother us, Daddy? You know, with regulations and all that?"

"That's his style, son. We'll just have to wait and see."

———

On a hot sticky night with mosquitoes, the Friday starting off the weekend before school was to begin, I went out to visit with Buster.

I did that when the concession was slow, and it was slow right then because the first run of the movie, *The Cry Baby Killer,* was near the end and everyone was waiting to see the climax. Or have a climax; I was now old enough to understand why some cars parked out near the fence were rocking.

Richard stayed to help with concessions. He seemed comfortable around the family, and right now, comfort was good.

Pretty soon, I found I was telling Buster all about Richard and his daddy without even being asked. It jumped out. Maybe it was information I shouldn't have shared, but I couldn't help myself.

Buster shook his head sadly and clucked his tongue.

"Older I get, Stan, more I wish I had a family and hadn't messed up the one I had. Drinkin' didn't do me no good. You know, I haven't had me a drink since that day . . . with you and Bubba Joe."

"Do you feel better?"

"I feel miserable. I think about drinkin' all the time. Near come off the wagon least once a day every day. Make that least every hour. It ain't easy. Main thing with me these days, is I'm finally startin' to feel old."

Buster removed from his shirt pocket a folded piece of yellow paper. He gave it to me and I unfolded it. It was the chief's report on Susan Stilwind and her father.

"Why are you giving this to me, Buster?"

"Old Man Stilwind starts to give you trouble, it might come in handy. Guess you could say it's a kind of insurance. You might want to make a copy of it and show it to the old man, tell him the real copy is put away and you got another copy written out and with a friend. That would be me. Here's the address where he's stayin'. I had Jukes get it for me."

"Is there anything Jukes can't find out?"

"My exact age, and that's about it. You do this thing, I think your problems with that old Stilwind cracker will be over."

———

NEXT MORNING, I awoke to find Richard lying on the floor of my room, twisted up in a blanket, clutching his pillow. Nub had taken his spot on the bed, and was lying on his back with his feet in the air, his tongue hanging out.

I got up, grabbed some clothes, went to the bathroom,

brushed my teeth, combed my hair and got dressed. I came back to he room to find Richard sitting up, looking bewildered.

"Don't like sharin' a bed?" I said.

"Nub kept licking me."

I got the piece of paper Buster had given me out of the sock drawer and took a pencil and paper and copied down word for word the police report. I put the original back in my sock drawer.

"I got to go into town today," I said, folding the copy, poking it into my pants pocket. "I'm going to go before Daddy or Mom asks about me. I'll be back soon as I can."

"I'll go with you . . . If that's okay?"

"I guess . . . Listen, maybe I ought not tell you this, but if you go with me, you ought to know. I need to have someone else who knows anyway, as a kind of backup."

I took the folded piece of paper Buster had given me out of my sock drawer, gave it to Richard to read.

When he finished, he said, "I don't get it."

I explained it to him. I told him a lot of stuff. One thing that can be said about me, I'm a regular blabbermouth. But I didn't tell him about Buster and Bubba Joe. I didn't even remind him of the night we had been chased together.

"So, you're gonna give him this, way Buster told you?"

"I'm going to give him a copy of it. That's what I was writing."

I took the paper from Richard, folded it, and returned it to the sock drawer.

"Well, let's get to doin'."

"First, you go wash your face, brush your teeth, and comb your hair. I've got a toothbrush and a comb for you. Rest is in the bathroom downstairs."

———————

As USUAL on a Saturday, the town was bustling. Since Richard didn't have a bike, we walked. We went by the picture show, and I walked fast as we went, tried not to look through the glass doors to see if I could see James, but I couldn't help myself.

I didn't see him.

We walked over to the hotel where Mr. Stilwind lived. In the lobby, we looked around and wondered what to do. A young man behind a counter smiled at us and beckoned us over. He wore a black suit and white shirt and his hair was slicked down flat against his head. He looked like the kind of guy Callie might find attractive.

He said, "May I help you boys?"

"I need to see Mr. Stilwind."

"Are you kin?"

"No."

"I believe I should call him. May I tell him what this is about?"

"Tell him Susan and her baby."

"Susan and her baby?"

"Yes."

"Should I elaborate on that?"

"No. He'll know."

"Very well."

He called up, spoke what I had told him over the phone. When he put down the receiver, he said, "He'll be right down. Would you like to make yourself comfortable."

We went over and sat in some big soft chairs. After a moment, the elevator dropped, opened, and out stepped Stilwind, all dressed in black, looking as if he were about to go to a funeral. The only thing missing was his hat.

He saw me, startled, then came over. "You," he said.

I hadn't really noticed before, and maybe it was the harsh sunlight slipping between the great hotel curtains, but up close his face was as marked with wrinkles as a henhouse floor with chicken scratches. He looked ten years older than I had first thought him to be, and I hadn't thought him to be a spring chicken then.

"I got something for you," I said.

"An apology from your father . . . He decide to take my offer? It's still open, you know."

"No, sir. He would want me to tell you to cram your offer where the sun doesn't shine. I have a copy of something. This was written by Chief Rowan. It has to do with you and your daughter Susan. We have the original put away in a safe place. This is a copy I made."

I gave it to him. He read it. His face turned pale. He held the paper in his hand as if he had suddenly discovered a snake there.

"That's your copy," I said.

"I assume this young man knows about it?"

"As well as others."

"If everyone knows, why should it matter to me?"

"Not everyone knows. Me and a few others."

"Adults?"

"Yes. I told enough people so I'd have backup. I want my family left alone."

"Your father put you up to this?"

"No. If my father wanted to do something about this, he'd come over and beat you and throw you down the stairs and drag you through the street and set you on fire. He doesn't know about it."

Stilwind's face moved, tried to find an expression, settled on a sneer.

"How do I know you have the original?"

"How do you think I made this copy? Think I'd give you the only copy?"

"How did you come by it?"

"That's my business."

"You know the chief?"

"Never met him, never heard of him until recently."

"He isn't in on this?"

"No."

"You want money, of course. Money for your silence."

"No. I want you to leave my family alone. No made-up safety problems for the police or the fire department to inspect out at our drive-in. No problems from you of any kind."

"I can't be responsible for anything you think might be my fault."

"That's your problem."

"You sound awfully grown-up for a kid. Awful mean."

I did sound grown-up, and I was proud of it.

"I'm not mean. You made a threat to my family. This is a way of keeping things where they belong. The only thing left is your son, James. He better never come within fifty feet of any of my family."

"And what about this boy?"

"You don't need to know who he is, but he counts too. You stay away from him."

"Gladly. Is that all, you little worm?"

"Yes, sir. That's it. The Worm has spoken."

––––––––––

OUT ON THE STREET, in the hot sunshine, I was ecstatic. What I had done had been Buster's idea, not mine, of course, but I was proud of myself. I liked the way I had talked, the sound of my voice. Richard was very impressed, and told me so.

"Man, you had him by the short hairs."

"The short hairs? What's that mean?"

"I don't know exactly, but I've heard it. You were really good in there."

"Thanks."

As we walked past Harriman's Feed and Seed, Mr. Chapman came out. He was wearing a sweat-stained brown hat and was carrying a large bag of fertilizer. He didn't see us at first. We froze. He eased down the steps to the curb and dumped the bag into the back of his old rickety black pickup, made it companion to a half dozen other bags there.

When he looked up, he saw us. There was something about his face that I can't describe. A kind of blankness as far as his features went, but his eyes, they were as dark and nasty-looking as a dying animal's.

"You," he said to Richard. "You had a punishment."

"I ain't gonna take no more of that," Richard said.

"Say you ain't?" Chapman said. "Say you ain't?"

"No, sir, I ain't."

Beside me, I could feel Richard tense.

Chapman glared at me. "And you and your high and mighty daddy, and that little Jezebel of a sister—"

"Shut your mouth," I said. "I'll tell Daddy if you lay one hand on me or Richard. And he'll come to your house and beat you like a dirty rug."

"He will, will he?" Chapman said.

"He sure did the other day," I said, "and he wasn't even trying."

"I ought to whip your proud butt with my belt," Chapman said.

"You ain't gonna whip either our asses," Richard said. "You laid your last hand on me, old man."

Chapman glared. "By the Lord Jesus Christ, you ain't no son of mine. Not no more."

"I never was," Richard said.

Chapman cackled like some kind of creature out of a storybook, turned, got in his truck, and drove away.

I peeked over at Richard. His chin was nearly on his chest, his shoulders slumped. He looked as if he were being held up by an invisible noose around his neck.

I took him by the elbow. "Let's go home."

22

THAT NIGHT, as Richard lay on his pallet on the floor, I heard him whimpering, and now and then he would sob. Nub, lying beside me, sat up, looked at him.

I rose up and took a look. I called Richard's name softly, but he didn't answer.

I pulled Nub close to me and went back to sleep.

———

SUNDAY, Drew came by, asked if Callie could go for a drive. Daddy studied Drew for a moment. He looked very different from Chester. He was neat, with a white sports coat, tan slacks, and a dark shirt and white shoes.

Dad said, "She can go, if you take Stanley and Richard."

Drew tried not to show it, but his face fell like a cake.

"Daddy," Callie said, "I don't want them to go."

"Be that as it may, I want them to."

This, of course, was just Daddy's way of messing with Drew, making sure that Callie and Drew were not alone all the time. It was a losing battle, but one caring fathers all over the world participate in.

Still, this deal had to have our cooperation. "You boys want to go for a ride?" Daddy asked.

"I don't know," I said. "I think I'd like to just stay here and play chess with Richard. I'm going to teach him how."

"Richard?" Daddy said.

"Yes, sir. I think I'd like to play chess. I mean, a ride would be okay, but I don't know."

"Looks like it's the couch and television," Daddy said.

Drew knew a bribe was in order. "I'll treat us all to a sundae at the Dairy Queen. Then we'll just ride around awhile."

Richard and I looked at one another. I said, "Sure."

"I don't want Callie in too late," Daddy said. "Tomorrow's school."

"Yes, sir," Drew said. "I thought we might go to the movie downtown."

Before Daddy could answer, Callie said, "I don't believe I'll be going there anymore."

"Why is that?" Drew asked.

"I'll tell you sometime," Callie said. "Just not right now."

"All right," Drew said. "We'll just have a soda and drive around."

"And you know to respect my daughter, of course?" Daddy said.

"Yes, sir."

In the car, Callie sat on her side, but when we drove up from the drive-in, made the corner into town, she slid over beside him.

I looked at Richard and we snickered.

Callie looked over the seat at us. "You won't think it's so funny when you start dating."

"I hope that isn't any time soon," I said.

"Well," Callie said, "in your case it may be never."

We stopped at the soda shop and had sodas. Tim wasn't working. A fellow with pimples was. I kept thinking one of them might have popped in my malt, and the idea of it sort of put me off the drink.

When we finished, we drove through town a couple of times, then on out to the lake. The sun went down and up came a beautiful night with the moon hanging high. The light of it spilled all over the streets and woods like milk froth.

Callie and Drew were sitting very close now, what Daddy called the two-headed monster when he saw kids in cars pass us sitting close together.

After a while, I said, "You know, at the top of the hill where you live, that old house? They say the old lady comes back there."

"How's that?" Drew asked.

"They say Mrs. Stilwind comes back," I said. "She lost her mind and comes back. Her daughter died in a fire right behind where the drive-in is now. But Mrs. Stilwind saw her ghost in the house on the hill. Guess she comes there hoping to see her again. She leaves the old folks home when she wants and goes there. We could drive over and see if she comes home. There's a hill behind the house, and some woods. If there's a road—"

"There is," Drew said, and he seemed happy about the idea.

We drove over there, went up a red-clay road and wound around amongst some trees and came out on a hill that overlooked the great house.

In the moonlight, from that distance, you couldn't tell the

house was run-down. The swimming pool, with the light of the moon filling it, looked to have water in it.

"When is she supposed to come?" Drew asked.

"I don't know," I said. "It's just a chance you might see her. She might be in the house now. She might not come at all."

"I know," Richard said. "Let's go down there for a look."

Drew said, "Why don't you two go look?"

"I don't think so," I said. "Not by ourselves."

"You chicken?" Drew said.

"Yes," I said.

Drew laughed. "That's honest. Oh, hell, let's all go."

Drew pulled a flashlight from under the seat. We walked down the hill, past the pool. We pushed open the back door. The only light was the moonlight that came through the windows.

Inside, Drew pulled the door closed, and there was an explosion of sound like dry leaves being run over by a herd of elephants.

"Bats," Drew said.

I couldn't see them, but I could hear them, fluttering up near the high ceilings and at the top of the staircase. In the beam of the flashlight, I could see the floor was littered with bat guano. It hadn't been there at the first of the summer.

Drew played the light on the ceiling. There were large rafters and from the rafters hung bats, but just as many bats were fluttering about the house.

With a burst, the remaining bats on the rafters let loose and joined the others and swirled about. Then with a rush and a flutter, they made a stream of shadow. Drew's light followed, and they exploded through a place where the roof had rotted and fallen in.

"Oooooh," Callie said. "Let's get out of here."

"What a shame for such a nice house to go to pieces," Drew said.

"Come on, Drew, let's go," Callie said.

"In a moment," Drew said. He shone the light on the stairs. "Let's have a quick look up there. How much of the house have you seen, Stanley?"

"About what you see now. I didn't stay long. I thought I heard and saw someone up there."

"It could be a bum," Callie said. "Anyone."

"I think it was her. Mrs. Stilwind. That's what Buster thinks."

"Buster doesn't know," Callie said.

"He knows more than you think about most everything."

"It won't hurt to look," Drew said.

"It might," Callie said.

We went up the stairs, clustered together like grapes, Drew shining the light. The stairs creaked as we went. We came to a hallway. Along it were a number of doors. We opened one and Drew shone the light about. It was an empty room. The wallpaper was peeling in spots, and as we entered, dust rose up from the floor like a mist.

We checked a couple of other rooms. Same situation.

Finally, we entered a room and found a bed inside. There was also a nightstand with a mirror and the mirror was broken, only one piece of glass still in it. It was in the right-hand corner and was a very small piece. The rest of the mirror was on the floor, spread out like pieces of silver.

There was a brush on the nightstand, and there were long gray hairs in it. The bed had wrinkled dirty sheets on it and looked as if someone had been sleeping there. Up close, we saw there were gray hairs on the pillows.

"Wow," Drew said. "Maybe she does come back here."

"Come on," Callie said. "Those bats make me nervous."

"They're gone," Drew said.

"Come on," Callie said again, and there was no sweetness in her voice.

We left out of there, half expecting to meet Mrs. Stilwind at the door.

Drew drove us home, Callie moving to the passenger position as we came closer to the Dew Drop.

———

Up in my room, me and Richard went to bed early, preparing for school the next day. I was both excited and worried. At least I had one friend there. Richard. And he'd be going to school with me.

I was thinking about all this, lying wide awake, when Richard raised up on one elbow from his pallet, said, "Stanley?"

"Yes."

"Your family has been good to me. Thanks."

"No problem."

"But I've got to go."

"Do what?"

I sat up in bed. So did Nub. He seemed annoyed. He didn't like his sleep disturbed.

"What do you mean go?" I asked.

"I have to go home."

"You can't go there. Your father doesn't want you there."

"Not to see him. Or my mama. I was thinkin' about that story you told about that old woman wandering back to her house, looking for her daughter's ghost. My daddy and mama don't even care about me and I'm alive. I'm not going there to see them, you can bet on that."

"Then why?"

"I want my bike. That's the main reason. I'm going to go over there and get it. I don't get it, Daddy's gonna sell it or throw it away for spite."

"Do you have to do it tonight?"

"During the day they'll see me, and if I wait too long, he'll get rid of it. May have already."

"You could get another bike."

"I made that one out of old bikes I got down at the dump. He didn't give it to me. They ain't never give me much of anything besides a beatin' and hard work. I've had more clothes give me since I been here than I got all them years from them. I didn't even have no underwear till your mama gave me some."

He stood up, took off the pajamas Mom had given him, started pulling on his clothes.

"You're just going to go over there and get your bike?"

"Yeah. At least that."

"What does that mean?"

"I'll be back."

I don't know what I feared he might do, why I thought he might need a backup, but I said, "Wait up, and I'll go with you. Just wait until it's later and we're sure everyone's asleep, then we'll both go. You'll have to hide the bike nearby. Out behind the house in the woods. We'll get it tomorrow, say we went over and got it after school. They see it tomorrow, they'll know we went out tonight."

"Ain't no need in you going," Richard said.

"I know. But I'm going."

———————

I GOT MY HOPALONG CASSIDY flashlight and snuck silently out the back way. In fact, any noise we might have made was covered by Rosy's snoring.

With only one bike, we walked. Nub went with us, trotting along, sniffing the ground. There was a cool, late August wind, and it gently shook the trees on either side of us and made the shadows of their boughs cut back and forth across the road as if they were sawing the earth in half.

When we could see the old sawmill, we stopped. Nub sat down in the road and let his tongue hang out, dripping drool onto the ground.

Richard said, "I feel like that little colored boy under all that sawdust and nobody giving a damn. 'Cept I ain't dead. If'n I was dead, maybe it would be easier. Maybe he's got it lots better now."

"Don't talk like that," I said.

"I don't know any other way to talk. Come on, we'll go behind the sawmill, slip over to the house, out to the barn. There ain't no dog to bark, so we can get up there pretty easy. I can get a shovel there."

"A shovel?"

"Yeah. I want to dig Butch up."

"Say what?"

23

"WHAT IN THE WORLD are you talking about? You came here to get your bike."

"That too," he said.

"Why would you dig up a dead dog . . . Your daddy's dead dog?"

"That's the one. I'm gonna dig it up because it meant so much to him. He cried over that dog. I ain't never seen him cry over nothin'. He sure ain't cried over me. I ain't never seen him like nothin' enough to even say so 'cept that dog. You know I oncet pulled cotton all day, and I filled bags good as a grown man, and I was only nine, and he didn't even say good boy, but he always told that dog how damn good it was. He never said nothin' to me. Not a thing."

We walked on toward the sawmill. Nub deserted us, ran off into the woods to pursue dog business.

"Sometimes people don't know how to say those things," I said.

"He knew how to say it to his dog."

"What good will digging up the dog do?"

We passed the sawmill, turned in the direction of the Chapman home.

"I want to put that dog on the back porch. Want to dig it up 'cause he cried over it and he ain't never cried over me. He went to all that trouble to bury it, and I'm going to unbury it."

"Richard, this is weird."

"It ain't weird to me. Now be quiet."

We were near his house. We stopped for a moment and looked at it, bathed in shadow from the trees that surrounded it.

"Daddy sleeps light. Used to claim he could hear a dog run across the yard, and I reckon he can."

"That doesn't sound promising," I said.

"We're gonna go out to the barn. There's a shovel there."

"I don't know, Richard."

"Listen here, Stanley. I didn't ask you to come. I appreciate you did. But I didn't ask you."

"You said we were going to get your bike."

"I am."

"You didn't say anything about this dog business."

"I didn't know I was gonna do it till I was standing out there in front of the old sawmill. It just come to me. You want to go home. Go. Ain't gonna hold it against you. But I'm gonna dig that dog up, and I'm gonna drag it on that screen porch. He'll know I done it, and that's enough."

"How will he know?"

"Because I'll leave him somethin' that lets him know."

"What?"

"Well, I ain't figured that yet. But I will. And even if he don't know, I'll know I done it."

I sighed. "All right. Let's do it."

THE BACKYARD WAS BRIGHT with moonlight, so bright you could even see where chickens had been scratching in the dirt. Out by the barn, the hog snorted once at us, then lay down in its wallow and went silent.

Richard and I removed the bar from the barn doors and heaved them open. Inside, the light from the moon was full in the doorway, but the back of the barn was as black as the devil's thoughts.

I pulled the small flashlight out of my pants pocket, and flashed it around. On the far wall of the barn hung a large cross. It looked to be splashed with dark paint. On either side of the cross were pages torn from the Bible and pinned to the wall. I remembered now what Richard had told me about the barn being a kind of church and Mr. Stilwind thinking he was a preacher.

I pointed my light at the pages on the wall.

"What is that about?" I asked.

"Daddy sticks them on the wall, underlines them, makes me and Mama learn 'em. I had to stand in front of them and memorize them."

"You never told me that."

"Would you tell that on purpose? I wouldn't tell it now, but there it is."

"Tell me that's paint on the cross."

"It's mostly animal blood."

"Why? . . . Mostly?"

"He butchered a chicken, hog, anything, he smeared the blood on there, let it dry. Didn't never clean it."

"Why?"

"Thought of it as a sacrifice to the Lord. You know, thanks

for this here fryin' hen. This here batch of pork chops. One time, when he whipped me across the back with his belt, he wiped the blood off and rubbed it on that cross, and he didn't even say thanks. I wasn't even as good as a fryin' hen. He said, 'And here's the blood of a sinner.' So it ain't all animal blood."

"Tell me what religion he is so I can stay away from it."

"He says there ain't none of the religions doin' what they're supposed to do. What they're supposed to do is what he does."

"I don't think they'd keep too many in church."

"Havin' to hear his preachin' might run 'em off too," Richard said. "It's mostly about dyin' and goin' to hell and burnin' up and stuff. And how we have to serve penance all the time."

"What's penance?"

"Kind of sufferin' and hurtin' for what you believe, to show how much you believe it."

I waved the light around. On one side, in a stall, was the mule. Its eyes in the glow of the flashlight looked like huge black buttons. On the other side, on wooden racks, shiny and clean with filing and oiling, hung all manner of tools. Scythe. Axe. Hoe. Posthole diggers. A shovel.

Richard stroked the old mule's nose. "Hello, boy. How are you? He worked this mule hard as anyone. I ought to let it out, but it wouldn't have nowhere to go. It'd just come back, or die somewhere."

"I'm afraid your parents will see us," I said.

"Yeah," Richard said. He gave the mule a last pat, took the shovel from the rack on the other side.

We pulled the doors back, slid the bolt across them as silently as possible, headed for the woods where the dog was buried.

LEAVES SNAPPED under our feet, and in the woods it was dark. The flashlight batteries became faint, and I had to shake the flashlight to make it work. Finally it quit altogether.

"Hopalong might ride a horse good," Richard said, "but he makes a shitty flashlight."

Due to lack of a flashlight, the grave was hard to find. But finally the trail, which was little more than a single footpath, widened and the trees broke, and there in the moonlight, under the sky, was the mound of dirt where Butch lay.

"I'll do the diggin'," Richard said.

"Suits me."

"Figured it would."

"I feel like someone in one of those monster movies," I said. "Ones with Bela Lugosi and Boris Karloff. The one where they were grave robbers or ghouls."

"You be Boris, and I'll be Bela," Richard said, and he started to dig.

"I wonder what Nub is doing?" I said.

"Chasin' coons and night birds would be my guess. Or squattin' behind a bush."

The dirt was not too hard, but it seemed to me Richard had to dig deeper than before. I suppose that feeling had to do with standing in the middle of the woods while you watched your friend dig up a dead dog in the moonlight.

Before Richard reached the dog, the smell reached us. It was so strong I thought I was going to lose my dinner, but after a moment I became accustomed enough to it to stand it, long as I held one hand over my mouth and nose and didn't breathe too deeply.

"There he is," Richard said, scraping the shovel along the length of the grave.

Sure enough. There in the moonlight was the head. No eye visible, because it was gone. Richard cleared the length of the body and you could see it all now, from tip of nose to tip of tail. Head and body had shrunk, as if it were a package from which items had been removed. The dog's snout had shrunk up so much, the teeth it contained seemed bared.

"It sure stinks," Richard said.

"How are you going to haul it?"

"Drag it on the blanket."

"Richard. I think you ought to just cover Butch up and let's get your bike and go back to the house. All this is going to do is make him angry."

"He will be mad, won't he?" Richard grinned big and the moonlight danced off his teeth.

Richard slammed the shovel into the ground next to the dog's grave, and there was the sound of dirt being parted, then something being cut.

"What was that?" I asked.

Richard pulled the shovel up, went to work digging. After a moment he lifted out something on the shovel. At first it looked like a mound of dirt, but when he dropped it onto the ground, most of the sticky wet dirt shook off of it, and we both knew what it was.

A human skull.

———

WE LOOKED CLOSELY at the skull. The shovel had split the top of it and gone deep. On the side of the skull was a hole, and the far side was shattered, bone poked out as if the brain had turned rabid and kicked its way free.

"That looks way a shotgun blast looks," Richard said.

Richard dug more, soon uncovered a rib cage from which clung red clay. Then some other bones. And two skulls. He dug around and came up with a bone that he pulled free of some roots, said, "This here bone goes in the neck, the spine. See the way that bone is? That's from a cut went into it."

"You don't know that for sure."

"I've seen plenty of animals butchered. I don't think people are all that different."

"We've found an old graveyard," I said.

Richard dug down again, came up with another skull. When he dropped it on the ground the dirt shook loose and I could see the teeth. One of the front teeth was silver.

I had a sinking feeling.

"My God," I said.

"What?"

I told him about Rosy Mae telling me that Margret Wood had a silver tooth.

"We've found her head, Stanley. The one the ghost has been looking for."

Richard poked around with the shovel some more, unearthed an arm. Meat was still on the bones.

"Jesus," he said. "This'n is recent."

Richard poked around some more, uncovered the rest of the body, and finally the head, which was cut free of it, tucked under the corpse's right arm as if it were a joke. Though much of the flesh was gone, there was enough on the face and enough long black hair there to make out it had been a woman.

"That there is the Mexican woman Daddy hired to do some house- and fieldwork. I think her name was Normaleen. She didn't speak much English. Daddy told me she run off. It was maybe a month before we seen him buryin' Butch out here."

Richard sat down as if someone had kicked his legs out

from under him. "I think these here are all people worked for my daddy. I think . . ."

"I think so too," I said.

"He said they quit or run off or he fired 'em. God, Stanley, he was murderin' them people."

"I wasn't murderin'."

Richard jumped to his feet and I spun. Mr. Chapman was standing at the mouth of the trail, where the woods cleared, and he was holding the scythe I had seen on the rack. He had his overalls on with no shirt. He had his shoes on without socks. His hair was like an explosion of dark sprouts. The wind moved it like it was alive. His face was sallow and wrinkled; I couldn't imagine the handsome man that had once been there, the one Rosy talked about.

I realized that Richard's remarks about his father being able to hear a dog run across the yard had not been exaggerated. Mr. Chapman had heard us, gone out to the barn to get the scythe, and followed us.

"You ought not to have dug Butch up," Chapman said. "I put him to rest."

"Did you murder him too?" Richard said. "Did he bark when he shouldn't have?"

"Butch never let me down. As for the others, God lets a righteous man make decisions about such things. Did you know God come to me and told me to do you like Abraham was told to do Isaac? I had to take you out and kill you. 'Cept God didn't come to me and tell me to turn my hand. I just didn't do it. Your mother didn't think it was the thing to do. She thought people would come to us, and want to know where you was, and that you'd be a strong worker. You remember any of that, boy?"

Richard, trembling, said, "No, sir."

"Naw, you wouldn't. I took you on a little squirrel huntin'

trip when you was five. And I was gonna shoot you in the back of the head 'cause God told me to, have a little hunting accident, but I didn't do it. I was supposed to. It would have made life easier. Raisin' you, that didn't do me and your mama no good. The world would have just thought it was a little huntin' accident. God was testin' me, seein' what I was made of. He never told me to stay my hand. I just did. And I shouldn't have. Only time I ever let God down. I didn't let him down with these others. When he come to me and told me what I had to do, I did it. But you were my son, so I didn't do it. Now it comes back on me. You're gonna turn me over to the infidels, ain't you?"

"For what?" Richard said.

Chapman laughed. "That was quick, boy. You're quick like your mother. You know, from the time I took you out and didn't kill you, 'cause I had your mama's thinkin' on the matter in the back of my mind, things have gone bad. Crops ain't good. World is changin'. Niggers is wantin' rights. All manner of evil. Can't abide it. No, sir. I won't. Your mama, I make her pay for it every day. Not because I want to, son, but because God expects it, and in spite of her mistake, she's a righteous woman, she is, and she takes it. She know she ought to. I ain't killed none of these people 'cause I wanted to, but because it was right. It was the will of God. You're my only mistake.

"And you, son," he said looking at me, "I reckon you're just in the wrong place at the wrong time. But you are from a sinful family. I can see that. Your sister actin' like she's got the rights of a man. That daddy of yours whippin' on me when I was seekin' out my own son. Givin' him refuge. Runnin' that movie house. That's wrong."

"You killed these people to save money," Richard said. "I think that's why you killed them. Because you're cheap."

Chapman snorted. "You think that? Well, you would. Some

of them people were drinkers, and fornicators . . . That silver-toothed one there. She was a whore, and ran with that Stilwind girl in a manner a girl ain't supposed to go. I tried to witness to her. She wouldn't have any of it."

"You witnessed to her by the railroad tracks?" I said.

"You witness where you find the need."

"I think you wanted her," I said. "You didn't want anyone else to have her. So one night you followed her . . . with that scythe, and killed her. Brought the head back here."

"You ain't no man of God," Richard said. "You ain't better than me. You ain't as good as me."

Chapman's face turned sad. He looked at Richard like the last morsel on a plate.

"You killed Margret, and you burned up the Stilwind girl, didn't you?" I said.

"You don't know what you're talkin' about," Chapman said. "And I ain't gonna talk no more."

That's when Richard flicked a shovelful of dirt into Chapman's face.

Richard bolted. "Run!"

I didn't have to be told twice. I went after Richard. We started back in the direction of the sawmill.

We zigzagged through trees and finally broke out to where we could see the old mill and the road beyond. I glanced over my shoulder, saw that Chapman was catching up. Spit was trailing out of his mouth in a way that made it look like foam.

I realized we weren't going to make it to the road before he caught up.

Nub chose that moment to burst out of the woods, and when he saw me running, and Mr. Chapman after me, he broke straight away for my pursuer, barking.

I shouldn't have stopped, but I turned and yelled for Nub. It was too late. Nub hit Chapman's ankle hard, and though he didn't get in a good bite, Chapman's legs got tangled and he went down, the scythe flying out in front of him.

While he was getting up, I yelled for Nub in as hard and as insistent a voice as I could. Nub barked at Chapman, and chose to obey me for a change. He came running toward me happily, as if it were all a game.

I bent down, held out my arms, and Nub jumped into them. I turned and started running, sneaked a look over my shoulder, saw Chapman was up now with his scythe, and he was picking up speed.

Ahead of me, Richard was almost to the sawmill. I was coming up on his tail, panting with the weight of Nub and the weight of fear.

When I reached the sawmill, Richard was at the base of the old ladder that lay fastened alongside the building and led to the upper platform. "Go up," he said.

Going up didn't seem smart to me. We would be trapped like a rat in a matchbox, but I couldn't run anymore. My sides felt as if they were about to split.

Richard pounded up the ladder before me. I tossed Nub over my shoulder with one hand, then started climbing, nearly losing my grip on the ladder and my grip on Nub, who was squirming like a snake.

"Come on! Come on!" Richard said.

The ladder was about eighteen feet high and I felt as if I were slower than a ground sloth, but I made the platform ahead of Chapman, set Nub on it, and looked over.

Chapman had laid the scythe across the back of his neck, balancing it, and he was climbing up. Nub stood on the edge of the platform and barked furiously.

Richard disappeared through the open door that led into the second-floor room, came back with an old busted two-by-four.

"Daddy. Go down now."

Chapman looked up. "I'm not your daddy. You have no daddy."

Chapman continued to climb. Richard launched the two-by-four forward with all his might. It caught Chapman in the top of the head, knocked him backwards to the ground, sent the scythe skittering over the leaves, the blade winking in the moonlight like death's smile.

Chapman shook his head, put a hand to it. I could see something dark oozing between his fingers.

"You child of the devil," Chapman yelled. "You wicked boy. I will chastise you."

Richard sat on the edge of the platform, kicked at the top board. It creaked. He kicked again and it came loose and fell.

"Hang on to me," he said. I grabbed his arm and he swung down and tried to kick loose the next board, but it was too late, Chapman was screaming. He grabbed the scythe and swung it high and the blade passed just beneath Richard's foot.

"Pull me up," Richard said.

He didn't have to tell me twice. I tugged him up.

Chapman was coming up again, and I knew that one missing board wasn't going to stop him.

"Come on," Richard said.

I grabbed Nub and we went into the old sawmill room, the moonlight cutting through rotted spots and slashing beams across the floor.

"That there in the middle is rotten," Richard said. "Stay close to the wall over here."

We eased along the wall and the whole structure wobbled. Richard said, "Worse comes to worst, we can slide down into that sawdust. But that's the worst. I don't know we'd come up out of it."

"We're trapped, Richard."

"Stay away from the middle. Stay right here."

We had reached the far side of the building, near the mouth of the sawdust chute. Chapman's shadow filled the doorway, then he was moving forward.

"You have just given yourselves to God's mercy."

"God can kiss my ass," Richard said.

Chapman roared, came across the floor. The entire building shook and the floor screamed and rose up and buckled and there was a crack, and Chapman's right leg went through. It went through so fast his left leg, which stayed on the flooring, bent under him and went backwards and twisted in a way that it hurt to see. A piece of bone had torn through his flesh, ripped through his overalls, and it stuck out like a muddy stick. I could see too where the floor had broken up and made a barbed piece of wood and it had gone into Chapman's lower abdomen. He had dropped the scythe.

Chapman screamed so loud I thought the building would collapse from the noise. "You beast," Chapman said. "You devil. God curse you for the bastard of Satan you are. O, merciful God, deliver me from this pain and this boy."

I glanced at Richard. A spear of moonlight lay across his eyes and nose. I could see tears in his eyes. He eased forward. The floor creaked.

"Careful, Richard," I said. "Be careful."

Richard picked up the scythe. He said, "Stand to the side and give me room, Stanley."

"No," I said. "Don't do it."

"Move aside."

"Don't do it, Richard."

"Then you better watch the blade as she comes, Stanley. Daddy, God is gonna grant you one last wish. You ain't gonna have pain no more, and you ain't gonna have to worry on me none."

I leaped back against the wall and there was a whisper and a glint of silver and the sound of Nub barking insanely.

The blade appeared to have passed in front of Chapman, and for an instant, I thought Richard had missed. Then Chapman's head rolled to the side and fell through the hole his fall had made. There was a burst of darkness from his neck and it splashed warm across me and Nub and Richard. Chapman's body bent forward, the boards creaked, cracked, and he fell on through, leaving a great gap in the center of the room.

Richard dropped the scythe and it went through the hole. He turned, looked at me, sat down on the floor next to the wall. Sat down so hard I thought the whole rotten building would fall. It shook and sagged and squeaked and creaked, finally went still and silent.

Nub stopped barking. He lay passive in my arms, his ears raised. Outside, gradually, I began to hear what had been going on all along.

Crickets.

An owl in the distance.

Somewhere, the howling of dogs.

24

THERE'S NO WAY I can tell you the type of commotion all of this created. You have some idea, of course. But in 1958 a crime like this was a sensation. Or should have been. It got little play outside of Dewmont, however. It didn't get picked up all over like you would expect. That was due to the town fathers, and Mr. Stilwind, who owned the newspaper.

Me and Richard missed a week of school. The police quizzed us for a few days and we were under a kind of mild house arrest without the arrest, if that makes sense. But it was made clear we weren't supposed to go anywhere until they said so.

The police tried to play the idea that we had gone in together to murder Richard's old man because of some sort of grudge Richard held for being thrown out.

But we kept to our story, which was the truth. About how we dug up the dog because Richard wanted to put it on the back porch to make his old man aware of how he felt.

It was such a dumb story they couldn't help but believe it. Besides, it was true.

Then there were the reporters. Each one trying to make the first big scoop of their lives. Pieces of it ended up in the paper outside of Dewmont, but it was downplayed and it didn't hit the big news much. A piece in the back of the Houston paper, a stamp-size square in the Dallas paper, and a few sentences in the Tyler rag. I think some money might have changed hands.

I told the police about the graveyard, of course, and Richard told them about the bodies and how they were people who had worked for his father. I told them about Margret. I told them that he may have killed Jewel Ellen. Mr. Stilwind later got wind of that and made a public display of the story about Jewel Ellen being murdered by Mr. Chapman.

That part did make the papers, and most of what you heard later was how this man had been killed trying to kill two children, and how he was responsible for the death of the daughter of the town's premier citizen.

Margret got lost in all of it. So did the workers, black and brown, that Chapman killed. It was all about Jewel Ellen Stilwind. Everything else was a footnote.

Mrs. Chapman said she loved her husband and had no idea he did such things. No one wanted to listen, and certainly didn't believe it, when Richard said she had to know. They didn't want to believe about the beatings she took and liked either. She was asked to move, however, and she obliged, and to the best of my knowledge, no one ever saw or heard from her again.

As an adult, I've often wondered about her. How much had she really done to accommodate her husband? What did she do after she left Dewmont? Sometimes, thinking about that, I get the creeps.

Out in the Chapman barn, a number of items were found

that belonged to the people he had killed. Like a magpie, he had collected things they had owned, gathered them up and made a nest. Wallets and rings and scarfs and even a pair of shoes. No one knew what he did with those things, or why he kept them in a greasy box beneath straw at the far end of the barn, and some of us didn't really want to know.

Richard was given a lot of sympathy for a while. He stayed with us and started school. He and I didn't get closer, like you'd think. We sort of drifted apart. We went to school together, we talked some, watched a little TV, and he helped out at the drive-in and slept on his pallet near my bed, but there was something missing. It was as if God had come down from heaven and driven an invisible wedge between our spirits.

Then, one afternoon, when I was to meet him after school, he didn't show. I learned he left at lunchtime. Just walked off. He hadn't gone home, and no one knew where he was.

My dad tore the town apart looking for him. We went out to the Chapman place, found it burned to the ground, house and barn and all the sheds. The animals had long ago been sold and Richard had been given the money.

I guess Richard did the burning, but he was nowhere to be had. The police sifted through the fire, the wreckage, to see if he had gotten burned up himself, but no bones were found.

After a few weeks, we decided he had done what he told me he was thinking about doing. Caught a train out of Dewmont, rode on somewhere where he could get a job and start a life. Being near us, even if we did care, was just too much for him.

———

BUSTER STILL RAN the projector, but into the school year he decided he had to cut back. The walking was really getting to him. I took over on Fridays and Saturdays. The rest of the week the job was his.

One night, a Thursday, I went out to see him in the projection booth. He had a big RC and was sipping it. When he saw me, he smiled, said, "It's just RC, Stan."

The cardboard box full of paper clippings and police files was on the floor beside him.

I said, "Guess we need to turn those back."

"Know what," he said, "only if you want to. Figure it don't matter none. This stuff is forgotten. You want to keep it, you can. Or you can toss it. I ain't gonna try to return it. Jukes done quit them jobs. He got him work over at the railroad making twice what he was makin'."

I sat down in the spare chair, said, "Richard's not coming back, I guess."

"Hard to say. But I doubt it."

"He took my Roy Rogers boots with him."

"That's not good."

"He left a note that said thanks. I guess that was for everything."

"You think he owes you?"

"I don't know."

"I figure a boy like that, he's startin' out with enough debts. Ain't no need to give him one more."

"Yeah. But it was my Roy Rogers boots."

"That's too bad. But, you know, in a year, you won't care. And in twenty years, them boots will be somethin' you think about all the time."

"I don't understand."

"You will. It's about thinkin' you grown up, then knowin' you ain't."

"You said bad people don't always look bad. But Chapman and Bubba Joe. They sure looked like monsters."

"Sometimes I'm wrong. A lot of the time."

"I still don't know why Chapman killed Margret or Jewel Ellen."

"Sure you do. They was different, and he wanted them. Or he wanted that Margret anyway. That's the one he killed. I can bet you that. He laid for Margret, jumped her, had his way, and killed her."

"And Jewel?"

"Now, if you done told me all Chapman told you correct-like, he didn't say he killed her, now did he? Took credit for them others and was proud of it, but he didn't say he killed her."

"He seemed confused when I mentioned it."

"That's what I'm sayin'. Now, Chapman could have done it. Won't never know. And that's the way it is in life. There's gonna be all manner of stuff you never can find out the truth on and can only guess."

"So you still think one of the Stilwinds killed Jewel?"

"I do. I think it was a coincidence. Not all planned and clicked together like I said things will do, and they do some-times. But not this time, Stan. And let me point out, Stilwind don't look like no monster. Chapman was crazy, Bubba Joe was pissed-on stupid. Stilwind. He's the real monster."

"One of the Stilwinds could have killed her on the same night to make it look like the killer did it? It could be like that."

Buster grinned at me. "I don't think so. I don't think one could have known about the other quick enough for both crimes to come down in an hour or so. I think Chapman's hate, Stilwind's need for Jewel Ellen to keep her mouth shut, just come together in the same night."

"Coincidence?"

"That's right."

"Mystery books I've been reading say there's no such thing as coincidence."

"They're wrong. You live long enough, you'll find life is so full of coincidence it'll make you crazy."

"Well, it's not very satisfactory."

Buster grinned. "Now you're learnin'. That's life. Ain't always satisfactory, but sometimes the part that is, is pretty damn good. Thing to remember is, enjoy life, 'cause in the end, dirt and flesh is pretty much the same thing. You understand that?"

"I think so."

"Good."

———

As school went on, and I got involved with making new friends and trying not to get beat up by bullies, I saw less of Buster. At nights I took to doing homework or watching television, and it got so most of the time we just nodded at one another.

Then one cool night in October, he didn't show. I had to run the projector. Though it was late, when I finished, I talked Daddy into allowing Drew and Callie to drive me over to Buster's.

Driving down into the Section, Drew said, "They need some lights down here."

"I think they'd be glad to have them," Callie said, "but I don't believe the city gives them out down here."

Drew pulled up in front of Buster's house. It was dark. I got out and went on the porch and knocked. He didn't answer. I hesitated about going in. He hadn't been drinking of late, but it occurred to me he might have fallen off the wagon.

I finally bit the bullet and tried the knob. It was locked.

I went to the window on the porch, pushed at it, and it came up with a squeak. I got down close to the crack I had made and called his name, but he didn't answer.

I pushed the window up all the way and climbed in. Buster was lying on the bed, the covers up to his chin, his hands holding them as if he had just pulled them up.

I knew as soon as I saw him, he was dead.

25

DADDY HAD THE BODY put in the colored funeral home, and he paid for it to be embalmed. We tried to find the relatives Buster told me about, but no luck.

They buried him in the colored graveyard near where Bubba Joe had tried to kill me. They put him down without a stone between two other heaps of dirt without stones—recent burials.

I took the books the way he wanted. While I was gathering them, Callie, who was helping me, came across a note.

It read:

"Stan, you are my true friend. I give you my books, and my records. You're gonna like them. Enjoy your life. Buster."

"He knew he was dying," I said to Callie.

"I suppose he did," she said.

I DIDN'T GO BACK to the grave until some years later, and by then I couldn't find it. Grass had grown over most everything and there were no longer mounds and what stones that had been there were gone or broken.

After Buster's death, lots of things changed. There was a rumble in the air about civil rights, and there was much confusion and gnashing of teeth, but as the years went on, there were changes.

Colored didn't have to sit in the balcony at the downtown theater anymore. James Stilwind sold out and moved off.

Mrs. Stilwind was found one morning in the pool out back of the old Stilwind house. She had fallen in and had been there for a few days before she was missed, or rather cared about. What I remember most about the story was a boy at school saying "Crows picked her eyes."

Mr. Stilwind sued the old folks home, won, put them out of business, owned the place. He tore it down and built a subdivision there. He made lots of money and no one ever accused him of anything, nor his son, James.

Not long after the subdivision went up, Old Man Stilwind was found shot in his hotel room. No one knew who did it. Rumors were a young lady went up to his room to see him. More rumor said lots of young ladies did that. This one had a gun and a grudge. She shot him through the heart, then through the head four times, just to make sure he didn't rise from the dead.

She got out of there without so much as anyone realizing Stilwind was dead or even hearing the shots. All she left were some gloves, and all that could be determined from those was that the label inside said they were made in London, England.

I smiled over that one.

Until now, I've never told anyone but my wife who killed Bubba Joe. All these years after, now and then I have a bad dream about him. See him chasing me and Callie and Richard. Richard is lost behind me, and Callie's ponytail is flying in my face, Bubba Joe is closing, and the train is charging up the tracks.

Sometimes, in my dreams, he catches me.

Daddy bought the theater James sold. I thought that was ironic. He liked to joke he was Dewmont's picture show magnate, indoors and out.

Mama began selling *World Book Encyclopedia*s door-to-door, and she liked it. Rosy ran the drive-in, and I ran the projection booth. Rosy got her room upstairs. Along with an air conditioner. Air conditioners were put in all over the house. One for each bedroom, one for the living room that cooled it and the kitchen.

Drew and Callie dated seriously all through high school, but when Callie went off to a teachers college, they couldn't hold it together. Callie became an English teacher. Got married, got divorced, met up with Drew some years later. He was divorced too. They got married, moved back to Dewmont where she teaches school and Drew runs his father's hardware store, as if he really needs to. Drew inherited money. Lots of it. Callie dresses nice and no longer wears a ponytail. Men still look and sigh when she walks by.

Mom and Daddy went on fine for several years, then Daddy decided to close the drive-in down. It was just a home then. He kept saying he was going to take up the speakers and plant grass, but he didn't. The projection booth filled up with lawn mowers and garden tools that he used to keep the front yard nice.

The indoor theater did all right for a few more years, and Rosy Mae worked there behind the concession and Mama took tickets, then Daddy gave it up too, retired.

He couldn't stay that way, though. He and Mom decided to

get back in the movie business. They owned the first video store in Dewmont. She quit selling encyclopedias and they ran it together until Daddy got too old and weak to be there.

Daddy retired for real, and a year later he had the big one; his great heart played out. Mom and Rosy lived in the drive-in home for another three years, then Mama died, left me some money, left Callie some goods, and left the drive-in to Rosy.

Rosy rented it out to a fella that wanted to keep scrap metal and old cars there. He cut down all the speakers. Rosy paid on a little house with the money she got from the rental, and moved out. Now and then, coming back from Austin, where I live and teach criminal justice, I'd stop by her house for dinner.

Rosy learned to "read real good," as she was fond of saying, but she never read as well as she cooked. Now and then, for some reason or another, I'll get the taste of her fried chicken and light biscuits on the back of my tongue, and it'll be as if I just had them.

Last year, sensing time was playing out its string, Rosy quit leasing the drive-in and sold it to me for a song. I buried her on the far side of town in the graveyard where my parents are buried, the graveyard that just thirty years before only whites could be buried in. I bought her a headstone big as the one my parents had.

Bless her.

My wife and I have plans to retire to Dewmont, maybe open the drive-in again, as a kind of retirement lark. That's down the road a way. We'll see.

Chester, he who was slapped by Daddy in an attempt to raise his IQ, never did get any smarter. He married Jane Jersey, the girl who had slipped the prophylactic into Callie's room. They had a couple of kids. One night he came home drunk and set out to beat her, a regular occurrence, and she shot him. The law called it self-defense.

Nub is long gone, of course. But I think about him at least once a day. He was a good dog and lived a long life. I have another dog now, but I don't like him much. He's my wife's dog, actually. A poodle with a pink bow in his hair. He bites me at least once a week.

My wife and I wanted children. But it didn't work out. We put it off too long. I guess the poodle is her baby. Nonetheless, I love her. She loves me. It's a good life. The poodle's name is François. I want a German shepherd.

———

ONE CURIOUS NOTE, and I read this in the Austin paper, just a little piece in the back section. It was about my old hometown, so I was drawn to it. It was more of a curiosity item than anything else.

It said an old sawmill in Dewmont, or what was left of one, a wobbly piece of rotted wood and rusted tin, had fallen down and been removed. There was a blackened mound of sawdust there too, washed down to where it was nearly flat.

When the sawdust was scooped up, a skeleton was found. I thought of that black kid Richard told me about at first, but I thought different when I read on.

Along with the skeleton, all that remained that was identifiable were some boots with one pull-up strap that had Roy Rogers written on it in silver paint.

It's all over now. Some things answered, some things not.

As I grow older, and frankly, I'm not that old, late fifties, but still, the past is more important than the present. That may not be good, but that's the truth. Things were more intense then. The sun warmer. The wind cooler. Dogs better understood.

Buster wasn't always right, and he gave mixed answers sometimes, but the thing that sticks with me, the thing that always seems right, was what he said about how life isn't always satisfactory, and that in the end, dirt and flesh are pretty much the same.

Visit THE ORBIT, the official drive-in theater of champion MOJO STORYTELLER Joe R. Lansdale, located on the web at www.joerlansdale.com. Free stories changed weekly.